Old Three

and Other Tales

of Survival and Extinction

AMERICAN INDIAN LITERATURE AND CRITICAL STUDIES SERIES

Old Three Toes
and Other Tales
of Survival and Extinction

John Joseph Mathews

Edited and with an afterword by
Susan Kalter

UNIVERSITY OF OKLAHOMA PRESS : NORMAN

Also by John Joseph Mathews

Wah'Kon-Tah: The Osage and the White Man's Road (Norman, Okla., 1932)

Sundown (New York, 1934)

Talking to the Moon (Norman, Okla., 1945)

Life and Death of an Oilman: The Career of E. W. Marland (Norman, Okla., 1951)

The Osages: Children of the Middle Waters (Norman, Okla., 1961)

Twenty Thousand Mornings: An Autobiography (ed. by Susan Kalter) (Norman, Okla., 2012)

Also by Susan Kalter

(ed.) *Benjamin Franklin, Pennsylvania, and the First Nations: The Treaties of 1736–62* (Urbana, Ill., 2006)

(ed. with Hsuan Hsu) *Two Texts by Edward Everett Hale: "The Man without a Country" and Philip Nolan's Friends* (Lanham, Md., 2010)

Library of Congress Cataloging-in-Publication Data

Mathews, John Joseph, 1895–1979.

[Short stories. Selections]

Old Three Toes and other tales of survival and extinction / John Joseph Mathews; edited and with an afterword by Susan Kalter.

pages   cm. — (American Indian literature and critical studies series; v. 63)

Includes bibliographical references.

ISBN 978-0-8061-5120-5 (pbk.: alk. paper)

1. Animals—Fiction. 2. Nature stories, American.

I. Kalter, Susan, 1969– editor. II. Title.

PS3525.A8477A6 2015

813´.54—dc23

2014021368

Old Three Toes and Other Tales of Survival and Extinction
is Volume 63 in the American Indian Literature and Critical Studies Series.

This book is dedicated to the children and grandchildren
of John Joseph Mathews
Virginia Mathews
John H. Mathews and his children, Sara, Laura, and Chris
John Hunt and his children, Diana and Mead
Ann Hunt Brown and her children, Diane, Peter, Henry, and Sammy
his nieces and nephews
and all of their descendents

and to the children in my life
Sam, Naomi, and Annabel
Simone and Nicholas
Sabine and Sam
Ari and Talia
Lauren and Dane
and all those to come

Contents

Preface

FROM AN EARLY AGE, John Joseph Mathews was drawn to wildlife. He yearned to experience the world through the eyes of hawks, panthers, and other beings. All his life he observed and studied the habits of these and other wild animals. After he became a grandfather, he wanted to pass his knowledge on to all his grandchildren, and indeed to the world. His granddaughters Sara, Laura, and Christine lived in Maryland with his son, John, and daughter-in-law, Gail. Diana and Mead, the grandchildren of his second wife, Elizabeth, lived in Paris with Elizabeth's son, John Hunt. Diane, Peter, Henry, and Sammy lived in California with Elizabeth's daughter, Ann Hunt Brown. When Mathews made an arrangement with the *Atlantic Monthly Press* to work on a children's book, sometime in the early 1960s, it is certain that these children were uppermost in his mind.

Although few of his short stories have ever been published, Mathews wrote at least thirty-four during his long career. The nine collected here are unique in that he intended from the beginning to publish them together, in a book he increasingly envisioned as a boy's book. "I am not sure of myself in writing my boy's book," he confessed. Yet when he told his first-written story, "The White Sack," to Ann Hunt Brown and her husband and to her children in separate sittings in August 1963, the grandchildren clearly understood something about the story for which the adults had little appreciation. Diane, Peter, and Henry Brown were all held spellbound.

It is a shame that Mathews never found a publisher for this book or prematurely gave up trying. The stories in this collection speak to a wider audience than even he imagined—not only to children, but also to animal and nature lovers, environmentalists, as well as those interested in Mathews's work and Native fiction. Readers of the 1960s would have recognized and readers of today (of all ages) will recognize immediately those pearls he cast from the prairie, the blackjacks, and the mountains. Many of the stories individually, and the stories as a collection, are very moving, from "Singers to the Moon" to the climactic "Old Three Toes of Buffalo Fork." Mathews's long sentences flow beautifully, sustaining a momentum that propels the reader along with anticipatory interest. They are often built on the simplest of conjunctions, "and," which holds our attention, maintains the smooth, calm pace, and sustains a compelling rhythm, which when broken is almost always broken with purpose. Even his paragraphing is top-notch and inventive. And we appreciate immediately the enormous work of characterization that Mathews has poured into characters like Lineback, Three Toes, the mother heath hen, the little heath cock of destiny, Arrowflight, and many others. He figures place as character; his meticulous painting of place is among the best we will find in such stories. His plots are creative and often unpredictable and suspenseful. This volume shows that Mathews had even more literary ability than we had yet seen. He writes from close and expert knowledge.

Acknowledgments

I WOULD LIKE TO THANK all the dedicated faculty, staff, and students of the Western History Collections, University of Oklahoma, Norman, Oklahoma—particularly Kristina L. Southwell, Jacquelyn D. Slater, and Jacquelyn K. Sparks—who have assisted me throughout the duration of this project with the John Joseph Mathews Collection, the University of Oklahoma Press Collection, and their other collections. Thanks to the John H. Mathews family, as well as the Western History Collections, for their permission to publish these works, as Mathews originally intended to do. Work on this book was funded by the College of Arts and Sciences at Illinois State University through a 2010–11 Faculty Research Award and a timely sabbatical in fall 2010. Thanks to the members of the Council of the Department of English, the Faculty Status Committee of the Department of English, and the Research Proposal Review Committee of the College of Arts and Sciences for those grants of time and resources. Carter Revard and A. LaVonne Brown Ruoff also supported the project through letters of reference to an external granting agency. Finally, I would like to thank John H. and Gail Mathews and their daughters, Sara Dydak, Laura Edwards, and Chris Mathews, for their review of my preface and afterword and their generosity in sharing thoughts and family history with me.

Editor's Note

THE NINE STORIES presented here are based on manuscripts found in the John Joseph Mathews Collection at the Western History Collections of the University of Oklahoma Library in Norman, Oklahoma. The stories have been lightly edited to correct typescript anomalies such as spelling and unorthodox punctuation. Words have sometimes been added or changed, as where clarity necessitates an explicit antecedent or where logic necessitates a different conjunction; such changes have been minimal. Some inconsistencies have been left in order to remain truer to the original and in the hope that doing so will better allow readers to judge Mathews's writing on its own merits rather than having to guess frequently at authorial versus posthumous editorial decision-making.

Explanatory notes to the stories may be found directly after the last story. I have chosen not to insert note signals into the stories themselves so that readers may read the narratives as Mathews wrote them and aspired for them to be published.

Old Three Toes

and Other Tales

of Survival and Extinction

Singers to the Moon

C EDAR CANYON HEADS IN THE WEST PASTURE, and the water that flows down the watercourse in the bottom of the canyon flows into Bird Creek. Some of the elms, hackberries, sycamores, bur oaks, and pin oaks have tried to climb up the canyon from the creek, but the rich alluvium of the bottoms did not reach very far up the canyon and they never attained the height of their parents along the creek. The cedars of course did much better, and at the very head of the canyon there was a tremendous bur oak. He was on the edge of the prairie, and he must have found a private water supply.

The canyon was like a gash in the earth. It looked as if a giant had slashed the earth with his sword and the edges of the gash had fallen away like flesh when a venison haunch is slashed.

It would seem that after the giant's anger had passed and he had thrust his sword back into its scabbard, he had walked away, pleased with himself.

The elms, sycamores, hackberries, pin oaks, and cedars grew so thick in the slash canyon that the sunlight only dappled the water of the watercourse during the summer months and made fretwork with the shadows of the bare limbs and twigs in the winter. On each side of the watercourse, the canyon bottom was carpeted with leaves of several seasons.

It was a wild spot, and you could only get there by horseback or afoot. If you went there in the late afternoon and sat on the sandstone ledges and were careful to wear clothing that blended with the moss and the lichen of the rocks and the twisted boles of the cedars, and if you kept absolutely still, you might hear and see strange things.

First, about four o'clock, you might hear the "whoo, whoo-WHO-whoo, whoo" of the great horned owl. It is a lazy hunting call for such a savage bird and it would come at intervals and one might think that the owl was disinterested since his voice was so quiet and casual, but he was one of the fiercest hunters of the creek bottoms, the blackjack ridges, and the prairie.

Also, from the creek bottoms you might hear the much more fearful cry of the barred owl. One might think that only a very savage beast could utter such a hunting cry and in imagination might see him aprowl, and there might be prickles on the back of the listener's neck. Unless a listener had been assured that the terrific booming "whoo, whoo, whoo, whoo—whooo-hoo-ah-ah-h-h-ha" was only the hunting cry of the barred owl, he might believe that only the savage great horned owl could utter such a cry.

The smaller, round-faced barred owl was not savage at all. He had no great ear tufts as did the horned owl, and he really looked too sleepy and silly to be the frightener of birds and animals.

If you sat very still on your ledge of sandstone which formed the edge of the canyon and your clothing blended with the moss and the lichen and it was late afternoon and there was no air stirring, then a moss-spotted and lichen-splashed stone you had been looking at might suddenly move and become a grey-tawny animal with speckled belly and legs. He would be as large as a medium-sized dog whose tail had been docked and therefore had only a stub for a tail.

This animal would stop and look about him, then walk on in the gloom of the late afternoon, lifting and setting each foot down as if he were afraid to hurt the earth. Sometimes when he stopped to look about, his ridiculous stub of a tail would twitch. He would be interested in everything, smelling of the leaves and the twigs and investigating among the large sandstones that had broken off from the canyon's edge and had rolled down the flank, finally coming to rest near the bottom.

The hunter-cat would disappear up the canyon, and the observer, who had been so still so long, must now stretch his legs and change position. And anyway it would be growing late, and there would be only the sad little voice of the phoebe who had a mud nest under the edge of the sandstone outcrop, and he would start to scold you for being so close to his nest.

Sammy of the ranch came here to sit quite often. He had heard the owls from the creek bottoms and he had seen the bobcat coming up the canyon in the gloom of the later afternoon, and the phoebe had scolded him many times.

One day in May he came there to sit with his back to the sandstone ledge and wait for something to happen. He tied his mare, Peg, back on the shelf of land higher up. He loved her very much; they had grown up together and they had become companions, but when you wanted to hear things and watch animals and birds who didn't know you were near, you couldn't have success with restless Peg near you. She could certainly see movements you couldn't possibly see, and she could hear the faintest sound of a twig being stepped on, and best of all she could smell the faintest of musky odors. But that was no good when Sammy wanted to sit in his favorite position under the sandstone outcrop of Cedar Canyon. Peg would soon become restive, and prance about; then she would start pawing the earth, and if she were close to you she might sniff the back of your neck, and cause you to move clumsily.

So this day, as he did every day, he tied Peg a hundred yards back from the canyon, and he had sat for an hour when his eye caught movement at the head of the canyon. There by the bur oak stood a coyote. She had come softly to the tree and then stopped behind it and froze. She was watching something and he followed her gaze and there he saw two coyote whelps having a tug-of-war with a chicken wing. They tugged and tugged, and they might have been growling at each other, in play of course, but Sammy couldn't hear them. One was larger than the other and seemed very dark.

The mother was unseen by them and she stayed behind the tree and watched them for some time; then she showed herself and the two whelps left their wing and rushed to her, nuzzling the hair of her belly. She lifted her hind legs and stepped over them, and they followed her to the mouth of the den among the loose rocks, just under the caprock at the very head of the canyon. Here she lay down and the whelps had their dinner.

As she lay there, the great horned owl boomed from a nearby post oak that had had its top blown off by high winds. The mother coyote paid no attention to him, and certainly the whelps paid no attention.

When the whelps had finished, the mother got up and started off on her night's hunting. The little ones, now like furry balls with their bellies like little balloons, started to follow, then stood and watched her go. She stopped when a little way off and came back and stood and looked at them. They seemed to understand; they turned and disappeared into the den.

Sammy was happy. The coyotes had not the slightest hint of his presence and he was filled with his own importance. He rose and stretched and walked back of the canyon to the spot where he had tied Peg. He was careful not to go near the den; the mother would get the man scent when she returned and she would probably move her babies.

Peg watched him approach with her head high and her forelock over one eye. He refused to roach her mane, as one did with cow horses, so that there would be no interference with the rope. Her mane, like her tail, was too beautiful.

She had dug a depression in the earth with her hooves in her impatience over his absence, and when he had untied her, he had to rein her in a tight circle in order to mount. Before he got his right leg over and his right foot into the stirrup, she was off in a lope.

He reined her in when they climbed out of the west canyon, or she would have jump-walked up the steep, twisting cattle trail. On the divide she fought the tight rein and was shaking her head; then she noticed the full moon climbing out of the prairie and stared at it. A big red moon will often startle men and horses and other animals, when it first appears.

At this moment it began. It began with a wolf-like howl, long drawn out; then it broke into yipping, then a long-drawn-out yowl. Almost immediately there was a chorus, and then coyotes to the east and the north of the divide joined in. Suddenly the chorus near Sammy and Peg stopped abruptly, as if some director had brought his baton down sharply. After the coyote songs, the prairie seemed to be without life.

Sammy didn't get back to the head of Cedar Canyon as soon as he wished, and when he did the whelps had left the den. There were some bones there, part of the dried skin of a calf that had died just after birth in February. The skin had been a favorite plaything of the whelps.

The summer passed with lightning over the prairie that looked like trees upside down, and before each summer storm, the coyotes howled, moved by the low pressure, and when they howled in a certain manner you would say that there would be a change of weather within twenty-four hours. Sometimes they howled close to the ranch house and the two stockdogs and the bird dog swore at them, with the hair on the back of their necks and shoulders standing erect.

In August Sammy would often ride over the prairie with Sheb Simpson, the cowhand, who had great sport roping the young coyotes, who were now practically grown but not as smart as they thought themselves to be. When they saw one of the coyotes, they rode toward him; then Sheb with his rope whirling over his head would spur his horse after the young coyote and throw his loop. Sometimes the coyote would slip through the loop, but sometimes Sheb caught one, then played it as it pulled back against the rope. The cow horses of the ranch thought this to be queer business and they would snort and back up.

When Sheb was by himself, he would kill them and hang them from the fence posts so that people could see them from the County Road. This was probably a queer sort of boasting. However, when Sammy was with him, he turned them loose, seeming to agree with Sammy that it was much more fun running them with greyhounds.

That autumn Sammy was riding along the edge of the canyon, and he saw two coyotes near the den at the head of the canyon. They didn't see him since they were busy sniffing around the old den. Then suddenly he noted something he had not noted last May when he had watched the whelps tug at the chicken wing. He had noted then that, of the two whelps, one was much larger and much darker than the other and now he saw that the larger one had a black line down his back like a "coyote dun" horse. Peg stood still as well since she was watching the two coyotes intently. Here they were then, come back to visit their old den and there was the one with the black stripe down his back. He was very large for a coyote, and very beautiful, Sammy thought. Just then a blue jay saw the boy and the horse and came close to swear at them, and both coyotes raised their heads and looked in their direction, and almost immediately identifying them as man and horse, loped over the prairie looking back over their shoulders.

A few days later Sheb said as they rode along, "They's a lineback whelp uses 'round Cedar Canyon that looks like a mountain coyote—half wolf.

Why, when he gits his full growth, he'll be as big as a staghoun'."

A fear passed through Sammy, and he hadn't the least idea why. Then he realized that he didn't want anything to happen to this special coyote. They had ridden a quarter of a mile before his vague worry left him. It was cleared away with the thought that running hounds wouldn't have a chance to catch *his* coyote when he got to the breaks of Bird Creek. Surely he would have sense enough to make for the canyon when the great high-backed greyhound-staghound crosses of his father's ran him.

In November the trail hounds could be heard chorusing along the creek bottoms, and Sammy would go out into the darkness and listen, hoping that they were not after Lineback. As he stood convincing himself that trail hounds seldom made a kill, no matter what their owners said, he realized that he had named *his* coyote Lineback.

In the meantime, Lineback was learning fast. He and his brother and mother, and sometimes his father, formed a sort of pack, but it was not a close one. They were often together, but it seemed that they stayed together long enough for the young ones to complete their schooling for survival.

One night, all four of them, the father who was anything except a faithful father and mate, the mother, and the two young ones, were on the flood-plain of Bird Creek catching field mice in the long grass. Field mice were like oysters—an appetizer—but apparently they cherished them. They would cock their heads and listen intently; then, standing on their hind legs, they would pounce and land on all four feet close together on the mouse's runway, either catching him under their feet or blocking his run in both directions.

It was very faint at first, then became louder and increased in volume, and the father stood like a statue, as did the mother. Both became nervous and trotted off toward the prairie, but the young ones didn't want to leave the wonderful game of mouse-catching and paid no attention to the increasing volume of the hound chorus. They had heard them several times during the damp nights of the later summer and the early autumn, and nothing had happened.

Suddenly the yelping broke out after a silence of several minutes, just across the creek, only a few hundred yards away. The hounds had come upon the very warm scent of the family since they had hunted mice on the other side of the creek earlier. There was jubilance and high excitement in the yelping now and Lineback and his brother ran at full speed up the flank of a ridge and onto the prairie, but the pack were running with great excitement behind them.

They came to the County Road, but just as they were about to cross it, they were blinded by headlights; but fortunately the pickup stopped and they ran off north into the darkness. The men in the pickup had guessed that the race would go this way, and they were as excited as the hounds and almost in ecstasies when the pack crossed the road, hot on the trail; then, not daring to turn off the road, they sped at sixty miles an hour in order to get to a crossroad so that they could see the coyotes and the hounds again.

As the coyotes crossed the divide between Bird Creek and Sand Creek, their tongues were out and their fright was effecting their cunning as well as their speed. Lineback had left his brother a quarter of a mile behind by this time, and the brother, almost exhausted, turned down a ravine that flowed into Sand Creek.

Lineback could still hear the hounds behind him, at least part of the pack. As he came over a prairie ridge, he could see and smell cattle. They were standing around a salt block. He couldn't see them very well, but his nose led him to them and, as he entered among them, several swung around and faced him and several followed him a short distance, bawling. He paid no attention to them but kept on and came to the pond where they had been standing previously, and here he stopped for a moment to lap up some water; then he loped on down the ravine. He stopped. He was panting so hard he made a noise in his throat, and his front legs shivered. He climbed a little way up among the rocks of the ravine's side and there flopped down heavily. His panting interfered both with his hearing and his scenting, so he had to close his mouth on his lolling tongue and, with his ears forward, listen and point his nose toward his back trail. He could do this only for a moment before he had to break into a gurgling pant again.

He would rest and wait until the hounds were started down the ravine; then he would run on, so he closed his mouth at short intervals and listened with ears forward and held his nose high.

He heard the hounds as they came to the herd of cattle, and they were in full cry; then, with every nerve taut, he waited, but they came no closer than the pond. The cattle had milled there as well as around the salt block all the afternoon and into the night, and the earth where they had trampled was hot and heavy with beeby scent, and the air above the earth was heavy with the acrid odor of their droppings and the hot odors of their bodies and their slobberings.

The hounds became confused and couldn't find the trail of Lineback beyond the pond. Then the pack song dwindled down to a single forlorn howl of a flop-eared black and tan, and they finally gave up and waded out into the pond and lay down panting with their eyes shut.

Later when the hunters blew their horn, the hounds were too tired to respond, so they only came out of the water and stretched out in the grass and went to sleep.

Lineback could hear the faraway horn for several hours, but it came no closer, and his instinct must have told him it was no enemy, so he stretched his chin out on the grass and went to sleep.

He never saw his brother again.

During his second winter Lineback found a lying-up place on the rim of Cedar Canyon, where he could see in every direction except north, but since the winds of winter were chiefly from the north, he needed no view in that direction. He got every scent that the north winds bore that winter. Several times he had to leave his bed in a growth of sumac and slink down the canyon.

Bird dogs would range over the timbered hills and the ravines and canyons, and he lay quietly and watched them and the hunters stumbling along and felt relief when they had gone down the creek. He had no fear of bird dogs, since he could distinguish between them and trail hounds, and certainly he knew the difference between them and the high-backed running hounds. As for the hunters, he had no fear at all, but he avoided them.

Twice, however, he had slunk out of his day bed and had crept down the canyon, stopping to stand in plain view on the other side of the canyon, watching both men and dogs without either of them being aware of him. He was careless about his trail, knowing that the dogs would only stop momentarily to sniff at it while the hunters would never know that there was a coyote within a mile of them.

This second winter he howled often, alone. When as a whelp he had first left the den to hunt on his own, he stayed in trailing distance of his mother, but one day he had got lost from her and his brother, and he had stood on the prairie and cried from loneliness. Now in midwinter, especially when the earth was white with snow, he would stand black against the star-brightened snow and with muzzle to the sky howl like a mountain wolf. Sometimes he would meet with others and he would approach them and they would all touch noses and wag their tails lazily, not with dog-like enthusiasm; then, as if directed by some ghostly director, they would start their song. They would stop suddenly and each go off on his own business.

During this second winter of his life, he never saw his mother or his father, and he had no ties whatever, but when February came, with its mud and its dripping ugliness, he was filled with a strange excitement, and his howling had a strange lilting carelessness in it, almost like laughter.

He would go to his lying-up place on the edge of Cedar Canyon, after his night's hunting, and he would lie with his eyes half shut, but his senses were alert always. He missed no sound or movement or odor, and usually he stayed here the whole day, at least on clear days, and only hunted during the days when there was a mizzle or lazy flakes of snow.

But now in his second winter, in this love moon of the coyotes, he was driven by a deep urge. He would come to his lying-up place, early in the mornings, and perhaps fall asleep for a short time; then he would get up and turn around several times, like a dog making his bed in the leaves. He would lie down again with a contented look in his face; then the urge would come upon him, and he was compelled to leave the day bed and wolf-trot up onto the prairie, and when he came onto the prairie, there was a force pulling him toward a United States Geological Survey pin that marked the center of Section 12, and which would have been a corner of some neat little farmstead if the land had not been ranch land.

He approached the survey pin, with his tail hanging down in coyote fashion, to be bumped by the movements of his hind legs as he walked. On reaching the pin, he stood for some time "reading" the messages. Here and at other places, such as fence posts, and lone trees on the prairie and uptilted limestone, the wolf tribe would leave their messages in musk. Sometimes a trail hound, after losing the trail and becoming separated from the pack, would visit the pin and leave his message, and often a high-backed grey-hound-staghound cross of the ranch pack would stop in his graceful wolf trot home, to learn the "news" and leave his own message.

All these things Lineback could read, and if you had been watching him, you would have understood whether or not the news he received was pleasant or unpleasant by the slightest movement of his tail.

On this day of thawing snow during February, the love moon, he became excited and his rag-like tail moved ever so slowly and actually lifted a little.

He stood for some time; then he circled the pin, and with nose to the wonderfully scented earth, he wolf-trotted to the north, just at noon. The trail he followed was strong and very easy to follow, not only because the earth was damp with the thaw, but because the scent itself was especially strong and even clung to the dead broomweeds and the bloom stalks of the bluestem.

When he arrived on the flank of Prairie Chicken Hill, he stopped and nosed the grass, making a circle. His nose told him an unpleasant truth—that the female scent he was following was joined by another. In his circling he found the message of a male coyote on a broomweed. In fact, a warning.

He could only express his annoyance by pointing his nose upward and howling his unhappiness to the grey sky. He stood for some time, looking over the horizons; then he trotted on, following the trail of the female and the other male.

After trailing for two hours, he found himself on the breaks of Dog Creek. He stopped again and now his tongue was hanging out a little, and he began to whimper, like a disturbed dog. Then again he raised his nose and sang his song of bafflement to the unheeding grey sky. He trotted on, then stopped suddenly and gazed to the south.

There against the skyline were two hunters and at the heels of their horses were the high-backed hounds, following stupidly, not even attempting to see a coyote, depending on their hunting companions, the horsemen.

The high-backed hounds were not trail hounds, and he had no worry about their finding his trail, but he must remain invisible. He forgot all about the thrilling trail he had been following, and sank very, very slowly to the earth, hidden now by the tall bluestem which, in its winter terra-cotta phase, was perfect protection. But he must watch the hunters, and he pushed some of the tall bluestem aside with his nose and lay with cocked ears and waited.

As the horsemen and the hounds approached, there was of course no talking between the men, and the hounds trotted along behind the horses with their eyes down, stepping aside occasionally to investigate some scent that had been wafted to them, or to investigate some movement or the spot from which a meadowlark had lifted. They never made casts for a scent trail and always came back to fall in line behind the horses.

Lineback watched the hunters as they approached and it appeared that they might be coming too close, so he rose and, with his belly close to the earth, he slunk down the flank of the hill into a ravine, then in the water-course, keeping low, made for the head. When he arrived at the head of the ravine, he slunk to the divide, and here he turned to watch the hunters. They would not come his way, but they came quite close to where he had lain watching them without the stupid running hounds getting his scent to at least put the hunters on the alert by their actions, even if they couldn't trail.

He felt safe now and now curiosity took control and he allowed himself to stand upright so that he could see better. The hunters rode on, facing north and watching straight ahead, and he stood to the west of them.

Then one of the horses saw him and threw its head up and gazed at him. The hunters stopped and looked and the hounds raised their heads and, even though looking in his direction, couldn't see him. Now it was time to go, so he slipped over the divide and trotted down the ravine on the other side.

The hunters would have missed the statuesque coyote watching them if Peg hadn't seen him, and Sammy was filled with pride; when he saw Sheb looking at her with interest as they rode along in a lope, he could scarcely keep from boasting. They knew the pattern; the quarry would trot casually to the next ridge, then look back to see if the hunters were following and, if so, how close they might be. Coyotes seemed to be never quite sure that the hunters were serious. This perhaps had to do with self-confidence and racial memories and many other things. In their racial memories there was no enemy on the prairie able to outrun them, and they had not yet adjusted their instincts to the fact that the man-animal had introduced a high-backed animal that could match them in their great speed. But there was still racial memory confidence that they had more than their speed; they could almost always rely on their protective coloring. They could lie down or sit down and look exactly like a clump of weeds or bluestem grass or a sandstone rock.

This lack of adjustment to new conditions was a boon to coyote hunters. While Lineback was taking his time up the ravine, stopping often to look back, Sammy and Sheb were loping their horses up to the point where he had stood. Peg was fighting her bit and the hounds were stepping high and with heads high were looking forward.

When the hunters reached the top of the ridge where Lineback had stood, he had not yet come to the second ridge, so they all saw him as he speeded up on seeing them against the skyline. Peg shook her head and, throwing her slobbers, leapt forward. Even Sheb's workaday cow horse caught the spirit, and they were off.

Sammy had not worried about their quarry being Lineback since he had seen him only at a distance and this was not his range and they were far away from Cedar Canyon. He didn't know about the wanderings of lovesick coyotes.

Lineback ran down the flank of the ridge, then up the ravine, and when he arrived at the third ridge, he kept its crest. The hounds were running beautifully and gaining on the coyote, and Sheb became excited and shouted over the pounding of hooves, "Wouldn't be surprised if it's a wolf—look at the size of 'im."

Sammy felt a pang of unhappiness just for the moment; then he immediately convinced himself that this was not Lineback's range and that Cedar Canyon was several miles to the southwest. It was easy to see nevertheless that the quarry was bearing southwest, running the ridges in plain sight.

The hounds were gaining but slowly, and already Sheb's cow horse had begun to huff, huff, and even Peg was tiring, despite the fact that her flaxen tail stood straight out like a banner and her flaxen mane whipped Sammy's face as he stood in the stirrups.

The hunt had to halt at a barbed wire fence, and as they walked their blowing horse to a gate, one of the hounds came limping up to them, having run into the lower strand of the fence. The hunt was ended for Sheb and Sammy; by the time they had gone through the gate, they could never hope to catch up to the hounds, so they stopped on a high hill and got off their horses, dropped the reins, and sat in the grass and waited. The horses' bellies were moving like bellows.

During this time Lineback was running for his life. He didn't dare even look back over his shoulder, and anyway he could sense the closeness of the hounds running silently. He knew how close trail hounds were by the volume of their voices, but running hounds gave no voice. He ran down into the Sand Creek bottoms and ran up the bank looking for a place to cross. He had no fox tricks in his racial memories about water-killing a scent trail, especially through swimming. Also, wet hair would have weighted him down. And anyway his pursuers were hunting by sight and what good would water be to him if they kept him in sight, and they had kept him in sight.

As he reached the divide between Bird and Sand Creeks, he was almost beaten. The earth that had thawed under the day's sun was now refreezing and this made the going even more difficult. His feet were now heavy with muck, and the trees and rocks of Cedar Canyon were still far away, and just behind Lineback was Ole Buck, the three-quarters staghound, snapping at the long hairs of his hind legs. There were only two of the pack in view now. With any other two members of the pack Lineback might have been able to hold his own in a fight, but if one of the two were Ole Buck, there would be no hope for him, despite his youth and his great size. Miss Blue, the other hound who would be in on the kill, was part whippet and the fastest member of the pack when the running was not too heavy.

Lineback's heart was pounding within his chest as though it might wish to leave his body to escape the death that seemed sure, and now he felt Ole Buck snapping at his long upper shank hairs, definitely, and he whisked his mud-heavy tail in a circle, momentarily blinding Ole Buck. As he did this, he turned sharply at right angles and Ole Buck rushed past him and crashed into the running oaks of the Bird Creek floodplain. By the time he recovered, Lineback was completely lost in the running oaks, the leaves of which were exactly the terra-cotta color of his coat.

Ole Buck walked about with head high trying to locate his quarry, and when Miss Blue came up with him, they both stood high-headed looking about them, paying no attention whatever to the hot scent that Lineback had left. They were running hounds who hunted by sight, not by their noses.

Their tongues were out and they panted with throat noises, so they flopped with groans to rest.

Lineback had kept going down the creek's floodplain, completely protected by the color of the running oaks' leaves and by their height of three or four feet. They had been friends in his tragic need.

He was almost too tired to climb halfway up the flank of the ridge on the other side of the creek, but he had to do it. He must not rest until he could have a clear view of the running oaks through which he had come. He lay there panting for an hour, with his ears cocked toward the direction from which he had come.

That night the hounds came to the ranch house, singly and in pairs, and Sammy examined the white chest hairs of each one of them for blood. When he found none, he was strangely happy. He knew now that Lineback was the object of the afternoon's race since their coyote was not an ordinary coyote.

It is doubtful if racial memories had guided Lineback to the running oaks, but the next time he was the object of a race, it was experience that guided him, and very naturally, he became famous in the next several years, and Sammy's name stuck. He became "Ole Lineback," and every owner of running hounds in the country tried for him, but he always sought refuge in the rock-strewn canyons where the running oaks grew.

He had learned how to evade trail hounds. He ran among cattle herds lazily ruminating on the prairie and killed his scent, and one time he ran through a herd of range horses, and being frightened or pretending to be frightened, they ran along with him, one of them playfully kicking at him. This drowned his scent completely.

Also he had another way of killing his scent and in this he was guided by racial memory again. When he set out for the night's hunting, he would visit the carcass of a bull that had been killed by a rival and he would roll in the rancid rib cage, he and others having eaten most of the flesh. Now there was not much chance for the trail hound to get wind of him since he masqueraded his scent: they *must* cross his trail. Semi-fresh cow droppings were better, in which to roll himself in order to kill his scent, since hounds would not have the least interest in the odor of cow droppings.

Running before the trail hounds was never so frightening as running before the running hounds. He was so full of the joy of living that he sometimes enjoyed a race with the trail hounds. At least Sammy held this theory. He knew the mountain-wolf voice of Ole Lineback just as everybody knew it; you couldn't mistake it. He reasoned then that if he didn't sometimes enjoy the race with trail hounds, why did he swear at them? After the hounds had been mouthing for several hours, you could suddenly hear the bass challenge of Ole Lineback from the point of a ridge south of the ranch house.

Sammy didn't know that, when Ole Lineback's mate or one of his whelps of the year were being run by the hounds, he would cross the trail and show himself, and if this didn't turn the hounds from his mate or one of the whelps, he would stay close to them; then during a lull in the mouthing, he would howl close by to attract attention to himself.

Trail hounds were much more friendly than running hounds. One morning while Ole Lineback and his mate were tearing at a steer carcass, a sad-faced trail hound appeared. He stood apologetically and very stupidly, and waved his tail slightly. He was lost from the pack of the night before and he was limping and very hungry. Lineback looked at him for a moment, then advanced toward him, holding his head very low, with his tail close and with the hair of his body erected. This was the coyote bluff posture, and apparently the hound understood it since he turned and limped away with the point of his tail touching his belly.

Trail hounds were to be feared only when they were on the trail and mouthing, but the staghound-greyhound cross were to be avoided at all times, even when alone and limping and lost. They would overrun and kill anything that would run from them in the form of cats, dogs, or wolves.

But Ole Lineback and his mate paid no attention to bird dogs, except when they got too close to their den; then the mother, who was always close, would run them off.

One day the ranch bird dog came nosing about within fifty yards of the den, and Lineback's mate saw him. She lowered her head and raised the hair along her back and advanced toward him, but the bird dog only stood and watched her advance and began to bark excitedly. The mother kept advancing with head low and eyes turned up to the dog. He ran a short distance and stopped again. He misread the bluff. It meant that he must run away from the coyote's den and never, never, come near again. The mother coyote became angered, and every hair on her body stood out until she looked like an angry porcupine, and with her tail straight out and fluffed like a great swab, she ran at the bird dog. He turned and, with tail between his legs, ran hard for the ranch house, with the mother coyote just behind him. She could easily have outrun him and caught him, and perhaps killed him, but why do this when her bluff was working so splendidly. Spot, the bird dog, expected to be killed momentarily, however.

This ridiculous race ended at the horse trap, but only for the mother coyote; Spot ran on and crawled under the porch.

When the whelps were young in early summer, Lineback and his mate worked well together, and even during February, a time when he was not always a faithful mate, often trailing other females. However, he would hunt for the mother and the whelps and often bring home a rabbit or a chicken. It was in February, the coyotes' love moon, that they got their bad reputation for calf killing.

Sometimes the cows would give birth to weaklings, and they were never able to rise to their feet to suckle. The wise pair knew about such calves, and when they came upon a range cow standing over a sick calf, they sat in the grass and waited for it to die; then they must wait for the cow to leave before they could feast. When these carcasses were found, Sammy's father and other ranchers jumped to conclusions and cursed all coyotes as eternal enemies. But when an agency of the Federal Government who had to do with such matters as varmint control suggested that they place chunks of poisoned horse meat here and there on his ranch, he thought of his hounds and rejected the plan.

But these energetic people in the spirit of efficiency placed chunks elsewhere in a twenty-mile radius. They placed these poisoned chunks in February, knowing that the coyotes would be wandering over an extensive area.

Racial memory couldn't protect Lineback since there had been no such planned poisoning in the history of the species, before man. When Lineback and a young female were trotting together across the prairie one February night, her nose led them to a chunk of the poisoned horse meat. He only tasted of it, but she was hungry and feasted. Later when they trotted off together, she became thirsty and led them to water. After lapping water, she turned and fell, then crawled on her belly into the weeds and died.

Lineback became ill, but before he could go back to the pond to quench his thirst, he heard the trail hounds. He ran hard for a short time, then became very sick. He stopped and vomited, then lay down for a short time and then ran on. After he had vomited, he felt better and easily eluded his trailers.

The next day he was well again, but the hounds never returned to their master, who had paid no attention to the notice in Spanish and English that poison meat had been put out.

The next time Lineback came across a chunk of horse meat, Experience was at his side holding up a warning hand, and he only sniffed it and left a musk message on it. Now trail hounds and running hounds and poison were futile against him.

His fame grew with the years; then one day when Sheb was riding the west line he saw a dead coyote. He got off his horse and kicked it, and the body was still flexible. He turned it over and there was a black line down its back. He picked the body up and hung it from the corner post, again in view of the County Road. This was truly an important boast since Lineback's nose almost touched the ground.

A short distance from where he had found Lineback's body, Sheb solved the riddle of his death. The earth had been disturbed where Lineback had dug down to a "cyanide gun." He had dug down to the strong love musk of a female, and this was February again, the love moon. He had tugged at the cotton, and when it had come out, the cyanide exploded into his mouth and he had died within a few yards.

There had been neither Racial Memory nor Experience to hold up a warning hand, but that night within a quarter of a mile from where he hung, the coyote chorus began in a long-drawn-out yelp, then reached its apex in a jolly, rollicking, lilting song that sounded very much like laughter.

Grus, The Sandhill Crane

H E WAS HATCHED IN MAY in Saskatchewan, Canada. He was of the species of crane called the Greater Sandhill Crane, and the scientific name for the species is *Grus tabida*, and since he was destined to play a very important part in the world of aviation, he surely deserves to be called Grus.

He was not noticeably larger than other baby cranes, and he bore no distinctive markings and was not more clever than others hatched that year or any other year, but his distinction would be great.

His parents had come all the way from Mexico where they had spent the winter, and they had found a perfect place to make their nest among the reeds and sedges and muskeg among the marshes that bordered a wild lake on the prairie. There were a few stunted birch trees and tall reeds and that was all in this great expanse of sky and prairie.

His parents took turns brooding the two buffy-olive eggs spotted with purple and black dots. One would brood for several hours and then the other would come to relieve, and this went on for twenty-eight days.

During that time the parents had to be ever on guard. The nest was built on a bit of raised earth surrounded by waters of the marsh and it wasn't much of a nest. There were sedge and cattail stems and reeds and arrowhead plants, which formed a very untidy little platform, and the platform was protected by the same type of growths. You might have thought after looking at the carelessly built nest that the parents weren't much interested in nest and eggs.

But they were. They weren't worried about their neighbors, the redwing blackbirds and the marsh hawks and the Canadian geese and mallards. As a matter of fact, the redwings and the marsh hawks were much more worried about their neighbors, the sandhill cranes, than the crane family could worry about them. The parents of Grus had never annoyed either the redwing or the marsh hawk, but the two species had a racial memory of egg-eating and nestling-eating sandhill cranes. So when one or the other of the cranes flew low over the marsh to relieve the one on the eggs, the marsh hawk would fly just above him, darting occasionally, in order to keep him going across the marsh and away from his own eggs. The redwing didn't seem to have much reason for his racial fear since he built his nest in the swaying reeds, often above the notice of the ground feeding of the tall cranes, while the hawk made his nest on the ground and the cranes might fly over it and spot it at any hour.

Whichever crane was on the eggs, he or she would sit with head high, just showing above the reeds and sedge, and note everything that moved. But if he or she saw or heard something and knew it to be dangerous, the brooder would lower the head and stretch the neck so that it lay flat; then when the danger was quite near, the parent who happened to be on the eggs at the time would rise and walk off the nest and run through the shallow water of the marsh and pretend to be crippled, with one wing hanging and one leg seeming to be too weak to support the bird. This often deceived a fox or a coyote or a wandering dog, and they would give chase, and when the crane was far enough away from the nest, it would fly and flap over the marsh, away from the nest, sometimes making a sound like a feeble young one, again inspiring hope in its enemies.

There was not much danger from coyotes or exploring dogs since they usually preferred to do their hunting or their exploring on dry land and shunned the marsh water. The fox would not go into the water to hunt, if there had been foxes there. And anyway the cranes had a way of dealing with foxes; they would lower their heads, spread their wings and make them quiver, and walk boldly toward the fox, their dagger-like beaks thrust forward. This bluff usually worked.

After twenty-eight days, Grus and his nest mate were hatched, and they were little balls of down stuck on stilts. Their legs were long and couldn't support their weight until twenty-four hours had passed. However, if the parents had been disturbed much by dogs and coyotes or even men, they would lead the little ones from the platform they called a nest and hide them in the rushes. If the water of the marsh had risen a little, they swam across to a little peninsula. They didn't need to be taught to swim; this was a racial memory. Many millions of little balls of down on stilts had been hatched on a platform of sedge and sticks, surrounded by marsh water, and this necessity and ability was deep in their racial memory.

The parents of Grus and his nest mate led them to the land that bordered the marsh and there they found grasshoppers and earthworms and spiders and tubers and sometimes the parents would catch a frog and beat it into little pieces and give the pieces to the little ones.

But here on dry land they had to be more cautious. The coyotes would hunt here, and one or the other of the parents would stand with his head high above the reeds and grasses, and even above the stunted birch, alertly on guard.

The food was plentiful and there seemed to be few enemies. The man-animal was growing things far away, and he had no towns near. There was only a rare golden eagle and a few hunting coyotes and the wolves came seldom and not in family groups now since their whelps were too young to hunt, and they travelled across the prairies as if they had something in mind. They stopped to nose here and there, then went on in their tireless wolf trot, not stopping to make a thorough hunt. The parents of Grus and his nest mate had been nesting in this territory every spring for several years and they had never seen a wolf, only coyotes and eagles, and rarely a man-animal.

The family of four sandhill cranes had every reason to be happy, and they were. They couldn't sing to express their happiness, like songbirds, or even make running-water sounds like the redwing, or whistle sadly like the curlew, but they could dance. They danced on every occasion, like the Masai warriors of Kenya in Africa, not only in the spring during the mating season like the prairie chicken and the sharptail grouse. It was far from a quiet expression of the joy of being alive, but yet had the dignity of a minuet.

One morning the parents of Grus began to dance. His father bowed and danced around his mother, and as he did so he picked up a reed stem and almost touched the ground with it; then he spread his wings and tossed the stem into the air and caught it as it descended. His mother flapped six or eight feet into the air and, with her neck stiff and held back over her body, feet dangling, wings balancing her, she sang the only song she knew: "Th-RR-RR-RR—Ga-Er-Er-Ga-ER-ER."

Then as she landed, having floated down like a parachute, her mate jumped into the air and with neck stiff and backward-slanted, almost over his tail, he flew over her and landed on the other side and bounced like a rubber ball.

Then they stood still for a moment, as if they thought this display a bit too frivolous in the presence of their young ones. Maybe they stood motionless for a moment to determine whether their joy-dance had attracted the attention of some enemy.

Suddenly again the father picked up several dead reed stems and again bowed low with his beak almost touching the ground; then as his mate raised her head with beak pointing to the sky and with drooped wings, he threw the stems into the air and caught them as they came down and they flew up to six or eight feet together, with their necks so far back that it seemed they might become unbalanced backward.

A mockingbird in the southern edges of his range, when he has not seen fit to migrate farther south, will utter sad little notes from his refuge in a cedar when the ground is covered with snow, and a tanager in his winter home in the tropics will sing sad little songs of bright summer memories, but the sandhill crane will dance with the same joyousness the year round, and unexpectedly. His dance is graceful and courtly.

Grus and his nest mate had watched their parents dance, but they had no urge to try in imitation as they might have imitated them in many other activities. But one late afternoon, before the four waded out into the marsh to stand and sleep the night through almost "knee" deep in water, a tremendous thrill came over Grus; his blood surged with emotion, and he had to dance. He was a little more than a month old, and his wings were nothing more than downy tabs with blood quills that weighted them so that he must allow them to hang at his sides. His legs were long now and his "knees" were large knobs. There were a few blood quills in his tail and his body was still covered by down, with the breast feathers just beginning to show.

He spread his ridiculous wing tabs and flapped the blood quills and ran with his head high and his beak pointing to the sky. As he ran on his stilt-like legs, he tried to jump, but couldn't get off the ground. He stabbed a fallen birch leaf with his beak and tried to toss it into the air, but it wouldn't leave his beak and finally, when he did succeed in tossing it and tried to catch it in midair, it floated away from him.

But he kept on dancing with his quill-heavy wing tabs flapping and his long legs lifting his body no more than a foot off the ground and his ridiculous head far back over his body and his beak pointing to the sky.

Soon his nest mate joined him, and they danced until their parents gave the alarm signal and they froze where they stood; then the parents called them and they hurried out into the edge of the marsh.

The days passed. The redwings had stopped singing and they had begun to flock and talked like people before the opening of a town meeting. The crows began to flock. The young mallards would take wing and fly about over the lakes and the marshes in pre-migration training, and the young geese would stand and work their wings for minutes, preparing for the long flight southward.

And now in September the sandhill crane families from all over the province had begun to join other families and soon there were flocks of cranes, flying high above the marshes, flying in circles like roller skaters, and their trumpeting floated down from the sky, and you couldn't know whence it came. It even seemed to come out of the marshes at times. This call of the sandhill crane was not in the least beautiful, but it was wild and fascinating, and when it floated down from the clouds from hundreds of throats, it truly was the thrilling voice of the solitude of the wilderness and inspired you to vague happiness.

Around and round they flapped or sailed far above the marshes, trumpeting. They could sail for minutes with no objective whatever. Not only did Grus and his nest mate join hundreds of other May- and June-hatched birds in training for the southward migration, but the old birds joined them in circling, side slipping, sailing, and trumpeting their happiness in being alive.

The mallards and the geese had purpose in their flights, and the yellow-headed and the redwing blackbirds came together in flocks and they certainly had purpose, judging from the manner in which they chattered, but the cranes seemed to be playing some game and were as purposeless as school-yard children.

Then one day in October, Grus and his family, along with hundreds of other cranes, left the marshes. They had circled and trumpeted for several hours above the marshes; then they flapped and sailed south, and there seemed to be no leader. They formed into a V, something on the order of the Canadian geese formation; then almost immediately they fell into what looked very much like disorder, and some of them circled and some side-slipped and some allowed their legs to dangle momentarily, but they soon lifted them and flew or sailed on as cranes should fly, with neck stretched out and legs straight out behind them.

They were often seen against the sky like great pieces of paper floating high above a tornado, and sometimes the migrants took the form of a kite string that had been severed high above the earth; then soon they would flock like blackbirds. But on and on they flew south at about thirty-five miles an hour, hour after hour. Far below them was the autumn-touched earth, and lakes and rivers that looked white, and yellow sand hills and bro-ken earth that cast inky shadows, and the yellow of the hackberries and the cottonwoods and the willows made the streams into yellow arteries of the earth.

Since they flew over the Great Plains, they saw few flaming maples and no yellow aspen, but that group of the migrants who turned southwest and flew over the Rockies and the Sierra Nevadas to the San Joaquin Valley of California saw the golden aspen and the red mountain maples that looked from their altitude like blood-oozing wounds in the mountainsides.

But Grus and his family flew with those that kept to the Great Plains. Sometimes they rested during the day on some marsh or wet prairie. The Platte River of Nebraska had some good stopping places since it was flat and wide and white like a crinkled, frazzled silver ribbon that had been dropped carelessly among the sand hills.

Sometimes they traveled at night, and there were interested people in Saskatchewan, the Dakotas, Nebraska, Kansas, Oklahoma, Texas, and

Chihuahua who sat through the night under their flyway, with telescopes and binoculars, hoping to see them against the moon.

Over Kansas they ran into a storm and they lifted higher and higher and were finally flying at fourteen thousand feet over the prairie-plains, and the farmers and ranchmen of Kansas might hear their trumpeting even through the clouds.

Again the flock split and part of them flew southwesterly to New Mexico to winter near Bitter Lake and some dropped off in the Panhandle of Texas to spend a pleasant winter at the Muleshoe Refuge. But Grus and his family with others flew on to Mexico and finally settled on a very large rancho in the state of Chihuahua. Here was grain and water, but the man-animal had a different attitude, and he sent boys out into the fields to scare them away. Men sometimes shot at them, but they were never allowed to get within shotgun range. The sentinels, with their necks stretched, stood watching while the others ate. Sometimes they didn't even have to fly but could walk away, just keeping out of range of the shotguns.

They flew from the marshy artificial lakes each morning at sunrise to the grain fields, circling, trumpeting, sailing, dipping, seeming not even interested in the very serious business of eating. There were always many on the ground, and as many in the air over them, playing some aerial game.

After they had fed, they flew back to their lake edges and there preened and rested until about 4 P.M.; then they went to the fields again.

And, despite this hard business of living with shotguns in the hands of optimistic Mexicans and despite coyotes and golden eagles and hungry people who knew their roasted excellence, they played daily in the sky and danced even as they foraged in the fields, or some of them suddenly awakened from their preening or dreaming at the lake's edge and started dancing.

In the fields, Grus and the others would suddenly stop eating and stand like painted cranes on a canvas or a screen, in a long line, all facing the same direction. Two or maybe five would drop from the sky and set their wings to land among the statuesque ones, and immediately a dozen or more of these would bounce into the air, with stiff necks slanted backward and with dangling legs, and fly over several of the others, landing and then bouncing. Several would pick up sticks or wisps of grass and throw them into the air after bowing to their nearest neighbor, all the while croaking.

Grus had a faint little baby squeak in his voice yet, and among the coarser croaks or trumpeting you could distinguish the current year's birds.

Grus was as tall as his father and was from all appearances just an ordinary Greater Sandhill Crane. There was nothing to distinguish him from the hundreds of others as they foraged or preened or danced. There was no distinguishing white feather in his wing, nor was he taller or stronger or more alert or more courageous, nor could he dance with more vigor or grace or with more joy than the others so that he might be more conspicuous than other sandhill cranes. Nevertheless he was a bird of destiny.

During the latter days of February and through the early days of March, the great flocks became restless, and they flew up and circled aimlessly high against the sky and among the spring clouds, and they danced even more, during longer periods and with more enthusiasm.

Then one day, after circling and dipping and sailing for hours, they all floated and sailed and circled away to the north.

Cranes from the Muleshoe Refuge joined them as did birds from Bitter Lake in New Mexico, and they flew on in groups of perhaps several hundred birds.

The Spanish oaks of Texas were greening, and there was green among the red hills of the Red River, making a beautiful pattern. There were great emerald blankets of wheat in the Panhandle of Texas and in western Oklahoma, but they didn't stop. They flew over Kansas with its arterial system of rivers now yellow-green, almost smoky, as their trees dominated them.

Then one day the silver, crinkled, raveled ribbon that was the Platte River with its fringe of elms and willows and cottonwoods lay under them. Its brightness in the sun and in the moonlight made the sand hills that bordered it seem even more sterile and brown.

Now they circled high over the village of Elm Creek and the town of Overton, Nebraska, and high over the stream of cars along Highway 30. From the height of eight and ten thousand feet and from three thousand to two hundred feet, they circled and trumpeted, but the cars sped along the highway not even knowing that the sky above them was filled with cranes. The people of the village of Elm Creek sold their bread and their potatoes and their gasoline, and the truck drivers from the south kept their eyes on the road. The farmers and stockmen went about their business with the din of the circling cranes in their ears, and to them it was ordinary and natural, like the winds of spring.

Grus and his family circled with the thousands of others, and they landed with legs outstretched and wings like parachutes and sometimes bounced a little or ran several steps. They walked in great dignity with their heads high, or searched for cutworms or grain left from last season's harvesting, and they danced with high emotion. They suddenly began dancing in the fields as they foraged, and they would just as suddenly start dancing during their rest periods in the middle of the day. They stood in the fields in long statuesque lines, and when others came to alight with them, several dozen of them began to dance, picking up sticks and straw and bowing, then flying up stiff-necked and hopping over each other to land and bounce, all the time trumpeting.

This was the mating season, and the paired ones as well as the not-yet-paired ones were in a fever of emotion. However, Grus and the near yearlings felt no fever of mating. They danced with the usual enthusiasm and fed greedily on cutworms and scattered grain, but they stayed with their parents, who were concerned now only with their own emotions.

There is no bird more wary and solitary than the sandhill crane, and he seeks the wilderness of great marshes and wetlands for his nesting and walks sedately away from danger or flies from it croaking and, from his great height standing, watches for enemies, yet for one week or more in his life, he stops among the sand hills on the floodplains of the Platte River of Nebraska to dance his mating dances, in sight of a great highway with cars speeding along both ways, in sight of great white farmhouses and red barns, only a short distance from a lively village. It is like the ancient Indian sanctuaries of the pipestone quarries in Minnesota and the Great Salt Plains in Oklahoma. There seems to be an understanding among sandhill cranes, as well as between man and sandhill cranes.

After a week of ecstatic dancing and joyous flocking with thousands of other cranes, Grus, his nest mate, and their parents flew on to Saskatchewan. The four landed on their old domain among the reeds and the scrub birch and on the muskeg, and they were the only cranes in all that expanse of marsh, lake, muskeg, and sky again. Grus and his nest mate stood about with no spirit of the spring and nest building, and this seemed to annoy their parents. Either the mother or the father would run at them with head lowered and rapier-like beak thrust out, and the young would be compelled to walk or run away. This went on for several days and between the runs at their young, the old ones built a nest not far from the one they had built last spring. When the nest was completed, the parents became more short-tempered and doubled the harassment of their young.

One morning, the two young cranes stood for some time; then they danced for perhaps three minutes; then as if it had all been pre-arranged, they ran a few steps and lifted into the air. This time they flapped to the south, and for reasons unknown to themselves, they veered to the east; then on the third day, after resting on the way, they saw below them a great flock of cranes. They circled trumpeting and those from the ground answered them and as they came near to land, the flock began dancing excitedly. The newcomers landed and from that moment became members of a flock of yearlings, who would not mate until their second year.

They foraged and they rested and preened and danced, but they had only the joy of living and none of the fever of mating that made the world about them throb with song. They had flown across the International Border into the state of Michigan.

One morning when five of the yearlings waded out of their marsh and walked to a nearby ridge, they saw a strange object; it was a house trailer pulled by a half truck. There were men about it. The truck was too far away to be a menace, so they foraged grasshoppers and one or two of them caught field mice, hammering them to bits, then throwing each bit into the air and catching it on the descent, allowing it to pass on down the gullet.

They went each morning to this area where they could fill up on grass-hoppers and the bulbs of a certain marsh lily, and one day when they walked leisurely to their feeding area, there was a small brown object, grown like a mushroom overnight. They stopped and watched it intently; then when it made no move to attack them, they moved on but foraged as far away from the little brown object as they could.

In four mornings, the brown object, a pop-tent, had not moved and they finally decided it was harmless, and came closer with confidence. One morning Grus chased a little lizard and lost him in the grassroots; then he cocked his head to one side and listened to the interesting workings of an earthworm, ready to jab the earth with his beak.

Just then, there was a boom, and he was aware of something over him. It was like wind-blown dust or swirling leaves, but there was no wind. He instinctively jumped into the air, but he became entangled and fell to earth struggling, with one of his long legs through the mesh of a great net, and his great wings helplessly entangled. He struggled frantically; then when he saw some man-animals coming, he became still, with his heart pounding.

There were two others of the flock caught under the net with him, and the men came and extricated them very carefully. Grus jabbed at them with his sharp beak, but they finally subdued him and the other two and carried them away. The men had shot the net out a little specially made cannon, and it had dropped over the three cranes.

After being jolted in a truck most of the day, and then kept bound in the darkness of a little house, the three cranes were taken to a very large cage with a very high ceiling and there released.

The ceiling was of strong fish netting and when they flew up to escape, they were thrown back. They were fed on cornflakes and lizards and meat balls and kaffir and millet, and the water ran constantly through their cage, but always there were man-animals watching them, and they became used to the churr of cinema cameras and the click of still cameras.

The three of them grew fat and lazy that winter and the man-animals became as trees to them, but March came, and this was their second year and there was a queer thrill that came over them. Grus stood long like a statue with head turned and one eye searching the sky. Then they began their mating dances, and at that moment when one of them was suspended above the others, like a parachute momentarily stopped on its floating descent, the man-animals grew tense and shouted to each other, and all the cameras pointed toward them into the cage began to churr and click.

When the high-speed motion pictures were projected in the great, shiny projecting room, grave men shook hands with each other and went with their films and slides to the engineering designing room.

It was the 24th of March when Grus and his companions were released from their prison. They flew high over a great city in a southwesterly direction, and within a day's time, they saw the silver ribbon of the Platte below them. They circled and trumpeted, and when they were just above the long grey line of resting cranes, part of the line became excited and began to dance.

That spring Grus found a mate, and they flew off to Saskatchewan, but for several days she kept pecking at the band on his stilt-like leg, but finally grew accustomed to it even if it did flash in the sun. Engraved on it were the letters "N.E.D." and following this, the blurred date, and then, quite clearly on the second line: "Grus tabida." The pictures of Grus had been the ones that had been sent to the aeronautical engineers, and from these pictures they devised a system of tiny holes along the leading edges of the wingtips of jets through which high-speed jets of air from a compressor attached to the turbine can send a high-speed flow of air and which has the same effect as the spreading of the tip of the wing feathers of Grus on landing, increasing lift and resistance. So that the jets can land with much less speed and within much shorter distance than before Grus gave the aeronautical engineer a hint.

Alfredo and the Jaguar

ALFREDO LIVED WITH HIS FATHER and mother and sisters and baby brother in a house with a grass roof on the shoulder of the Sierra Madre Mountains in Mexico. The house was perched on the shoulder like an eagle's nest, and they had few visitors. Once a month, Padre Francisco, the priest, came to see them, and to eat with them. He came on his burro and wore sandals, and both summer and winter he wore a black robe. On hot afternoons before starting down the steep trail, he would sit under a tree and fan himself with his stiff-brimmed black hat. Alfredo would stand off and watch him. If he nodded his head, then let it hang over his shoulder or let it fall back against the tree which supported his back, Alfredo would go down to the potato patch and pull the weeds that he and his father could not reach with the hoe.

But if El Padre sat fanning himself on a summer's day, just after the noon meal, and seemed to be planning something as he looked out over the plain below, Alfredo would go to him, and stand until he was noticed; then he would say, "With your permission, Father," and El Padre would say to him, "You may sit, my son." Then El Padre would tell him again of the Boy in a faraway land who had been born in a manger, and later of his wisdom at the temple, but he never quite reached the crucifixion again after the first telling. Alfredo did not want to hear about that again, so he would ask questions to which he knew the answers so that the story would never reach that point.

Alfredo's father would always bring the burro, already saddled, just as the clouds began to shroud the mountains, as they did almost every afternoon. Father Francisco did not like to travel down the steep, twisting trail in the cloud fog.

Then there was the Hacendado, the master of the Big House, the Casa Grande, down on the mesa. This was the Hacienda Santa Rosa and Alfredo's father was a tenant. When Don José came, the Hacendado and his father talked of the horses and other things, but mostly of the horses, and they rode out to see the new colts, and they talked of the jaguar, which everyone called El Tigre.

Don José would ask if El Tigre had come back since killing the colt, and Alfredo's father would answer that he had not, certainly. He would say this in a manner which would indicate that he, Carlos Predregales, had shot El Tigre. His manner indicated that one may be assured that when he, Carlos Predregales, shot things, they died—if not on the spot, then they went very unhappily to die elsewhere. He actually imagined that since there had been no cougar or jaguar down from the mountains to take Don José's colts that El Tigre must certainly have informed all the cougars and jaguars of that part of the savage Sierra Madre Mountains about the mighty noise made by the man who lived on the shoulder of the mountain and which had caused him to die, even as he was warning them.

These stories about El Tigre didn't bother Alfredo in the least, and he carried on with his trips for wood up into the mountains. Three times a week, he would tie the homemade packsaddle on his burro, and he would ride up into the mountains. He would then find broken limbs and chunks of wood, fasten them well on the saddle, and then drive the burro down the trail to the house.

He usually went up in the mornings, before the hot air from the Gulf of Mexico came in contact with the cold air of the mountains and caused a cloud fog and almost always rain. And this was the reason he had no fear of El Tigre since everyone knew that El Tigre, like El Diablo, the devil, hunted at night.

But sometimes he went up in the afternoons, and sometimes rather late, and the clouds would form in the afternoon and the familiar cliffs and trees would not be familiar in the ghostly light; they would be like trees and cliffs in a strange land, and this frightened him a little, and because it frightened him he was thrilled by it, and often let the burro graze on the very green mountain canyon grass, which was much better than the grass near his home since the goats kept it eaten to the earth there. He had even had to drive them some distance from the house so that they could browse and graze, but this was dangerous because the eagles would fall upon the kids and carry them away.

When the clouds made the mountains into a strange land of dreams, most of the birds stopped singing, but there was one which people called *jilguero*, and its song was one of the happiest songs of the mountains. Sometimes when he sat very still with his back against a tree, he could hear the brooklets that the rains fed daily, talking and laughing as they hurried down the watercourses. Almost always as he listened, there was a bird that seemed to be imitating the song of the brooklets. It was as if it had learned its song from the laughing, gurgling brooks. The people called it the *clarín* since it suggested a flute or a trumpet.

Alfredo went to school in the winter at the consolidated school on the mesa, and his teachers there had given him the material upon which many of his dreams were based, and as he sat in the eerie light of the cloud fog, with the heavy silence broken only by the *jilguero* or the *clarín*, he watched the very faint breath of the air very gently wave the moss that hung from the trees. The moss was like the beard of an old man who had come to their school to teach them about snakes. He was an old man and his beard was grey. Alfredo would imagine that he could see this old man without his clothing, lying on a limb, and the moss would be his beard. The old man was an Americano, an American, and the people said he was crazy. His body was very white.

Alfredo was so fascinated by the clouds that were like a fog in the higher mountains that he would go for wood so that he would be in the higher altitudes when the clouds formed. Each time he would stay longer, just sitting, dreaming and watching the waving of the moss which was like the beard of the old Americano. There was moss hanging from many of the trees and soon he imagined an old man in each tree and the moss became their beards. When the clouds came, there were beads of water in the "beards." The bird which he called *clarín* would sing in the ghost light, and the *coa* would sometimes call, but one afternoon, when the cloud fog was very thick and moved through the trees like smoke, he heard another voice. It came from up the canyon, and it sounded very much like the bawl of a bull calf that is just becoming a grown-up bull, like a boy who is just growing into a man and his voice is still squeaky.

He knew there were no young bulls up here in the mountains, but he thought there must be one, certainly. He was thinking, "I must tell my father," when out of the mists came a beautiful animal. He was spotted with rosettes, and he was limping in one front foot. Alfredo was sitting where he usually sat, with his back to a tree, and he was very still so the animal couldn't see him.

But the burro was a little below where the grass was like emerald, eating greedily since he knew soon he would be loaded with wood and he would be driven down the mountain, and he would sniff about over ground where the goats had been, his nose wrinkled with disgust.

Alfredo was fascinated by the great animal, but suddenly he saw him stop and fall to his belly, and he wrinkled his lips, and his long tail writhed like a snake. He had seen the burro.

Poor Macho, the burro, was not very clever. When he was in the mountains, he thought of nothing except grazing and it seemed that he depended on Alfredo to see for him and hear for him and scent danger for him. He could do these things much better than Alfredo because wild animals must be alert every minute of their lives, but poor old Macho had lost the instincts for protecting himself which had been handed down to him from his ancient ancestors. Although Alfredo was only fourteen years old, he was considered a man by all wild animals and birds, and they ran or froze or flew away when he appeared. Macho became accustomed to protection by one from whom things fled.

So poor old Macho kept his nose to the earth grazing, and the large animal lay watching him, and Alfredo was fascinated and frightened at the same time and was afraid to move. He wanted to shout to Macho, or say to the animal, "Go away," but his throat was dry, and he had lost his voice through fear, suddenly. The great animal spotted with rosettes was El Tigre, the jaguar.

El Tigre rushed at Macho and, with one paw over his shoulders and one clutching his throat, he bit through the back of his neck and severed his vertebrae, and poor old Macho kicked a few times and lay still.

Terror came to Alfredo. He ran to the trail and down it. He couldn't run down the steepest parts, but jumped like a buck deer. He lost his sarapé, the blanket-like roll which he carried over his shoulder wherever he went since it was his bed, a raincoat, an overcoat, and a jacket.

He couldn't stop to pick it up, but ran and jumped on down the trail until he could see the grass roof of his home. His father was patching the roof with palmetto leaves, and Alfredo being Indian did not shout, but his father saw him running down from the mountain, and he knew that there must be something terribly amiss.

Carlos Pedregales let himself down from the roof, and Alfredo came up to him with his thin chest pumping, but he came with great dignity and said through his heavy breathing, "My father, I have seen El Tigre."

"El Tigre," questioned his father, "truly?"

"Yes, truly."

Carlos, the father, walked over to a tree and sat down with his back to it so that he could think with clearer thoughts. He thought for some time; then he said to Alfredo, "My son, what has passed is that you have seen not El Tigre, but the devil."

"But," said Alfredo, "does El Diablo bawl like a bull calf?"

"Yes, it is true, he can do that if he wishes."

"Does El Diablo then eat burros?" asked Alfredo.

Carlos's wooden face showed emotion, and he asked with anxiety in his face, "Is it the truth that he eats the burro?"

"Yes," said Alfredo, "even now he eats the burro."

Carlos did not become excited and rush into the house to tell Maria, his wife, but sent Alfredo to get his mule, Mercedes; then he went to tell Maria. A great fear came over her face and she called the little girls, and they each made the sign of the cross, and as Carlos left with his sarapé over his shoulder, the eldest daughter, twelve-year-old Mechy, walked over to the baby as he lay on his back on a pallet and made the sign of the cross over him.

When Carlos arrived at the Casa Grande on the mesa, they told him that El Padre was at the sick bed of Jaime Lobo and couldn't leave, and Carlos was almost in despair when Don José asked him his trouble.

"Then," Don José said, "you did not kill El Tigre with that old rifle, eh? You have but wounded him, and now he can't catch deer and javelinas and must catch that which he can catch."

"It is only that he is dead, and El Diablo has found the body and crawled into it, and my bullet is now burning in his bowels."

"Perhaps," said Don José, "but the man we want now is not El Padre but El Tigrero."

It was true that which Don José said about El Tigre being wounded and unable to hunt his usual prey. El Tigrero knew this as well. He was called El Tigrero because he was a professional jaguar hunter.

The jaguar, after being shot by Carlos months before, had climbed back into the mountains to lie for a day licking his wounded paw, but the ankle bone was broken and when he set out to satisfy his hunger, he could bear no weight on his right front foot and had to walk on his ankle bone. He had lain in wait for some wild turkeys, but when they had come close to his hiding place and he attempted to make his famous rush, he became overbalanced, fell, and rolled over, and the turkeys flew up into the trees and looked down saying "pert, pert" with great wonderment.

When he tried to rush deer, he remembered his ankle, but he was too slow and clumsy and the deer jumped away, waving their white tail flags and blowing through their noses.

So he wandered through the mountain jungle each night, very hungry and very short-tempered. Sometimes he caught a mouse and often he found a great snake trying to look like a limb, but these things could not satisfy the appetite of a great hunter-cat. He prowled the dark jungle trying to find something to eat, limping, and he grew so hungry that he couldn't sleep during the daytime, so began to hunt during the day as well.

He had seen Alfredo several times as he rode his burro up to gather wood, but he had only crouched on an overhanging cliff and watched every movement, his great hunger urging him to attack the burro. He was afraid of men, so he only crouched and watched. When you came near men there was a great blast and pain stung you, so now when he watched Alfredo he only laid back his ears and became more angry at the thought of the terrible gun noise hidden somewhere inside Alfredo.

But the afternoon he killed the burro, his hunger had driven him into a sort of madness and carelessness, and he had limped down the canyon roaring. Then suddenly he came upon the burro, without ever seeing or scenting Alfredo. But in his anger he didn't care and he would have attacked Alfredo as readily.

Alfredo came up into the mountains with El Tigrero to show him where the burro had been killed. He rode behind El Tigrero on his fine bay mare and had been very proud as they left the house since some of the other tenants of Hacienda Santa Rosa had heard and had come to see El Tigrero depart. This made El Tigrero very proud as well, and he was very deliberate and casual in preparing to depart so that everyone would have a chance to see the great Tigrero.

He must give instructions about his hounds, which were to be left at the house, how they should be fed and when, and he kept examining his 12-gauge shotgun, pretending that he must be sure it was ready. He looked at the people watching silently and pointed to his shotgun. "Americano," he said proudly, "a present from an American, very rich," then looked closely into each face to find appreciation there of his greatness.

When the two arrived near the place of the kill, they could see that much was left of the burro, and this is exactly the way El Tigrero wanted it. He was lucky too since there were bushes at the foot of a cliff, within range of his powerful shotgun. He was very serious now and was not showing off when he looked about him, mostly to the front since he would be sitting with his back against the foot of the cliff.

He sent Alfredo back with the mare, then made himself comfortable for the night. An Aztec thrush sang beautifully and he felt a mild happiness. Even an ignorant Tigrero could appreciate the song of the thrush since he was an Indian.

Everything was in his favor; the moon was shining, and he could just make out the dark hump that was the carcass of the poor burro, but nothing whatever happened all night. He was motionless all night, except when he very gently and very slowly moved a leg, ever so little, or shifted ever so slightly his body.

The dawn came and the birds began to sing; the *jilguero*, the *clarín*, and the *coa* called the thrush. Down the canyon, a Mexican jay began his vulgar call, and El Tigrero began to curse the jay's mother under his breath. Jays were gossips and if one saw El Tigrero, he would tell the world of the jungle mountain that there was a strange animal sitting at the foot of the cliff, and this would tell El Tigre that there was danger, and he would make a great circle, until he came downwind; then he would know what the danger was, and his curiosity would compel him to creep slowly, slowly through the bushes, until he could actually see El Tigrero, and he would not show himself, and there could be no shooting of El Tigre.

Then El Tigrero had another thought: What if the jay was telling the world that El Tigre was coming up the canyon? El Tigrero faced down the canyon now, waiting, but the jay stopped his cursing, yet still he waited for El Tigre to come for his breakfast at the burro's carcass.

Hunters of long experience have a sixth sense—the sense that tells them they are being watched or followed—and suddenly El Tigrero was filled with tenseness. The back of his neck was prickling, and he knew. He knew that El Tigre was watching him, and he knew that he was within rushing distance, and he knew if he turned his head to see, El Tigre would spring. As long as he pretended he didn't see him, El Tigre would crouch and wait for movement, certainly until he was discovered, and then he would rush and kill.

El Tigrero was a very clever hunter. He had killed many a bayed jaguar with his spear, making them fall on it as they sprang for him, but now what should he do? He remembered from yesterday that there was a shallow cave to the right rear of his position but he had thought nothing of this, yet now he knew El Tigre was in that cave watching him, waiting. There was a palmetto to the right and even if he were quick enough to swing his gun, the palmetto would interfere and El Tigre would have his fangs in the back of his neck before he could shoot.

He knew that El Tigre didn't want to kill him and that he was really afraid of him, but now El Tigre felt that his life was in danger and he must kill this dangerous man-animal, who could produce the nerve-shattering blast, in order to save his own life, but perhaps the dangerous man would go away and never see him; then he could sneak away and lose himself in the dappled shade of the jungle.

He had not intended to go into this shallow little cave when he had heard the mare's hooves clinking against the stones. He knew that the noise was made by a horse and he could smell this wonderful odor of the flesh he loved so much. Alfredo and El Tigrero had been silent, and somehow he also failed to smell them. Perhaps because the odor from the sweating mare was so very strong, it drowned the man odor. He also heard a most unusual sound, almost like the squeaking of a mouse or chipmunk, and he wished to know what that strange squeaking sound could be. He couldn't know that it was the stirrup straps of the saddle, which needed oiling.

But it was too late now; waiting by the burro's carcass to which he had come in daylight for another meal, he smelled that dreadful odor of man, and the clicking of the mare's hooves against stones was so loud now that he slunk into the shallow cave and waited for the men to pass. But they didn't pass and El Tigrero had put his sarapé down and laid his shotgun across his legs.

El Tigrero was thinking. If he could get his feet under him so that he could make a quick jump, then turn quickly to fire at the cave, his gun would be above the palmetto. He felt sure El Tigre would reach him before he could fire, but what could he do? Soon, El Tigre would become so hungry and so frightened, he would spring anyway, even if El Tigrero didn't look in his direction, or even if he didn't move quickly.

He thought of praying, but first he had better think of some way to escape, then ask El Señor the Lord for help.

Then he saw a movement and there in the morning light was Alfredo. Alfredo handed him a small package in a clean cloth: "My mother sent these tortillas."

El Tigrero was more frightened than he had ever been in his life. Would the coming of Alfredo frighten El Tigre into rushing now?

"Sit down," he said in a whisper, "and look at nothing except the carcass of the burro—nothing more, nothing, nothing, nothing. El Tigre will be there," he lied.

They were so silent and motionless, sitting there, that a squirrel wondered what they could possibly be. Squirrels are as inquisitive as jays. When these strange animals didn't move and made no noise, the squirrel came closer and stared with his beady eyes; then he raised his tail and swished it in anger, and then he began to bark at them, really swearing at them, because they wouldn't let him know what sort of animals they were.

His curiosity took complete control of him and he came close and was so interested in them that he came out on a very slim twig, which swayed under his weight, but he failed to notice this and swore terribly at the silent forms.

El Tigrero wondered if the jaguar was watching the squirrel but he was afraid to risk a shot, and his fear now was making his knees weak, and he knew he had to do something almost immediately. Just then the squirrel came too far out onto the quaking branchlet, and in the middle of his terrible swearing, the branchlet broke and he fell to the earth below. El Tigre was distracted for a moment by the falling squirrel and the outbreak of a strange nerve-shattering sound, and in this moment El Tigrero whirled and, forcing his gun barrel past the palmetto, fired into the mouth of the cave.

The strange, nerve-shattering sound when the squirrel fell was the loud laughter of Alfredo. The falling squirrel and the loud laughter were too much for El Tigre. He had never seen a squirrel fall and he had never heard man's laughter, and in that moment of his distraction El Tigrero had shot him.

El Tigrero took off his sombrero and, as Alfredo looked at El Tigre, rolled a cigarette and lit it.

"Look," he said to Alfredo, "he is dead truly." He puffed thoughtfully, then continued, "And why, my little Alfredo, is he dead?" He took several more puffs. "He is dead, little Alfredo, because El Señor," and he pointed to the sky, "could see that we had nothing else left for saving our lives, and He sent down laughter. He gave only men laughter, and that is the weapon He has given men to defeat El Diablo. We are alive because you laughed. When man is laughing, his enemies will be defeated."

The White Sack

T HE GREEN-GREY WORLD SEEMED TO BE ASLEEP. There was no palpable air current, and there was no stir of life. The glinting quartzite and mica chips, left by the erosive processes through millions of years on the slopes of the mountains, were the only hint of animation.

The grey of the sage and the faded green of the cactus and the scattered junipers filling the ravines and washes and climbing up the slopes of the mountains dominated the scene, even though there were cool green pines on the higher altitudes, pines growing along the crests like the hackles of an angry beast, and even though there was the dark green of stunted pines scattered down the slopes among the grey of the sage, like picnickers.

The sun was hot, penetrating, causing discomfort during this midday in western New Mexico. Stressing the impression of emptiness was the total absence of the voices of insects with their complaint to the sun.

But far down on the lens-shaped, grey-green flat something moved. It was obviously an animal, but it could never be taken for a wild one because it moved slowly, clumsily, more like a broken-winged eagle at a distance than anything else. But the figure seemed to have purpose, and moved along toward the mountains with the carelessness of a skunk, and therefore did not in the least express the bewilderment of a suddenly grounded eagle.

As the figure approached the mountain slopes, there was something about it, outside its clumsy movement, which pulled all eyes to it. It was almost like a heliographic signal, and as the figure came closer, it began to look like a great beetle walking upright, with a color like sand and with a patch of glaring white on its flank. Soon this little patch of white swinging at the flank of the figure became the center of the world of grey-green.

Slowly the figure came toward the hot, glinting slopes of the mountain with only its upper half showing over the grey-green brush. Sometimes it disappeared into a ravine or a wash, or was hidden by some bushy cedar at the foot of the slopes, and at such times the world waited for it to appear again.

During a moment when the figure was completely hidden, a wolf that had been sleeping away the day under a juniper halfway up the mountainside and had been startled into rising when the glaring white had come to his notice now became uneasy and looked back over his shoulder nervously, as if he would make sure that his ways of escape were still open. However, when the white flashed in the sun again, he felt more secure. He might not know the nature of that which held his interest, but he knew where it was and what it was doing at that moment. His gaze was steady and he was afraid to flick a fly from his ear.

A Clark's nutcracker that had been alternately preening and looking about him alertly in the sun-protected lower branches of a tall pine caught the flash of white down among the grey-green brush of the flat and immediately flapped to the very top of a pine on the steep slope of a gash ravine which gave upon the flat, where he could get a better view. His move was prompted by curiosity alone. He was of the jay-crow-magpie family of renowned gossips. He was called Clark's nutcracker for Lieutenant Clark of the Lewis and Clark expedition.

Being a big bird and ordinarily flock-protected, he had no need for silent wings, and his balance-flapping as he attempted to perch on the tiptop finger of the pine caused a big mule deer buck, lying under a juniper on the ravine slope, to become alert. The buck looked up at the big bird, then began to move his great mule-like ears from front to back, then back again, like sound detectors on an airfield. But really one ought to say that the sound detectors on the airfields were like mule-deer ears since man had taken the hint from animals' movable ears. For some time he moved only his ears, leaving one forward and one backward for a moment, then switching them so that they moved past each other constantly. He strained to pick up the slightest sound in the sun-deadened air without moving from his comfortable bed, which he had pawed out under the juniper.

The big bird was in the process of absorbing information about the strange object moving over the flats, approaching the gash ravine's mouth, as eager gossips must do when they feel they have insufficient details for their self-glorifying recitals. He was finally badly balanced and he sat like a mounted specimen, with his left eye held upon the great beetle with the white flank. He would wait until he determined the nature of this strange animal before flying off to scream the exciting news to the world.

The man came on slowly, then stopped to wipe his glasses, and far up on the mountainside, the wolf, blending into the dappled shade of the juniper, had an intenser light in his eye as he saw the fluttering white handkerchief, but still his fear was not great; he could see the strange animal, and just as man is afraid of the unknown, so was the wolf afraid of the unseen and the unscented.

The Clark's nutcracker was now well balanced on his pine finger that bent beneath his weight, and he had no fear at all, but he was intense with puzzlement.

The big buck had swallowed his cud some moments after the nutcracker had flapped to the top of the pine to peer down the ravine with intense interest. It had flowed down his throat with the impression of a darning ball passing to the toe of a long stocking. The uneasiness inspired by the unknown made his search for something in the sun-deadened air urgent; he must find something in the air with his sound detectors that would give him release from his uneasiness. His hind leg twitched ever so slightly as if he would rise; then it stilled and he remained absolutely motionless. Unlike the wolf, he did not stretch his muzzle forward in vain to test the air, but kept his great ears moving back and forth, back and forth, with that slow movement under the dappled shade of the juniper which was scarcely a breaking of complete immobility.

After wiping his glasses, the man put them back on with a slight grimace; then he reached for his quart canteen hanging from his shoulder. When he found that he couldn't drink and hold his rifle as well, he looked around for an object against which to lean it. To the left of where he was standing was a large sage bush, and he walked over and laid his rifle against it. He had been warned in camp against getting sand in the works of his rifle. He then lifted the canteen and drank.

The rattlesnake, which was coiled under the sage bush close to where the man had been standing as he wiped his glasses, felt relief by letting his flat, ugly head move back to its former position from the one it had assumed immediately over the center of the coil. The pits at the sides of his nose had received the warm-blood message from the man when the man had suddenly stopped to pull out his handkerchief, but even though he felt relief by the man's movement away, he remained alert from the effects of the fear-message that the pits had sent through his body. The message of warm mammal blood from this animal that he could not hope to swallow demanded defense and inspired fear. He didn't want to harm the man, therefore, but fear would have urged him to do so. Besides, he had a terrible temper and thought he ought not ever be disturbed. He made no attempt to locate the danger which had passed out of the range of his sensitive pits, and he would await further information from them, knowing instinctively that his muddy-colored diamond blotches blended perfectly with the light and shade of the sagebrush under which he was coiled and motionless. Even at this time, the first week in November, he dared not expose himself to the direct rays of the sun, but daily he and others writhed stiffly from their winter dens in an abandoned prairie dog hole, to lie during the warm noon hours; then they would crawl back with summer suppleness to protect themselves from the cold nights. With his forked tongue darting like a horizontal-working, slow-moving stitching-machine needle, he had "heard" the animal move off several of his own lengths away, and his pits brought him no more fear-messages.

The nutcracker suddenly flapped away up the little gash ravine, talking excitedly to himself, rehearsing that which he would say to the flock higher up on the mountain, and the buck knew immediately that the strange unknown must be approaching the little canyon's mouth from the flat. He wasted no more time testing with his great sound-detector ears, but gazed down canyon with both great ears forward. He heard the slightest click of a pebble; then he arose very slowly, growing higher inch by inch, and he disturbed not one granitic pebble. The nutcracker's interest in something the buck could neither see nor scent made him extremely alert and highly nervous. He rose slowly, slowly, until he stood in full stature.

He stood and waited, looking down the ravine that was not yet become a canyon toward the spot where it entered upon the grey-green flat. He divided the animal world into two classes: enemies to be guarded against every minute of his life, and others to be ignored as if they didn't exist. He had no friends; he had only his mule-like ears, his keen eyes, his great speed, his coloration that was indistinguishable from the pine shadows and light flecks that played on the pine needles when the breezes flowed; more than these, he had his keen nose, and the reactions of other animals, both protective and investigative, when strange scents and sounds came on the air currents or when strange things appeared. He made use of the reacting range cattle all staring in one direction, the slinking coyote, the wolf trying to look like a cloud shadow, the gossip and excitement of the pine squirrels, the chipmunks, the Rocky Mountain jays, and the Clark's nutcrackers.

The buck had watched the nutcracker for information and the wolf high on the mountain slope had waited for the scent of the strange animal of the sage flat, but even when he had extended his muzzle and tested the air with deep concentration, he failed to get it. The flexing and relaxing of his nostrils in the constant testing of the sun-deadened air of noon had given him no message. However, he had kept his yellow eyes upon the great "beetle" that walked across the flat on its hind legs.

Suddenly the primitive fear of the unknown came over him and he looked back over his shoulder again nervously. The strange upright beetle had suddenly disappeared into the mouth of the gash ravine, completely hidden by its screen of stunted pines and junipers. The wolf thrust his muzzle farther out in the direction of the spot where the strange animal had disappeared and raised it slightly, as though he would make one last super effort to solve the mystery. He expressed his frustration and his fear of the unknown now by lowering his bushy tail and slinking off with his belly close to the ground. He slunk off transversely up the mountainside in the opposite direction to that which the strange animal had taken. Had there been fleecy clouds casting their moving shadows up the mountainside, not even a professional wolf hunter could have seen him, and even on the sun-splashed slope, no one except an accustomed hunter could have seen him.

The buck's great ears, now motionlessly erect and forward, caught the faint click of pebbles, and then the scrapings of the man's careless feet. Because of the careless treading of the man, the buck's curiosity came to balance with his fear, and he continued to stand like a cast iron monument on a Victorian lawn. There was no necessity for the least movement of his ears now, and as he waited, the careless sound of the man's walking allowed his curiosity to almost devour his fear. No enemy would be out prowling at midday, and no enemy of deer would come so carelessly. Only the range bull could be so indifferent and arrogant, and the buck actually moved his nose up a little to get the beefy scent he expected to come, or the acrid scent of droppings which he had often investigated and which he associated with all cattle. But he could see nothing yet, and the dead air brought nothing to him, and there were still only the arrogant movements which a bull would make for his information, a bull walking among the waterworn rocks of the dry watercourse of the ravine. He now waited to hear the great boasting roar of the bull. The nutcracker's reaction to the approaching man served only to put the buck on alert guard and make him nervous; he couldn't reason that the bird could not possibly become excited by the sight of range cattle, which he saw often.

As he waited, the buck felt a growing pugnacity. It was the rutting season and his neck was swollen and his own musk was strong. He had an impulse to stamp his sharp hoof in rut arrogance at being disturbed by this lumbering fool of a bull.

Then the sting of fear went through him, surging up and overbalancing the curiosity and the feeling of pugnacity, as something white flashed through the brush and the man appeared in full view. At the same time, the scent waves hit him full in the nose. The waves came in concentric circles from the sweating man like ripples from a pebble tossed into a calm pond, forcing themselves out from the heated body upon the currentless air. It was too late to run now, too late to lay his antlers back along his backbone and sneak out among the shadows of the pines. He had only two defenses left now: depend upon his protective coloration and maintain his complete immobility, or jump high out of his position over his bed and charge off down the side of the ravine in very high, stiff-legged jumps of ten and fifteen feet, leaping high across the ravine's bed where it was clear of brush, and then bound up the other side to finally lose himself in the timber of the opposite slope. This defensive jumping would be protective confusion, as well as enable him to see above the brush, and he would be gone before the surprised, nervously excited hunter could even take aim, and even if he did fire, the long noisy leaps, the high head, the tail up like a flag to distract the eye, and the nose emitting breath like escaping steam would complete the hunter's nervous confusion so that he would certainly fire wildly.

But it was the arrogance and surliness of rut that urged him to depend upon his immobility, so thus he stood like an ornament and watched the man as he began the slight ascent up the bed of the ravine. He followed him by the slightest, absolutely impalpable movement of the head, and there was no infraction of protective immobility here.

When the man drew opposite the buck, he stopped and looked over the side of the little canyon. He took off his glasses and wiped them again carefully; then he put them on with the same grimace. He looked again over the slope where the buck stood, his eyes passing over the statuesque buck without seeing him, without taking in a single detail. They saw only the steep slope of a little canyon, on which the pines grew tall and the Douglas firs lifted their crowns high toward the sun. At the feet of these tall trees were bushy cedars and fantastic little junipers, stopping only a little way up the slope and at the feet of the tall trees, as if they were too tired to climb farther.

The man felt that it was cool here in the shade of the larger firs and pines, and the sweat from his hatband was now like ice water as it evaporated in the dry air. He looked then up the left slope of the canyon and climbed out of the bed of the gash ravine ten or fifteen yards up the side and laid his rifle against a fallen Douglas fir. He ducked out from under the strings of the white laundry sack and pushed his hat back, then sat down. He swung the canteen off and drank again, then laid it aside. He then reached into the white laundry sack and took out an apple.

As he ate, his eyes were level with the buck standing on the opposite slope of the little canyon, exactly fifty yards away, but he saw nothing but flecked light and moveless shadow. And anyway his thoughts had begun to blot out eye messages, as if they were window shades blotting out the world. When he had finished with his apple, he reached into the sack for another and bit into it. His hunger was a rodent in his stomach, and the apples were not in the least effective; they could not stop the gnawing. He had been aware of self-pity over his sacrifice in refusing the lunch laid out for him by the camp cook early that morning, and now he was so full of self-pity that he must glance at the new hole in which his belt buckle fitted, two holes from the metal-stained, well-worn one nearer the tip. He had told the boys at the court building, when they had come into the District Attorney's office to wish him luck on his hunt, that he intended to lose some of the blubber he had picked up. He told them that he was tired of carrying his big stomach around and of not knowing when he needed a shine except by peeping over it.

He smiled to himself when he realized that everyone really appreciated his humor. But it was true; he was serious about his stomach. Women voters wanted virile-looking men, just as they voted for men with shocks of hair and good looks and preferred them over bald-headed men. He had plenty of hair, but a trimmer body would be good for a few more votes in the governor's race the following summer.

His winning the office of governor was almost a sure thing. He had won a great reputation as a clever District Attorney in the Paglioni gambling racket case. He believed there were grounds for the public's appreciation of his wit and his ability. When it came to that, he could almost tell what a witness or a juror or a judge even was thinking by watching his little mannerisms and noting his inflections and his face. Funny thing, he was getting so he could look through the rear window of the car ahead of him and tell what kind of a fellow the driver of the car might be by watching the back of his neck as he drove along. He had a slight horror of car accidents and he had found himself, unconsciously for a long time, studying the backs of drivers' necks. Unconsciously studying the backs of drivers' necks had a fundamental purpose; it was protective, and aided him in his own driving judgment. He might have saved his own life more than once by knowing something of the driver in front of him, who knows?

And that's the way it was with judges and witnesses and jurors and lawyer opponents. In his intense desire to excel and climb the political ladder, he had made an unconscious study of the human mechanism, so to speak, and he kept ever alert to the least human manifestation that might be of aid to him, and it had paid off. Such alertness to survive the competition of the hordes of lawyers turned out each year by Harvard and Virginia and other law schools had paid off, he believed.

After the third apple, he felt better about the great sacrifice of the morning, and he felt the slight thrill of achievement as he cast his thoughts into the future, and his eyes carried no messages to disturb his thoughts as they rested on the sun flecks and the shadows on the other side of the gash canyon, where the deer buck stood motionless.

But soon he became aware of discomfort and, through the discomfort, he became aware of the scene around him but yet aware of no details. His sweat had cooled rapidly on his body and he actually felt a chill that was very uncomfortable. The boys around last night's campfire must have played a joke on him, he began to believe, by telling him that a foot hunter would have the best chance on the first day after the horsemen had stirred up the bucks. They knew that there wasn't a buck within five miles of the mouth of the little canyon and the mountain slopes. They had drawn a map for him and he knew that he had come to the right place. He believed he had never seen such a godforsaken country. He had seen and heard nothing.

The cool air from the shade of the pines and firs at the head of the little canyon or ravine had begun to flow downward now to displace the lighter, sun-heated air of the flats, exactly like water flowing down the bed of the ravine in the rainy season. He became cold and began to shiver as the down-flowing air currents whispered and hissed through the Douglas firs. The murmuring and hissing and sighing seemed ominous in this "lifeless" land, and the bed of the little canyon was even now in the late afternoon shadows. He thought of camp. They had told him that this little gash canyon headed at the camp's horse corral, and all he had to do was to follow it up the mountain.

He closed the mouth of the white laundry sack and hung it from his shoulder, swung his canteen over his other shoulder, picked up his rifle, and set out up the ravine dry watercourse. It was easier walking up the watercourse, but his ascent was spiritless.

All the time the man had sat on the fallen fir eating apples and thinking of his success and his hopes, the buck had not moved. His rut surliness was completely submerged by his curiosity and his instinct for protection. But when the man had disappeared among the scrub pines and was lost to view among the windings of the little canyon's bed, he left his position over his pawed-out bed and, with his antlers laid along his back, he crouched low and disappeared like a shadow down the canyon in the opposite direction. When he was clear of the canyon, he broke into a springy lope toward the heavy forest under the rimrock of Santiago Canyon.

————

While the renowned District Attorney sat with his thoughts and his apples on the fallen fir at the bottom of the little canyon, another member of the hunting party, a nuclear physicist, stumbled noisily over the rimrock of the same little canyon two miles up. He wore a bright red shirt and a red band about his ranger's hat. He found a spot from which he could command a good view up and down the canyon and from which he could penetrate the thick growth on the opposite slope. He noted that he was well screened by a thickset cedar that was shaped like a candle flame. He waited nervously, but he kept still, except for very carefully straightening out his cramped legs periodically.

The afternoon shadows had already absorbed the sun's light until the little cedar was just a dark substance with definite outline, the shadows dulling the brightness of the great physicist's shirt. He was shocked into alertness when he saw something white and thought only of the white rump of a deer. It disappeared; then he felt nervously for the safety catch of his rifle. He watched the spot where the white had disappeared intently; then he heard the slight grinding of gravel and the click of water-rounded pebbles. He felt of his safety catch again and kept his eyes on the spot where he had seen the flash of white.

His heart seemed to come into his throat and his hands shook a little when the sounds of disturbed gravel indicated that the buck must be coming right up the watercourse. Then there was silence. He moved again for a better view, keeping his hand on the safety gadget to make sure that it was on the "on" and his rifle ready. There was deeper silence, it seemed to him, and he moved again for a better view and, as he moved, a water-rounded pebble the size of a tennis ball was dislodged by his foot and went clicking down the side of the canyon.

The District Attorney had stopped to rest, and was standing, thinking of the distance to camp, when he heard the clack, clack, clickety-clack of the bounding pebble. He felt nervously for his safety catch and continued to stand still, and he could hear his heart pumping. He got down on one knee and looked up the slope under the screening lower limbs of the trees. He saw a movement behind the flame-shaped cedar and he centered his eyes, his mind, his heart, and his whole being on that bushy cedar. His vision of a glorious buck with antlers in majestic alertness was projected in his full-blooded emotion to a point just behind that bushy cedar so that the screening branches blurred the conformation of a hiding buck, but the more intently he gazed, the clearer the projected image outline became, like the suddenly appearing image on photographic paper, growing under the gaze. The cedar branches moved again, and he pulled up his rifle and fired. He didn't hear the bullet that whizzed past his own head because of the blast of his own rifle.

Something fell, and rounded pebbles came clicking down the slope as though a dying buck were kicking them loose. The rifle's explosion bounded and rebounded from the sides of the little canyon; then the sound died completely. Now the silence was profound. He stood with shaking hands and he could think of only one thing: a warning from the campfire that he must throw another shell into the barrel before approaching a fallen buck. He did this, and in his high emotion his fingers moved in involuntary sequence, and the second explosion came, sending its bullet into space at a forty-five-degree angle, and he was startled. He felt his face turn red and he had an urge to glance over his shoulder to make sure no one had witnessed his blunder.

Emotion flooded him and he started up the slope toward the little cedar. Halfway to it he stopped for breath where he had a good view of the little flame-shaped cedar and watched for further movement. He could see nothing, and he was sure that the buck was hidden behind the bushy branches.

Now his thought was a single one again, and it repeated itself over and over in a mind from which everything else was shut out: "I've got my buck, I've got my buck."

He couldn't wait to get his breath completely; he must go on toward the little cedar, but just as he put one foot forward, his eyes fell on an object a little way down the slope from the little tree. It was a hat with a red band around it. He felt no shock yet, and his mind was still filled with the thought that he had his buck. Then he raised his eyes to the base of the cedar, and he saw a pale hand at the end of a red-sleeved arm, thrown out with the irresponsibility of a sleeping child.

His knees weakened and his blood seemed to turn to warm water, which in turn seemed to turn his knees to water and they would no longer hold him up. He sank to the pine needles and sat there staring up the canyon with his mind as blank as cave darkness and his eyes seeing nothing.

Arrowflight,
The Story of a Prairie Chicken

H E WAS NOTICEABLE BECAUSE HE LIVED ALONE in the west pasture and because he loomed very large and black, on rainy mornings especially. He was larger than most prairie chicken cocks, and certainly the black barrings of his feathers were broader and of a blacker shade than those of other cocks.

He lived by himself all year, instead of joining a flock during the autumn and winter months, but during April he joined the others to dance each morning at dawn on the high prairie, and there he had a chosen beat, up and down, which he ran with wings spread and held against his body and his black, unspread tail erect. The sacs on both sides of his neck would be inflated and would glow in the early morning light like oranges; his pinnate feathers would be erected like horns above his head, and you could hear his booming for more than two miles. The pinnate feathers were the black feathers that hung on each side of his neck and covered the sacs when they were not inflated and the cock was not dancing.

When the fever of mating season began to pass, he would come back to the dance ground each morning and dance without enthusiasm, as if he were weary of it; then he would walk off with the other cocks, foraging. The hens had already begun to make their nests.

One morning in May, when the fever had died, Arrowflight, the great black-barred cock, flew back to the south, high over the grazing cattle, to the west pasture, and there he sat on a post oak tree for some time, and just gazed over his domain; then he dropped to the ground and sought the shade of a thick growth of sapling blackjack oaks and there he rested until late afternoon when he began foraging. He always slept on the ground and would find a spot which blended with the barred feathers of his back.

He was careful to select a spot where the tall grasses would not hinder his abrupt lift into the air if a coyote came too close or a great horned owl discovered him. Coyotes, skunks, and raccoons didn't bother him much since he could hear them coming through the grasses, and sometimes he would wait tensely, hoping they might pass without noticing him; he would allow them to come quite close, and then with a great flutter of wings almost fly into their faces, startling the animal trying to catch him. If the night were dark, he would rise and fly away from the trees, out over the prairie, perhaps flying for a mile, then come to earth and freeze, remaining wide awake the remainder of the night.

But the great hunter owl, the great horned owl, was another matter. He hunted everywhere. He would come up from the creek bottoms on the most silent wings in nature, flying like a ghost across the moonlit prairie, or he would alight on his favorite hunting station: a lightning-blasted blackjack, a power pole, or even a fence post. There he would sit for an hour or more, listening for the least sound, and if he heard no sound he would give his hunting call, "who, who-WHO-who, who." A frightened mouse would then lose his nerve and break his protective immobility and make a dash for his nest among the grasses, but he would never make it. The great bird would pounce, and there would be only a squeak.

The easiest prey of the great ghost hunter was the skunk. Nature has given the skunk a most effective defense—his musk gun just under his tail—and relying on this gun for protection he walks about during the night, and often during the day, as if he has not a care in the world. He doesn't think it necessary to look up, so he keeps his nose to the ground and waddles along looking for anything he can catch, his broad white stripes over his back, seeming to say, "Attack, if you dare." The great hunter owl dares quite often, and he sinks his talons into the back of the skunk, and there is a scuffle and soon the skunk lies dead, but the air for many yards about will be filled with the stench made by his musk-gun.

Arrowflight often heard the hunting call of the owl, and he could hear the scuffling when the great bird captured a skunk or a packrat or a field mouse. At such times, he would draw his feathers very close and remain completely frozen. The owl couldn't very well make out which was the back of the cock and which the surrounding grasses, weeds, and leaves, but he could hear the faintest sound. His ears were not like the great sound-detector ears of the mule deer but were tufts of feathers covering large ear holes. His sound detector was his great round face since his ears were really holes under the tufts of feathers. In some way his round face concentrated the sounds, like the sound detectors on airfields, and his head turned exactly like a radar detector. He couldn't turn his eyes as other birds and animals were able to do but must turn his whole head. He didn't depend on his eyes as much as he depended on his face, but might have if he could have turned them. In so doing, however, he might have moved them to look right or left and missed a very important sound with his radar-screen face. He pointed his face toward a sound as a mule deer moved his ears.

One night when there was a cold autumn moon and the shadows were black, the great horned owl came up from the creek bottom and alighted on a tilted limestone rock near the sleeping place of Arrowflight. The owl never chose a hunting station which was not free of leaves and twigs since he must be free of such interference when he must swoop down on his prey.

This night he sat for some time turning his sound-detector face, first one way and then the other, and the heart of Arrowflight was beating faster and faster, seeming to pound against his breast, as if it might free itself before the owl pounced, like a rat fleeing a sinking ship.

But the spirit of Arrowflight was not sinking. He was as tense as a drawn bowstring, and he stared at the shadowy form of the owl, not even allowing his eyelids to move.

They sat for some time, the owl unmoving on his limestone stone and Arrowflight with his heart trying to escape his breast. Then the ghostly hunter sang out, "who, who-WHO-who, who," and a mouse had nerve failure and ran frantically along his runway in the grasses, which unfortunately ran within a foot of the grass tufts Arrowflight had chosen for his sleeping place, and it was here that the owl intercepted the frightened mouse. The great bird saw Arrowflight as he made his first movement, and he left his mouse and sprang at Arrowflight. But the wily old cock fluttered into the owl's great round face and flew off into the moonlight with the horizon as his guide. He flew away from the small patch of blackjacks and high across the prairie. He knew better than to try to fly into timber, where he would be unable to see well and might fly into the branches, or even the trunk of a tree.

The owl was startled and confused, but he lifted and set out to catch the cock, yet he flew only a short way when he seemed to realize that he couldn't possibly catch Arrowflight. He turned gracefully and came back to his mouse, which was like an oyster compared with the feast that Arrowflight could have become.

One can't even guess the reasons for Arrowflight's desire to live alone for most of the year, without the protection that a flock could give him. He had to be his own sentinel and had for this reason to be more alert than other prairie chickens. Only the prairie falcon could outfly him; there were no goshawks hunting over the west pasture. The red-tailed hawk circled high above the prairie and the timber patches, but Arrowflight would stand in the open and watch him, without the least fear, and the harriers, called marsh hawks, would hunt the ravines, and he was not the least afraid of them.

One February, the love moon of the coyotes, the Fish and Wildlife people put out poison horse flesh and poisoned the coyotes. They overdid it with a sort of American business efficiency, and that spring, after the winter poisoning, hundreds of thousands of cotton rats swarmed over the prairie and through the blackjacks and stayed for two years. There had never been one on the prairie before this invasion, and there was no enemy to keep down their numbers since the coyotes had been poisoned. Where there are no enemies to keep a species in balance, they swarm over that area of the earth. The ranchers lost much of their stored grain, and the liberated rats came in the daylight hours, as well as during the nights, and they cut flower stems and green tomatoes off the vines, and when one was trapped, the others ate him.

The harriers called marsh hawks tried to take the place of the coyotes during the two winters. They came from all over the Great Plains and the woodlands and sailed over the prairie, hunting rats, but still the rats swarmed, and during this time there were no prairie chicken hatches since the eggs were eaten by the rats.

During the second April of the invasion, there were fewer cocks dancing on the booming grounds and they were molested. Swarming harriers, with their hunger satisfied and feeling quite playful, would dart at the dancing cocks and annoy them. They had no intention of eating them; they only wanted to tease them, many of them coming from parts where there were no prairie chickens, and this dance on the high prairie was fascinating to them and they had to do something about it. The cocks would stop dancing and look bored, or run a little way and then fly over the grass just in front of the bluffing hawks, who would then zoom, and circle for another bluff-stoop.

And old Spooky, the cow horse that had just been retired and was bored with his freedom, thought the dancing cocks a novelty, and when he saw the cocks against the prairie horizon he would trot toward them with ears forward; then when among them, he blew on them, almost pushing them along with the strength of his nasal blasts.

This was unusual. The dancers were never bothered by their enemies as they danced and boomed since every one of their enemies knew that an attack was useless. They chose for their dance or booming ground a high ridge or hill where the grass was sparse, and while they could be seen and heard by their enemies, they on the other hand could see in every direction. Even before the coyotes had been poisoned and after they came back to fill the vacuum by breeding and migrations from the north, a lone coyote would stand on some high ridge and watch the dancers hungrily, but knowing the uselessness of trying for them.

The Osage Indians gave Arrowflight his name since that is the name they gave prairie chickens in general. They flew over the prairie like flying arrows, they said. They flapped their wings for some time; then they set their wings and sailed and this sailing, from a distance, looks like an arrow in flight. Also the Osages say that their booming, when heard at a distance, is like the sound of a bowstring at the moment when the arrow is released.

The cotton rats disappeared as suddenly as they had appeared, and soon the coyotes were heard in their chorusing over the prairie, and the cocks were many again on the dancing ground, and the hens could hatch their eggs without being molested, and now the chicks were healthy and perhaps half of them would grow to adulthood. There had been hunger and disease when the rat swarm had eaten the ragweed seeds and other food upon which the prairie chickens depended. Flocks of them had flown to the Lewis ranch house and had eaten the green leaves of the privet hedge during February.

But now there were no rats to sit waiting for the hen prairie chickens to leave their nests to eat and dust-bathe so that they could eat their eggs, and the hens were not worried by rats trying to sneak under them to get the eggs which they brooded.

Where Arrowflight lived, in the blackjack patch and on the prairie of the west pasture, man was not his enemy since he was never hunted here, but still when a hunter did come into the west pasture to hunt quail, Arrowflight soon learned about bird dogs. When they came upon his very warm scent and had stopped, frozen, waiting for their masters, Arrowflight, unlike a quail, was perhaps forty or fifty yards away. He had immediately slunk through the grass and away from the dogs. If they followed his trail, trailing him as he stayed well ahead of them, he would finally become tired of the game and actually run for some distance, then rise and fly away, much to the puzzlement of the dogs. In all his long life he had never been stung by birdshot.

A man walking was easily avoided, and he feared him, but man as the projection from a horse's back, he feared not at all. He would walk out to the side to avoid the horse's hooves, then stretch his neck and watch the horse and rider pass, or he might squat in the grass, making no attempt to blend with the immediate background by freezing.

In January, quite often the flock from the high prairie would swish into the blackjacks of Arrowflight's domain to feed upon acorns, and this seemed to make him nervous. He would fly up into a post oak and watch, no matter if there was a sentinel on guard.

His size and his black bars did not make him famous, as they might have done if his chief enemy had been the man-animal and there had been gunners trying for him, or if he had become famous as a dog-deceiver or shot-evader. He was only known by the people of the ranch, especially because of his solitude. But soon a new flock had its beginnings in the west pasture.

One April the dancing was especially wild and exuberant. There were twenty-five cocks dancing and booming just as the sun came up, and they danced and boomed for two hours with little intervals of rest. Seeming to feel that the dancing and booming failed to express their intense emotion, they flew into the air perhaps three feet and cackled like domestic chickens. There were hens all over the place with their usual indifference to the parading of the cocks.

It was upon this April morning that a cock decided to take over Arrowflight's dancing beat. Arrowflight lowered his head, with the pinnate feathers still erect and tail elevated, and charged the newcomer in the middle of his boom. They flew together and hit at each other with their wings, since they had no spurs, and a few barred feathers floated off on the slightest of early morning air currents. They stopped flying at each other suddenly and stood looking at each other; then with beaks almost touching, they sat down and watched each other.

Then they arose and started flying high into the air, striking with their wings; then landing all fluffed and angry, they stood and looked at each other for some time. The smaller cock decided he had had enough, and he started to walk off, but Arrowflight wouldn't let him off so easily; he ran at him and the smaller cock ran, but as Arrowflight was about to overtake him, he lifted off the ground and flew just over the grass tops with Arrowflight after him. When he had chased him for perhaps a hundred yards, Arrowflight came back to his beat and danced more fervently and boomed more heartily.

This time when he flew back to his patch of blackjacks in the west pasture, a hen came with him. He ignored her completely, and didn't bother to know where she had deposited her eggs.

Now, since the rat swarm, the prairie chickens had only their old enemies to worry about, but here in the west pasture where the timber patches grew at the heads of the canyons, there was the great horned owl. On the high prairie where there were few hunting stations for the ghost bird, he might fly over sleeping prairie chickens or brooding hens without seeing them, but here in the blackjacks, cedars, and post oaks, he had many possible stations.

The hen went onto the open prairie to scratch out a nest and lay her clutch of eggs. She chose a tussock of bluestem grass at the edge of a growth of sand plum bushes, where cattle and coyotes would be little likely to explore unless the coyotes caught her scent, which when she began brooding was very faint, or perhaps even absent. No coyote would try to go through such a spiny plum thicket unless his nose informed him that there was something especially interesting there.

Every time the hen approached her nest, she flew to within fifty yards of it; then, crouching almost to the ground, she sneaked toward it, hidden by the bluestem. After she had gone perhaps thirty-five yards, she stopped and stood erect, with her feathers drawn very close, and looked first to the sky for falcons; then she scanned the horizons and listened intently. After thirty seconds or more, if she was not sure of a distant object or an unusual noise, she would crouch close to the earth again and sneak toward her nest. At about sixty yards, she stopped again and stood looking and listening; then after a half minute or more, she would continue her cautious approach.

When near the nest she would not stick her head above the grasses but would squat and listen and then, after a minute, she would crawl directly to her nest and adjust herself to the eggs.

Of course Arrowflight cared little for the dangerous experiences of his wives, and constant alertness was the price they must pay for existence. He had only the few weeks' glory of the mating season, and he lived the remainder of the time protecting his life. He, like the hens, had no moment of leisure as men often had, when they might forget the world, or as members of a flock had under their sentinels. His business or profession was the necessity to remain in the balance of nature, and he worked at it for twenty-four hours, night and day.

When the hen started her brooding out at the edge of the plum thicket, he seemed not to miss her, but continued on with his routine of living.

Perhaps every other day when she was brooding, she came off her nest to feed and dust-bathe. She would step off the eggs and, with her closed beak, scratch bits of dead grass, shriveled leaves of last year's plum, heaping them under her chin and bringing them thus over her olive-brown eggs so that they would not be seen by the crows. When she had her eggs covered to her satisfaction, she would sneak away from the nest hidden by the tall grasses;

then, when she was perhaps fifty or seventy-five yards away, she would fly away to feed, or to her favorite dust bath, knowing instinctively that her olive-brown eggs, made even more inconspicuous by the dead grass and leaves she had scraped over them, would be safe. There never would have been grouse called prairie chicken if they had laid white eggs.

Again when she came back she would alight, perhaps fifty yards away from the nest this time, but repeat the approach she made before.

Sometimes a cow would, in her grazing, suddenly come upon the brooding hen. She would stop, with grass still hanging from her mouth, when her tongue had stopped in its progress of pulling and pushing it back into the gullet. She would stand and stare at the brooding hen stupidly, then blow through her nose at the hen in what seemed much like contempt. The hen only stared back at her, afraid that she might be a young cow and suddenly become playful and try to butt her.

There was no hunting station near the nest for the great horned owl, so he did not become a menace, as he might have done had there been a convenient power pole, a blasted tree, or an uptilted limestone for his use. As it was, he flew over her brooding her eggs without seeing her.

The crows were a menace in the daytime and the coyotes during the night and early mornings. There was a cow trail not far from the plum thicket and each morning at dawn the hen could see a coyote trotting along, with his mind on getting home before the sun could point him out. Even if the wind came from the south, as it did often in the temperamental months of April and May, the coyote seemed never to get her scent.

But the crows were a different thing. They came to the prairie in pairs now, and sometimes in threes and fours, with always a sentinel standing erect watching the horizons, while the others walked about as if the west pasture belonged to them, searching for slugs and other crow delicacies.

The hen watched them intently; they were notorious robbers of other birds' nests. It was not likely that they would walk, hunting, into the thicket, but the danger lay in the possibility that one might fly directly over the thicket and, being always inquisitive, might discover that part of the dead grasses and shriveled last year's plum leaves actually moved. He would wheel and alight on a plum bush, even though he might have to flap his wings constantly to keep his balance. He would cock his head and then call to the others, "I think I've found something."

So when the crows flew up from their sedate walking over the prairie, the hen must watch their direction and freeze into absolute immobility if one came toward the thicket.

But at the end of the first week of her brood, there was fortunate activity in a blackjack that had ventured out to the edge of the sandstone. A pair of scissortail flycatchers began building a nest. The tree was perhaps forty yards from the nest, at the edge of the plum thicket, and no crow or hawk would be allowed near the tree. They even attacked the golden eagle, flying above the great bird and diving at him. He dodged them but lost his kingly dignity in getting away.

The flycatchers made noises like a mechanism made of wood which one whirled by a handle and creaked from want of oiling, and made their wings boom in their nuptial flight over the brooding prairie chicken. One would sit for hours waiting to chase crows, hawks, and even the great eagle away from their airspace above and some hundred-and-fifty yards each side.

The cattle liked the early spring grass that came before the bluestem got well started, so they had grazed about the thicket often during the late winter and had left their droppings, which by this time had dried into chips. Fat beetles and certain larvae lived under these chips, and both the skunks and the coyotes loved them.

One moonlit night, a skunk came rocking along with his nose close to the earth and his beautiful white-sprinkled tail dragging. There is nothing a skunk likes better than eggs of any kind, no matter what stage they may have reached in incubation, and he loved prairie chicken, no matter if she is a brooding hen who is no longer fat and juicy.

When the brooding hen saw him, she drew her feathers very close and froze absolutely. The skunk turned each chip as he came to it, and as he turned them and ate the beetles and the larvae, he came closer to the brooding hen. Three feet from her was the last chip on that side of the thicket, and as the skunk approached it, the hen was afraid to blink her eyes. A mite began to bite her, and she had to suffer the pain and annoyance. To have gone after the mite would have meant her death.

When the skunk had approached the last chip three feet from the hen, a lanky coyote appeared with the same business in mind which occupied the skunk. He was tall and very thin, and apparently had traveled far in his hunger. Possibly he had traveled some thirty or forty miles hunting and possibly he had come from a place where there were no skunks. There were still rags of winter hair hanging to him.

His hunger overwhelmed his coyote intelligence and caution, and just as the skunk was about to turn the last chip, he came closer and actually wagged his rag-like tail, to indicate his good intentions, like a fawning beggar.

The skunk stopped in his work and stared at him. He had no need for bluffing; he had no need to growl or hiss or raise his hackles since every animal including man knew that the very fact of the skunk was bluff enough—every animal except a coyote from the wheat fields to the north who had never seen a skunk.

The skunk, satisfied that the hungry-looking coyote must know about the tremendous respect due a skunk by all living creatures, went on about his business, ignoring the coyote completely. But just as he was about to turn the chip, the hunger-driven coyote bluff-rushed him, and as quick as a flash, the skunk turned, raised the rear part of his body with hind feet in the air, and balancing only on his front ones, pulled the trigger to his musk sac and the coyote fell, momentarily blinded, to the ground and began frantically to push his face through the tall bluestem with his hind legs, folding his front one under him as his face and chest slid through the grasses.

The skunk lowered his tail, turned again to his chip-turning, just as if nothing whatever had happened. But the terrific odor that filled the air for hundreds of yards saved the life of the hen prairie chicken—if not her life, at least her eggs—since the skunk couldn't possibly scent her through his own musk as he ate the beetles of the last chip only three feet from her. He then rocked on across the prairie looking for more of last winter's chips.

Nor could the hungry coyote from the wheat field of the north scent the brooding hen, and undoubtedly in his hunger he would have searched the plum thicket. And anyway, he was in no mood for brooding prairie chickens or beetles or anything else. When his sight returned dimly, he trotted off down the canyon to the creek, and there he would find some relief at the riffles.

One afternoon about 4 P.M., a blue-black smudge appeared in the north-west, and soon the clouds came over the prairie and became as rounded bags, like kidneys. As a matter of fact, such clouds are called botryoidal, which means kidney-like, and when they appear, the cowboys watch them since they may also mean a tornado or hail or both.

The brooding hen had been restless since dawn when the coyotes had howled near her nest. She was not especially afraid of them, but that which made them restless made her restless. This was the low atmospheric pressure which preceded a great storm over the prairies.

She didn't leave her nest for food this day, and was so restless that she kept turning on her eggs, and the mites kept her busy. They too were made restless by the low pressure of the atmosphere.

During this mid-afternoon, the prairie grasses began to hiss in the wind, and bits of dust were picked up and flew into her eyes. Then the great balls of ice started to fall and bounce, and one hit her. She stood up but continued to cover her eggs, yet her erect position had a purpose since she sloped her back and held her head high with beak pointed up. This made her a slim target for the hail, and it is likely that only one hailstone might hit her in this position where six or seven might have hit her broad back and head. But still not a hailstone hit the eggs.

Several stones hit her back and glanced off, but one glanced from her head and she slumped upon her eggs, yet just at this time the hailstorm was over, and the rain poured and revived her, and her dizziness left her.

When she had revived and the storm was spent, she began to preen her wet feathers, after settling again to her eggs. The meadowlark sang with silly joy, and the upland plover whistled mournfully, and Bird Creek roared.

On the twenty-first and twenty-second day of her brooding, there was a peep under her breast, and she stuck her head under her feathers and made soft sounds of encouragement. Then the next day when all the ten eggs had hatched, and after the dew had been burned by the sun, she led her flock away from the nest never to return. That night with the damp earth carry-ing even the faintest of scents, a coyote trotting by had his nose drawn to the edge of the thicket as if someone had pulled it with a cord. He stopped and nosed among the olive-colored eggshells, pushing them out of the nest with his nose. His curiosity satisfied, he raised his leg against the shells and the nest, then trotted off on coyote business.

The tragedy of the earth's balance began the moment the little prairie chickens pipped their way out of their shells with their little egg teeth. In the oak and cedar patch a week after the hatching, a Cooper's hawk swooped from his station on the lower limb of a post oak and clutched one of the chicks that was too slow in freezing on the mother's cry of danger and flew low through the tree trunks with it in his talons. The next day he caught another one, and the hen led her brood away from the blackjacks and onto the prairie where there would be no blue-grey shadows that turned into savage Cooper's hawks.

One morning a coyote trotted over the prairie, after his night of hunting. He had possibly had good hunting since he trotted in a straight line, but too close to the hen and her brood for comfort. She gave the alarum, then crouched close to the earth until she came to a tall spiderwort, whose stems and leaves she could use. Standing up straight and with head as high as she could reach, she would look like just another tall spiderwort to the coyote in the early morning light. She gave the signal to freeze and her chicks all faced one way, the direction away from the coyote, and they looked like bits of last winter's grass, small sandstones, or dead leaves blown from the patch of blackjacks during the March winds.

The hen, with feathers very close and her body very thin and her head held high, watched the coyote out of sight, then gave the all-clear signal and the little flock carried on with their food hunting.

By the time October came with the pin oak leaves red and shining in the sun and the white ash leaves bronze-purple, the mother prairie chicken and her eight chicks with Arrowflight were the beginning of a new flock and the west pasture became their province.

The chicks were grown now and were truly arrowflight birds themselves. The flock would fly from oak ridge to oak ridge over the prairie to eat the acorns, but when they left the patch of blackjacks in the west pasture they went without Arrowflight. He couldn't very well avoid being of the flock when they foraged in the west pasture, but when they flew across the prairie to the north, he remained behind.

But he had begun to depend upon the eyes and the ears of the hen prairie chicken, and there is no keener hearing and sharper eyes than those of a hen prairie chicken who has brought to adulthood eight children out of ten. He even relaxed when he was a part of the flock together and she sat in a post oak as the others fed.

One day, when the hen had led her children across the prairie to the north to feast on sluggish autumnal grasshoppers and Arrowflight was alone, the high circling of migratory hawks caught his eye. These were red-tails and harriers and Swainson's and he had no fear of them, but there were so many that his curiosity was aroused, and he stood with stretched neck watching them when he was suddenly aware that the ranch bird dog was pointing him, only a few yards away. He knew the ranch bird dog and knew what to do about him. He squatted and then ran through the tall bluestem looking back, but the well-trained dog continued to stand. Arrowflight stopped and raised his head above the grass to have a last look at the outwitted dog.

There was a flash in his brain and that is the last he knew of the world of prairie and blackjack and post oak and cedar. The boy came to pick him up, and then went proudly to meet the other boy, holding Arrowflight up. The boys were not trespassing. They had obtained permission to hunt squirrels. The ranch dog, seeing and smelling their .22-caliber rifles, had followed them to the patch of post oaks and blackjacks in the west pasture.

The relationship that had existed for so long between the man-animal and the prairie chicken cock lost its natural rhythm for only a moment, and Arrowflight had to die so stupidly.

When the boy who killed Arrowflight approached the other, he held him high and said, "Look, I've killed a chicken hawk—I guess it's a chicken hawk."

The Last Dance

T HE LITTLE HEATH COCK was a bird of destiny. His mother kept making her little clucking sound to assure him and his little brood mates that all was well, but he was the only one among the six that had been hatched this May day in 1924 that was active and vigorous, and it was because of this vigor, intelligence, and alertness that he became a bird of destiny. The other five seemed dull, and one peeped constantly and before they could leave the nest, died. There was a little brother with toes that pointed back toward the heel, and he walked jerkily, like a man with bunions, and the remaining little ones seemed to desire to stay in the little depression where they had been hatched when the mother heath hen stepped daintily away, careful not to step on any one of them.

Even when she called them to follow, only the little cock of destiny followed quickly and with joy. He even ran ahead of her and lifted his downy little wing tabs.

She waited for the others. Soon one came toward her, but had to rest on the way; then the other two came to the mother's call. This call was reassuring, and even though they had not heard it until this moment, it was a racial memory which had been handed down through the centuries, and they knew this call as surely as if they had been taught its meaning through repeated lessons.

The mother stopped and, with head high, listened and noted every movement of grass stem and leaf. She had no friends. There were house cats gone wild and hawks and other enemies on Martha's Vineyard, and the laws of nature are harsh. She stood for some time, stretching her neck, and listened for the least breaking of a stick, scraping of leaves, and saw every grass blade wave and every leaf move in the gentle air.

As she stood, almost ready to move on in order to get as far away from the nest as possible, she caught a movement in the corner of her eye. It was the vigorous little cock of destiny exploring on his own. He was facing a little field mouse, and neither one of them knew what he ought to do, so the little mouse stood up on his haunches and began to wash his face. He wasn't in the least frightened since he knew this perky little ball of brownish, yellowish down could do him no harm. But he wasn't quite sure just what he ought to do, so he washed his face.

Mother heath hen knew that the mouse was harmless as well, but she was annoyed with her chick for his boldness in going out on his own. She called sharply, and he came running back, not frightened, but with the joy of being alive surging within him. He lifted his little downy tabs, which later would be strong wings, and raced back to his mother.

The mother moved on slowly, clucking encouragingly, and her downy little ones followed: the splay-toed little male running jerkily and the other three, strung out behind, struggling with every weed stem and falling over every stone and fallen branch. The mother went on, crouching low to the earth so that her movements might not be seen, and the little ones followed, and walking with her, and at times being trod upon, was the strong-bodied, joyful little cock of destiny.

She was now in the thick growth of scrub oak saplings, and she knew a hawk would not be able to see her here, or even if he did, he wouldn't endanger his wings by trying to catch her.

There was an anthill there and she began to call her brood. She would pick up an ant, then drop it, then pick it up and eat it. The cock of destiny got the lesson immediately and imitated her, then began to pick up ants as they ran madly about.

Mother heath hen of course couldn't count, and she didn't know that her brood of five were not all with her at the anthill. But she knew suddenly when she heard the peeping back along the way she had come. She cared little about giving away her movements now, and rushed back toward the sound of the peeping, her feathers fluffed and her wings atrail. This was not her battle attitude, but bluff. All animals and birds bluff when they know they must face an enemy.

But there was no enemy; there was only a little ball of down, wonderfully colored so that it had the same pattern as that which the sunlight made on the leaves and the grasses. It was one of the little females, and she seemed too weak to climb over a fallen limb, over which the others had struggled without much effort; even little splayfoot had managed. Now the mother clucked and walked about helplessly. She touched the little one with her beak, and it stopped peeping, but when she looked back she saw that the others were trying to follow her back to the rescue of the little sister. They were in the open and moving, and even the odd little patterns of sunlight on the grasses and earth that would make them invisible if motionless were of little use when they moved in the open.

She was disturbed, so she shouted "kr-r-r-r-r-r," and they each one stopped in their tracks, squatted, and became motionless. Now you couldn't see them at all; their dappled patterns protected them.

The mother walked about the chick; then finally after walking several times around the limb, the little one followed her and they came around the end of it. On the way back to the concealed chicks, the little female stopped and began to peep, and again the mother heath hen fluffed her feathers and rushed to her, but this time only clucked and then went on and the little one finally followed her. When she arrived back at the hidden brood, she gave the signal and it was as if bits of stone and little tufts of grass might have come to life. The mother bent low and crept under some scrub oak saplings, then sat on the back of her "knees" and the chicks came under her for a nap.

Within a week, the cock of destiny had little quills coming out of the edge of his wing tabs, and they seemed to weight the wings so that he carried them lower. The same with splayfoot and the others. The little female that had been unable to climb over the fallen limb could scarcely keep her little tabs up because of the weight of her starting quills, and she was always the straggler, and often during the day when the family were foraging she would stop and peep until the mother would give the signal for the others to hide while she went back to determine what might have gone wrong. The mother was ever ready with her fluffed-feather bluffing, but she usually found no enemy to bluff, only the miserable female sitting, and too tired to travel farther. She might be caught in the grass stems through which the others had come without trouble.

But one day, after the family had been dust-bathing in the lazy hours of the spring afternoon, the heath hen had led her brood away from the dusting grounds rather hurriedly since the log with the lovely grubs was an eighth of a mile away and the shadows were growing long. In the area of the log, there was no place for hovering her brood for the night, so she must come back to the scrub oak saplings. She became impatient with the slowness of her brood, as well as with the cock of destiny, who always ran ahead, often too far ahead.

She would stop after twenty or thirty yards to stretch her neck and note every movement as she listened, even though she was in a hurry to get to the rotting log and its wonderful grubs. As she made the third stop, she heard the peeping of her unhappy little female. She gave the alarum to hide, then rushed back toward the sound, but just as she arrived, she saw a house cat gone wild walking off through the brush, his tail waving with contentment and self-appreciation. She fluffed her feathers even more and rushed at him, but he only turned his great moon face to her, and she stopped. He stood, drew his lips back, and growled, and in his mouth was the downy body of the little female. The cat's tail was no longer waving gently with self-appreciation, but was twitching with anger.

The poor mother came back to her brood and soon forgot the tragedy, and though she had only four babies with her, there might as well have been five since she couldn't count.

Another week passed, and every minute, each day and each night, this mother of the wild had to be on alert guard. At night the great horned owl hunted and paralysed the people of the grassroots with fear when he hooted. She herself would bring her feathers close about her, pressing closer over her brood, as if by growing smaller and shutting her eyes she would escape his ears. One night, quite close, the tomcat that had caught her little one made the slightest of noises and the great bird fell upon him and buried his talons in his back. The noise of the spitting and the yowling was so frightful that the heath hen, in making herself small, pressed too hard against her children and there were peeps of pain. The remainder of the night she hovered her brood, frozen, waiting for death.

Death did not come to her, but when she left the spot where she had hovered, another of the little females was dead. That afternoon it had lagged behind and only pecked at the food with indifference. When they went to the dusting grounds, it had not joined the others, but had sat at the edge of the dust bath and, with eyes shut, had allowed its beak to rest on the earth.

After the mother left with her brood, a crow came to the branches of a scrub oak, cocked his eye at the little body, then after looking at it from several positions on the tree, hopped down and picked it up, and flew to a limb higher up, and there hammered the little body on the limb until he had broken it into bits small enough to be swallowed. He would never have seen the protectively colored little grouse if she had been alive. Dead animals and birds have their own shapes.

The mother and little brood moved on. Now there were only three, but still she didn't know the difference since she couldn't count, but there was plenty of food, and soon there were feathers grown out of the little wing tabs, reaching almost to the little tails, which had sprouted their own little tufts of feathers; and when one day a farm dog came trotting by with his tongue out as if he were laughing to himself, the mother gave the hiding signal and then flew out over the tops of the scrub and toward the dog. She flew on in front of him and fell to the ground—in a clear spot where she would not be hindered—and assumed an agonized look and lifted one wing and made it quiver. The dog forgot his little joke, cocked his ears and closed his mouth, then bounded forward toward the hen, but just as he got to her, she with the greatest of difficulty got to her feet, ran a few yards, then, barely getting off the ground, wobbled over the tops of the scrub oak saplings. The dog came after her, tearing through the brush, but she kept just ahead of him. When she had led him away from her children, she flew off on sound wing. When she came back, she called and the little ones appeared—not all three of them; just two of them. The cock of destiny, on the alarum and seeing the dog in his keenness, had put his baby wings to use and flown into a tree and there froze against a limb, and when his mother called it was as if a piece of bark had come to life. In a tree you are safe from foxes and wolves and dogs, and his ancestors had sent this message to him through the centuries, and in him was the instinct that had protected his species through the ages.

Each day, each hour, each minute, the animals and birds of the forest, the woodlands, the plains, the desert, the mountains must be alert or they cannot survive. Nature will have no weaklings or slow thinkers, or those who cannot react or adjust. In the world of nature, where there is continuous struggle to survive, there can be no misfits, only the perfect ones, so that naturally not even the most cautious and alert mothering could protect little splayfoot and his dull little sister.

While foraging one morning the mother heath hen had seen a goshawk sail over the tops of the trees and she had given the alarum, and the little female froze where she was, and the mother ran to the bushes with the alert little cock of destiny with her, while little splayfoot became excited and tried to run to cover instead of freezing. The sailing goshawk, low over the scrub, saw the wobbling movement, spread his long tail as a brake, and then using it as a rudder, stopped and turned in midair, then fell like a plummet on the little splayfoot. He wasn't much of a meal for the big bird, but an appetizer.

The sprouting wings of the little female grew so heavy that the feathers dragged the ground each morning when the dew weighted them down. She sought food halfheartedly, and when she found a spot of sunlight, she stood long there with her eyes shut, and sometimes murmured with discontent, even while being warmed in the sun spot. But these sun spots were in the open.

One morning a house cat came along—a great, round-faced brindle tom who as a kitten had been left at the roadside in a sack, his owners so filled with sentiment that they could not destroy or give this unwanted kitten away but, by their sentimental action, doomed many a heath hen and songbird. The little grouse's protective color pattern escaped the brindled tom as she stood still with head in the air and eyes shut. He was about to pass with thoughts on some cat business that had to do with stranded fish at sea's edge, when his ears caught the faint little peep of complaint. He stopped and stood frozen for a minute, then the faint little complaint again, and he fixed his attention on an object that looked like an odd bit of earth. Then the bit of earth moved a little, and the tom crouched and drew his lips back and, very slowly, silently pumped his front feet up and down, alternating them, as if he would build the rhythm for the pounce.

The miserable little grouse peeped faintly again and moved as if to join her mother and brother, but the tom pounced and carried her off. Her peeps were so faint that her mother had not heard them, and the tom had cut off all sound so that the mother never missed her.

It was better this way. The little sick misfit could have endangered the lives of both her mother and brother by the very fact that she was unfit in the struggle of the scrub oak plains of Martha's Vineyard, Massachusetts. The cock of destiny and his mother were alone now, and they found abundant food: not only fruits and spiders and insects and green leaves, but there was a certain place on the Green farm where there was an ever-ready banquet of grain, kept fresh by their ancient enemy who had recently become a friend: man. Farmer Green was not the provider, but the state of Massachusetts. The people of Massachusetts had become concerned about the heath hens of Martha's Vineyard and had raised $70,000 to set aside a special reservation for them, and then had appointed special wardens to protect them.

When the cock of destiny and his mother felt the need of grain, they went to this opening in the reservation and there they met other heath hens. When the cocks saw the mother and her lucky child, they might lower their heads, inflate their sacs, and dance briefly, even in the autumn, because there were only seventeen heath hens in all the world, and only three of them female. The cocks were lonesome.

The cock of destiny grew into a fine cock and he went at mating time to the little opening in the brush where the cocks gathered each year to dance and boom. They came there in April of each spring, just at sunrise, and immediately began their dance to impress the females. They elevated the pinnate feathers above their heads, spread their wings a little, and held them close to their sides; then they lowered their heads and there appeared on each side of the neck a great orange-colored, orange-shaped balloon, and they boomed "oo-den-oo-den-OOO-o-o-o-o," and they stamped the ground with their feet. The sacs were deflated and the pinnate feathers, which had looked like horns, lowered, but the unspread tails remained elevated as the cocks ran for forty or fifty yards with heads down, then stopped and elevated their pinnate feathers, inflated their sacs, and boomed again. The hens sat about and watched, or walked about pecking at imaginary food to show their complete indifference to male vanity and parading.

The days passed. The oak leaves turned brown, and there was a new danger now from migrating hawks. However, when the cock of destiny saw his mother and several of the others that had joined them tilt their heads to the sky and keep one eye on a circling speck, he soon learned that this was simply a matter of curiosity, or for the purpose of assuring themselves that the circling hawk was one of the broad-winged species who circled high in the sky playing with the winds and was definitely not looking for heath hens. The grouse would stand and watch, sometimes uttering a little note of mild warning, which sounded like "er-r-r-r-r-r," which was to say, "Never take any bird of prey for granted; watch him." They stood out in the open as the hawk or hawks circled, only two tilting their heads while the others fed.

But the cock of destiny knew the goshawk well, and all the other of his kin whom the farmers called "blue darters." When these graceful hunters flew swiftly among the trees or sailed low, the heath hens squatted and froze immediately or ran for cover. When the falcons came, then you must freeze and hide and never in your fright leave the earth since the terrible and beautiful bird would fall like a plummet on a grouse's back and break his neck, and the body would fall to earth, a bundle of disheveled feathers, and the falcon would then circle and alight by the body.

So even when the cock of destiny and his mother were foraging, one or the other would stop after several pecks at the food and stand still to listen or cock an eye to the trees, which the goshawks would use as hunting stations. Often the two would draw their feathers close and stretch their necks to a ridiculous length to see better over the weeds and the brush.

Then there were the moonlight nights when the savage house cats prowled and the great horned owl hunted, but because of the mother's experience and age and because of the cock of destiny's racial memories, so vivid in his high intelligence, and because of his physical perfection and coordination and because of the warden's daily banquet of grain, they survived.

But there were only two heath hen females now in all the world, three years after the cock of destiny's birth, and the biologists and ornithologists and the members of the bird clubs and officials and wardens of the state of Massachusetts came and built blinds near the feed ground and near the dance grounds and they counted the birds as they came, and they counted the cocks dancing and they remembered that the brood which the cock of destiny's mother had hatched were the last heath hen chicks to be hatched. That was in 1924, and now in 1927 they counted only thirteen heath hens in all the world, and only two of these were females.

The year before the cock of destiny's mother had been shot by some boys from Tisbury. They had come out with a .22-caliber single-loader and shot at everything that moved, and had managed to kill a rabbit; then when they were walking along by the spot on the Green farm where the state was feeding the precious heath hens, the youngest one of the three carrying the rabbit, they were talking with excitement. One shouted, "Hey, there's a pheasant." The mother of the cock of destiny was sneaking through the brush, low to the ground, away from the clamor and the cracking of twigs. She was actually out of sight when the boy pulled the trigger, but by accident the lead barely scraped her back and hit her in the back of the head. Being head-shot, her flutterings were startling, and she was still pounding the earth with her wings when the boys came to pick her up and gloat. The boy with the rifle held her up. "'T'ain't no pheasant," he said.

They all three knew that it was a heath hen and immediately knew they were in very serious trouble. The *Vineyard Gazette* had taken up the cause of the vanishing heath hens, and even the lowest gunner, along with the sportsmen and the public in general, was interested in saving them. The situation was very serious. They couldn't leave her body there where she had been killed, since a warden would be sure to find her, and with the telltale twenty-two caliber bullet hole in the head.

They took the body to a small sand dune, after scattering the death-struggle feathers to the wind, and there buried the mother of the cock of destiny.

So when the heath cocks came to their dance ground to dance in 1927, there were only eleven of them and they danced for the last two heath hens on earth.

During the two Aprils of his youth, Cock of Destiny was not allowed by the older and stronger cocks to mate, but now he himself was the strongest cock on the dance ground, though the youngest, and took both the females to himself.

The season grew, and the other cocks became discouraged and drifted off, and Cock of Destiny grew disinterested in dancing after the two females went off to lay their eggs in simple nests which they had scraped in the earth. He wandered off with some of the other cocks, and they were friends again after the nuptial dances, but he never knew that the two clutches of eggs did not hatch. Even the perfect heath cock could not now transmit his strength, his alertness, his intelligence and perfect physical attributes, to future generations of heath hens. Through disease and inbreeding, the species was weakened. A fire that swept the island in 1916, driven by a sea gale, had occurred at a time when the heath hens were on their nests, on the 12th of May. The people of the bird societies, the biologists, the ornithologists, and the people of the state were happy before this fire since the heath hens were estimated by wardens to number two thousand, and they had only numbered two hundred in 1906, a year before the reservations were established through donations by the people.

But this terrible fire had thrown the balance of nature out, and that winter goshawks came by the thousands to pick up the smoke-blinded heath hens, and the cats wandered about in search of the charred bodies of the young ones and the rats ate these and the eggs that had been roasted in the nests.

The fire destroyed the birds and the insects and the rodents that had lived on the insects which carried the bacilli which caused the heath hen diseases. By 1920, the biologists and the ornithologists were picking up dead and diseased heath hens that not even the cats and the hawks could dispose of, and they counted only 314 heath hens alive, and the year Cock of Destiny was hatched, only seventeen.

During the winter of 1927, Cock of Destiny's mates failed to show up at the feed grounds since they had died, and there were only six males besides himself, and during the winter, the goshawks and the cats got all except three.

The species called heath hens was dying out: some dying of disease but most of them became so weakened by disease and through general stupidity that they were taken easily by the hawks and the cats.

But the cock of destiny, as strong and alert as ever, lived on, carrying within his perfect body the racial spirit and alertness of the centuries. He came to the dancing grounds in April of 1928, but there were no hens to see him as he strutted up and down his beat, booming with so much volume that he could be heard two miles away. There were only two other cocks booming and dancing at the edges of the area, too weak and weary to contest the cock of destiny. And anyway, there were no hens in all the world, and when the sun had climbed well above the horizon, the cock of destiny stopped his dancing, deflated his sacs, and stood like a mounted specimen, as if he were in great puzzlement over what had happened to his world.

The other cocks, who had lost their vitality, seemed tired of earth living, and they ceased their dancing and booming long before the cock of destiny had done. The latter shook his feathers, pretended to pick up food as if he would shake off his puzzlement and go back to the business of life. He cocked his head to the sky to see that all was clear, then walked over to the two other cocks, and they became friends again and began to search for food among the scrub oaks.

It seemed that when the two other cocks were with the cock of destiny they were safe, but when autumn came, and one day they were separated, feeding, a goshawk appeared, alternately flapping and sailing over the scrub. One of the cocks became distracted and took wing. The hawk had not seen him until this moment of nerve failure. He spread his tail as a brake and then swung it as a rudder and, folding his wings and drawing his feathers close, he hit the unfortunate cock from above and they came to earth together. The hawk flapped into the air, barely able to carry his prey. He settled on a fire-blackened stump and there ate one of the last three heath cocks in all the world.

In December of that winter, the other cock, weakened by disease and inbreeding and weary of life, died in his sleep by freezing.

And now the last heath cock on earth was watched by the wardens and the biologists and the ornithologists and the members of the bird-watching clubs, and the cock of destiny became the Last Cock, and there were stories about him in the *Vineyard Gazette,* and grave men sat about polished tables and talked of him and wondered if they should send to Wisconsin for female prairie chickens as mates for him.

On April mornings when he came to the dance grounds, now, there were men watching him from blinds with pencils and notebooks and with camera lenses trained on him.

One April morning he approached the dance ground with all his senses alert as usual. He stood at the edge of the dance ground for minutes, waiting, and the watchers in the blinds became impatient with him and squirmed.

Was he waiting for the hens that would never come again? Was he waiting for the listless cocks he had dominated in the glory of his strength? He stood and the watchers waited. Then he moved with great dignity to the middle of the dance ground and the cinema cameras churred and the still cameras clicked, but still he did nothing to indicate that he might dance. He pecked at the food placed there for him and raised his head and gazed about him. He cocked his eye at the sky; then, as if he were afraid to satisfy some urge within him, there on the ground, where he had always danced, he flew to the dead limb at the top of a tree at the edge of the dance ground and there, after gazing about him expectantly, he elevated his tail, lowered his head, inflated his sacs, and with his pinnate feathers sticking up like horns, he boomed several times. Suddenly he drew his feathers close and after looking about him, he flew down among the scrub oaks and was lost to view.

This April of 1932, he came again to the dance ground, and the lens eyes were on him from the blinds in the scrub oaks. The observers got their pencils and notebooks ready. He hesitated for only a short time at the edge of the dance area this time, then came directly to the middle of it, and there stood like a museum bird for a minute. Then, impulsively, he began to dance with great intensity. His sacs were inflated and glowed in the morning light, like polished oranges, and his pinnate feathers seemed even more like horns. His head was low, and the observers on this very quiet morning could hear his feet beat the earth.

Suddenly he stopped and brought his wings back to normal position. His pinnate feathers lowered and his sacs deflated, he shook himself violently. He was like one who had awakened from a dream. He walked sedately to the edge of the stunted oaks and was lost in the black shadows made by the early morning sun rays. Last Cock was never seen again. He had danced his species into oblivion.

The White Gobbler
of Rancho Seco

THERE IS AN AREA WHERE the Hondo River of southwestern Texas flows through valleys of its own making, where men have planted fields of wheat and some have milk cows and chickens and turkeys. There was one who raised White Holland turkeys for the market. In the upper reaches of the river, there were cone-shaped hills and steep ridge hills like mountains covered with brush, and this was cattle country.

A coyote from the hills wandered downriver one night and came upon the yard where hundreds of White Holland turkeys roosted on their huts behind a mesh wire fence. This was wonderful; he had been accustomed to have very hard hunting in the harsh hill country, and often went for days with the rodent of hunger gnawing at his belly. The odor of turkey was delightful, but there was the fence.

He tried scratching at the bottom of the fence but that was no good, so he trotted around it until he came near the house before he was aware, and there was suddenly a terrific clamor of dogs barking. They had smelled him.

He slunk away and when he had gone about a quarter of a mile he stopped and looked back. The dogs were still barking. He lay on his belly in the bushes to think things over. He was very hungry, and it was a terrible thing to have to leave all those silly, man-protected turkeys. The fools had not even said "perk-perk" when they saw him in the dim light of a new moon.

But the scent of turkey still filled his nose and he was separated from them by a quarter of a mile of bushes. He lay and then began to look around and there, only a few feet from him, he saw something ashen and he knew why the scent of turkey was so strong. There under a bush was a white turkey hen on her eggs. She had got out of the pen and stolen away to lay her eggs and now had begun to brood her clutch and would add the last egg within a few hours.

She said only "perk-perk," thinking that the coyote was a dog. He rose very carefully, then stood and looked at her. He would take no chances. He knew turkeys; they flew when you tried to catch them, so he stood very still and the silly hen stared back, saying "perk-perk."

He rushed suddenly and caught her by the neck. The struggle was brief, and he began feasting there on the spot. He ate most of her, and he was so full that he could only stretch out and pant for perhaps half an hour; then he went to have a look at the nest. He rolled several of the eggs out and then fell to his belly and began to play with them, hitting at them playfully with his paw. When one broke, he would lick up the contents, but he was not the least hungry of course, so after licking up the contents of the last one he broke, he walked a little way off where there were tufts of grass and, lowering his chin into the grass, he pushed himself along with his hind legs, thus washing his face.

The dogs had ceased barking sometime before and he stood as if in deep thought; then he took up the carcass of the turkey and trotted off for his cone-shaped hills, several miles away. When he arrived at a familiar spot, he laid the turkey down and sank to his belly and with his tongue hanging he panted, but he was not really hot. He seemed pleased with himself.

He got up and nosed the carcass, reaching inside the skeleton, and selecting the titbits—the lungs from the back, the liver, and the heart—and he nibbled the egg bag and sheath, and an unlaid egg rolled down a light incline. He followed it, and when it stopped by a thick, overhanging bush, he nosed it a moment, then went back to his carcass, picked it up, and trotted over the saddle.

The morning mists had cleared and the sun was well up when a wild turkey hen came crouched very low through the bushes. She would stop and look and listen, for perhaps thirty seconds, without even blinking her eyes; then she would crouch again and creep through the bushes, stop again for about thirty seconds and, standing straight up, with her feathers close about her body, would listen and watch for movement. Suddenly she crept to her nest, adjusted her body on her seven eggs, and became quiet. Then the egg from the carcass that had rolled down the incline the night before caught her eye and, thinking it was one of hers that had rolled out of the nest, she reached out with her beak and, hooking it over the egg so that the egg came under her neck, she drew it to her and pushed it beneath her; then, with a slight squirm, she was settled.

She had come to lay her last egg before beginning to brood, and from this day she would remain on her eggs and every day thereafter for twenty-eight days, leaving her nest only to eat every other day and have a dust bath.

Chip, the rancho foreman, was the first to see the white poult. He had ridden out into the brush to count the new quarter horse colts. He had to take dim deer trails through the kinikinik, the live oak, and the cedars, and he had to climb the steep hillsides and stop to allow his horse to rest and get his breath many times during the search, so he had plenty of time to look over the country, and at such stops he often could make out the great ears of a nervous doe, gazing intently at him and wondering what she ought to do—run or stand without even flicking one of those big ears. If she stood, perhaps this dangerous man-animal would not see her. This time of the year in the spring, she was very nervous, and had to know what every sound meant and to test the air with her nose every few minutes. Her spotted fawn hidden in the bushes would have many more enemies than she herself had before it arrived.

But Chip pretended he didn't see her so that she wouldn't run off and wave her white tail flag to tell the half-wild mares that he was coming. The horse made enough noise as it was.

As he followed the hoofprints of some mares with colts at their sides, his chaps would scrape the live oaks; when his wise horse stepped to the side of the trail in avoiding a pear cactus, the scraping became louder and this was entirely too much noise. The mares were not really wild, but they were afraid that he might be coming to drive them back to the ranch corrals. They were happy with their freedom.

Then suddenly Grulla snorted, lowered his head as if he might buck, and threw Chip against the pommel of the saddle. The live oak brush had suddenly come alive with wild turkeys. A turkey hen, frightened by the scraping of the bushes, took flight into a Spanish oak with her half-grown poults, and there they sat stretching their necks, seeming to be quite surprised that the thing making the terrible noise was only the man-animal and a horse.

Chip swore at Grulla. "You crazy old fool," he said. "Haven't you ever seen a turkey hen and her young ones before?" He touched the horse with his spur and started to ride on when he saw an object of white in the very tall Spanish oak. White objects in the Temperate Zone will attract the attention of all animals because white is unusual where all birds and animals must blend with their surroundings so that their enemies can't see them if they also remain immobile. This white object was immobile, but it called out to be seen by all, seeming to shout, "Look at me."

"What is that white rag doing in that tree?" thought Chip, and he reined Grulla toward the tree to examine it. People, like the lower animals, *must* know the nature of white things in the mountains and the deserts and plateaux of the Temperate Zone, and certainly in this sun-dominated region of Texas.

After leaving the trail, he could scarcely see the young turkeys and certainly he couldn't have counted them since they were very still and even blended with the leaves and the bark of the oak, but he kicked Grulla through the brush since he must determine what that white thing was.

Then something happened: the white thing took wing and flew, wobbling a little, and lost itself in the leaves of the trees. Soon the hen and then the others followed one and two and three at a time, taking the same direction.

All Chip could think of as a solution for this strange happening was one word and he uttered it to himself, "Albino." That night he told his wife about it. "When the hunters come out this November, that white'un is a goner. Ever'body will be awantin' 'im—if he is a gobbler, and I guess he is judgin' by his size."

Chip was right about the white poult being a gobbler but wrong about his being an albino, and it never occurred to him to wonder why he was the first one to leave the tree and lose himself completely in the trees of the hillside. Why would one poult fly before his mother gave the signal while the others sat frozen and waited for the signal?

From the day he was hatched, the white tom had to adjust to the fact that he was different, and in this adjustment he learned things faster than the others because he had to do so to preserve his own life. And all of this was due to the fact that he was white, and from the day of his hatching he seemed to shout to the world, "Look at me." The struggle to survive was much more difficult for him than it was for the others, who were protectively pattern-colored; and they were not compelled to use their wits every minute of their lives and therefore they were not as sharp as the white gobbler. He had already learned much because of his whiteness by the time Chip flushed his family on the hillside.

The day he was hatched, he came out from under the breast feathers of his mother along with the others and pecked at her eyelids and her wattles, but immediately she noticed him and was uncertain about him. She said something like "yok" and pushed him away with her beak, but he came back; then she pecked him, and he rolled over on his back, and when he had got to his feet, he with legs wide apart stood for a few moments. He wanted to join the others, who were still pecking at mother's wattles, but he was afraid. He had begun to learn, from the very hour of his hatching, the harshness of the struggle to survive.

He made one more attempt to join the others, who stood just outside her breast feathers, and the newly hatched ones who peeked out from under them. The hen pecked him and again he was sent rolling. This time he stood for a long time, until the air grew cold and the others had gone under the mother to snuggle under her warm body; then he went around behind the hen and crept under with the others.

When the hen stepped daintily off the nest the next day, each poult was ready to follow her. She said "tuke, tuke" constantly, as she led the way through the kinikinik bushes. After several days, she became reconciled to the white poult and treated him as she treated the others, holding up a grub for him, and held still while he took it from her beak. Sometimes when she ran to catch a fat insect, she might run over one or more of her children, but never the White Gobbler since he was careful to keep out of the way of her feet and her beak, and even though she accepted him completely now, when she squatted to hover them, the White Gobbler went under her tail to the nursery.

The scrub jays found him a novelty when he was still in his white down, and they followed the brood, hopping from limb to limb and flying from tree to tree above them, talking like scatterbrains about this white poult. Once, one alighted among the brood as they fed and attacked the White Gobbler. If the hen had not come to his rescue, he might have been killed. One day a squirrel ran at him and knocked him over, but before he could sink his great chisel teeth into him, the hen had intervened. Now he was ever alert for jays and squirrels. Neither one of them wanted him for food, but he was white and they had to do something about it.

Much later, when the poults had grown wings, the scrub jays would gather in a flock, like a gang in a large city; they would swear and tease and bounce above the flock, and once this brought a coyote sneaking through the brush. The hen was worried by the jays' fearful swearing, so she was standing with her neck stretched high and saw the coyote. She gave the "fly" alarum signal and the whole flock flew into the tree just in time. The coyote immediately saw the White Gobbler on a high limb, and he stood for some time watching him. When the coyote had trotted away, the hen fell from her limb and with heavy wing beats flew high over the ridge, the flock following her.

Chip saw the White Gobbler several times that summer, but he noted that, instead of standing still against the brush or against the lichened rocks of the hillsides or running as the others did, he immediately rose and flew over a ridge or a divide. The White Gobbler now knew or rather perhaps he now "felt" that his lack of color pattern not only did not protect him but was a curse. It was like the sun shining on chromium, drawing all eyes.

Chip sat Grulla for some minutes and watched the others of the almost-grown flock walk away from him up the hillside, taking advantage of the shadows and the cedars and the live oaks and the rocks so that their bronze-black-grey-trimmed feathers blended perfectly, and even with his keen eyes Chip was not sure that he saw them at times, and even then he could only see two or three of the flock of ten at one time.

Chip was a keen observer, just as all cowboys and hunters must be, but he was puzzled by the White Gobbler. That night he said to his wife, "Saw that white gobbler again today; yu know that albino? I can't figure what makes him so wild."

There was an incident several times each week which disturbed the area in which the White Gobbler, his mother, and his brothers and sisters foraged. They remained a flock, those who were left of the original brood of eight. Now there were six almost-grown poults, their mother, and three other hens who had not raised families. These hens had joined them during the late summer and later, in the early autumn, another hen with her five poults joined them, and there were now sixteen wild turkeys foraging over an area that might comprise a thousand acres during years when the live oak acorns were not plentiful or during years when the kinikinik berries did not produce abundantly. They didn't need this much acreage when these fruits were abundant.

They wandered about in search of food during the early morning hours and perhaps until ten or eleven o'clock; then they sought a spot where the cover was protective and there rested during the noon hours and until about three o'clock in the afternoon. They found spots within sight of each other where they would just sit and rest, or where those who chose to do so might dust-bathe.

But there was always a sentinel—always one or more of the old hens who stood completely alert for half an hour or an hour. They stood with heads high, listening, and noting every movement. On windy days, when the leaves rattled or the limbs of the trees swayed, the sentinels were nervous.

When a sentinel came to sit or dust-bathe, another took her place, with that understanding which man has never been able to fathom. The sentinel coming to sit and to preen, and perhaps to nap, simply left her post and another hen took her place. If danger was sensed, heard, or seen, she gave the signal, and from the inflection of her voice or by the nature of the signal, the others reacted. They slipped low through the brush, silently, with the dust of their dust-bathing still falling from their feathers. They dared not shake themselves when a danger signal was given. Then when they had sneaked through the brush for some distance, whether or not they took wing of course depended on the nature of the enemy, and from the alarum signal of the sentinel, they *knew* the nature of the enemy. If the enemy was a coyote or a bobcat or a hound, they would fly into a tree; if an eagle, they would freeze, and if a man, they would sneak out ahead of him and, keeping to cover, make of him a clumsy, stupid animal.

But this flock of sixteen were endangered by the whiteness of the White Gobbler. He was a big bird now and carried his head high and his breast was much broader than those of his brothers, and his alertness was equal to that of any of the old hens, but he was never trusted as a sentinel. Not because he was white but because he was in his first year and a gobbler. The hens with their broods never depended on the gobblers to warn them since, even now in early autumn when they happened to meet up with a flock of old gobblers, the latter thought only of showing off. One or two of them would lower their wings, lay their heads back on their backs, and prance about for a few minutes; then they would readjust their feathers and the two flocks would separate, the gobblers going one way and the hens and their broods the other.

And each night they chose a different roosting tree. Perhaps a great horned owl had called too close to the one they had been in, or perhaps they might feel the coming of low pressure, and one of the old hens would lead the flock to a tall tree in a canyon and they would fly to it from the rim. Here they would be protected from the autumnal winds and escape the full force of the autumnal rains.

One day a bobcat saw the White Gobbler from a cliff as the flock foraged up the canyon. He had the protective color-pattern of the hunter, and there on the cliff he was like a lichen-covered boulder. His spots were like the spots made by the sun on the leaves and the bushes and his stripes and bars were like stem shadows. He was a poor trailer, but he was quite able to keep this flock in view, with the tall white gobbler standing with head high as the others fed. The White Gobbler was like a crane.

He watched with great expectations since he knew how to hunt turkeys. As the flock fed along the floor of the canyon, they would, he knew, forage up to the very head of the canyon, and there he would be waiting for them.

He slunk back from the edge of the cliff and crept almost on his belly through the brush; arrived at the head of the canyon, he chose a leafy Spanish oak and climbed it, then waited.

He was very patient. Stupefied autumnal flies would cause him to twitch his ear occasionally, and some titmice and chickadees discovered him when he had to flick a stinging fly from his ear. They were not jays or squirrels, so they soon lost interest in this bundle of fur that remained so immobile, and a good thing too, since the bobcat could hear the turkeys talking among themselves as they foraged slowly up the canyon floor.

He became tense, and his lips were drawn back and wrinkled involuntarily. He could see them now, because of the White Gobbler. The bobcat moved his hind feet ever so little to make sure that the bark would not give way when he made his lunge.

The several old hens of the flock came on talking, and the young ones followed, all with their heads to the earth, foraging. They would come directly under the Spanish oak. They had only a few yards to come now, and the bobcat could make his choice.

But suddenly there was a "k-i-r-k-r-r-r-r-put-put," and each bird stood still, as if he or she had been galvanized, and then there was a muffled sound of wing beats, and early autumn leaves were sent rolling over the ground as the flock scattered to the four directions. The grown White Gobbler remembered his days of downy helplessness and the menacing squirrels and the nerve-shattering scolding of the scrub jays. He looked into the foliage of every tree and had seen the great lump in the Spanish oak which was like the swelling on some trees caused by a disease. He had stood with feathers drawn close and watched as the others foraged. One or the other of the old hens would stop and listen also, but were soon satisfied and resumed their feeding. However, White Gobbler sensed the menace in the hump on the tree that was like a disease, and he gave the alarum.

The bobcat, in his terrible anger and frustration, growled at a harmless little nuthatch that explored the bark of the tree. He would have torn it to shreds if he could have caught it. But he waited, and soon he heard, far down the canyon, the "yuk, yuk-yuk-yuk-yuk" of a turkey hen calling the flock together. There was an answer from the other side of the canyon, then another from another direction.

The bobcat knew they would not come near his tree as they came together again as a flock, so he came down and slunk toward the sound of the calling. He came across a trail and then another, but his sense of smell was so weak that he was only confused by the trails crossing each other. He finally gave up.

Now it was November, and the whitetail bucks were wandering about with their noses to the earth, trying to find mates, and the whiteness of the White Gobbler seemed to annoy them especially, and they would lower their beautifully antlered heads and walk toward him, or rear up and strike at him with their front feet. But they were not enemies; they were in a state of bad temper because this was the season for mating or rut. The White Gobbler was conspicuous in his whiteness and this whiteness annoyed them, especially at this time of year. He kept out of their way, but he would sometimes strut a little just to annoy them.

One morning as the flock were feeding, leisurely, there was a terrific sound that echoed from the cone-shaped hills, and the buck that had stood staring at the White Gobbler, wondering what he was, fell and kicked himself around in a complete circle, then lay still.

At the report of the rifle, the White Gobbler had gobbled, and another of the young toms had gobbled, but the flock remained motionless in the thick brush. There was no man-animal coming from the little brown house with a slit in it since the hunter in the blind was nervously waiting for the gobbler to appear. He was a push-button man from a large city, and he expected response from things. Soon, however, he convinced himself that the gobblers that had gobbled had gone, and he came out to stand and look over his buck.

The old hens seemed to know that danger lurked in the area of the little brown house, but it was located on a terrace which they had been passing over all year, and they had even come close to the little house and nothing had happened, but now the blast that was like thunder, the buck that had kicked the earth about, and the man-animal who had come out of the little house frightened them only a little.

It was almost time for their rest period, so some of them began to dust-bathe and two old hens stood as sentinels. They talked to each other all morning, and the man of many push buttons in the blind went into a mild frenzy since they would not show themselves. He was so disturbed that he couldn't even read the book he had brought along with him.

It was the third day after the shooting of the buck, and the old hens of the flock seemed to forget about the little brown house in their hurry to go up the canyon where there was an abundance of acorns. They had led the flock out into the open before they were aware of the menacing little brown house, but the White Gobbler was the last to come from the brush into the open, and just as he did, one of the young gobblers suddenly fell to the ground and started flopping, then another, and the others ran, then flew. The White Gobbler ran back into the cover; then after running a hundred yards, he also took wing and flew over the divide.

Now the flock shunned all the little brown houses scattered in strategic locations on Rancho Seco.

Sometimes a buck whitetail would get downwind from one of the little brown houses, and thus he could get the scent of the man-animal waiting there. He would blow through his nose, raise his tail and wag it like a flag, then bound high over the bushes away. This warned the turkey flock that danger was near, and they stole off through the bushes silently, in the same direction the deer was traveling.

Soon there were no more hunters in the little brown houses, but still the old hens of the flock stood for minutes watching before coming out into the open while the White Gobbler circled wide and remained in thick cover.

But he had been seen and he became the conversation around the fireplace each evening, as ice clinked in glasses. He had been seen from blind number 4, and each member of the party wanted a morning in blind number 4. Then he was seen from blind number 1, but always, always, it seems, beyond rifle range, not to mention shotgun range.

Thus he became famous while he was still with his mother, several other old hens, and poults of the year.

Then came March, and he saw his mother no more; the young of the spring before went off by themselves, the gobblers in one flock and the hens in another, or scattered here and there, listening with interest to the gobbling of the old gobblers. A strange restlessness came to White Gobbler and he found himself strutting alone in the bushes. The emotion would suffuse him and he would lower his wings, lay his head back, raise his tail, and make a great fan of it; then he would step daintily forward, dragging his wings against the earth, but no one except the winter mockingbirds and the white-crowned sparrows and the towhees saw him.

He had heard the gobbling of the old gobblers and he had been driven to the place where they were strutting by an uncontrollable urge, but as soon as he appeared, an old gobbler ran at him, stopped, and stood at full height and turned a side to him, flicked a wing at him, then, uttering a "K-R-R—Ruk," flew at him and spurred him. Spurless White Gobbler had to leave the gobbling ground.

When the hunters came the next year, they asked Chip, "Have you seen the white gobbler?" And Chip would answer, "Yeah, but he's the wildest thing on this outfit."

"What'd'yu 'spose makes him so wild?" and Chip would answer, "I sure don't know."

"Which blind'ud be the best one?"

Chip would shake his head and say, "I just don't know; I've seen him at all of 'em, but yu put a man in one of 'em and he's liable to come near another. I just don't know."

The man in number 4 got a shot at him with a rifle, but he was too far away and he missed, and he said the White Gobbler looked back at the limestone rock the bullet had powdered as he went into the air as if it were a spook.

The hunters took home twelve turkeys that year, some of them great bronze beauties with long beards which they could pull and stick in the bands of their stalking hats, but the talk on the last night was about the White Gobbler, as it had been during the four days of hunting.

By the fourth year White Gobbler had established his own gobbling ground—not exactly his *own* gobbling ground since there were two other toms with him, all strutting and parading before the hens that had come there from other spots. When the hens arrived, you might wonder what had happened to the urge that compelled them to come. At the gobbling ground they seemed to be indifferent, perhaps a little weary.

The gobbling ground was about four acres in extent and was among the oaks where there was no underbrush to hinder the toms in their showing off.

This year, after the mating season, White Gobbler went off with the old toms and they stayed together all summer and all winter and ignored the hens until the next March.

White Gobbler was a handsome bird now. He was the largest gobbler on the Rancho, and he gobbled at every thunderclap and at every rifle or shotgun shot during the hunting season, but now he was seldom seen by hunters since he had learned that from the little brown houses came terrific blasts. He was as much of a menace to the old gobblers with whom he flocked now as he had been to the flock of hens and poults, but of course the great toms didn't have as many enemies as the hens and poults might have. The young golden eagle that claimed the ranch for his domain would sit on a fence post and watch them, not caring to attack these great birds. He would wait for the hens and poults. The barred owl would sit on an old corral fence just at dusk as they walked by in the direction of the roosting tree. He eyed them with unconcern, and while he might have liked turkey meat, he would wait for a fat rat, a rabbit, or even a mouse.

The White Gobbler was a menace to the gobbler flock, but also he was their constant sentinel. Sometimes during the early autumn, one of the flock might feel an urge to strut, and he would do so half-heartedly, but in the open the White Gobbler never took his eyes from the trees, the sky, the bushes.

But the dark hours were the hours of fear. There were the bobcat, who could climb a tree, and the great horned owl and White Gobbler's whiteness screamed out to both of them, endangering all. Only a stupid turkey need be taken by a bobcat at night. He could be heard climbing the tree and the turkey had only to fly out into the moonlight, whether dim or bright, but if the hunter-cat came on a dark night, the turkey flew out of the tree blindly and only hoped to crash into the well-leafed top of another tree; otherwise he might land on the ground and would surely be caught.

The great horned owl is a tiger in feathers, but he usually came on moonlit nights or just before dawn when there was light to see by.

The fear of the great horned owl was racial, a species memory. It was not necessary to have an experience. The savage hunter had the power to scare his prey by his very presence or by his "who, who—*whoo*—who, who." He came always on silent wing.

One morning, during the darkest hour just before dawn, he came to the tree where the gobbler flock were roosting, and he came so quietly that even the ever-alert White Gobbler didn't notice him until he was beside him on the limb. He was so startled and frightened that he couldn't give the danger signal, and he also forgot he was white and drew his feathers close about him and grew small against the limb. He was too frightened to fly, and anyway he couldn't see, and that was part of the owl's plan—to move closer and closer until the gobbler must be pushed off the limb and then must fly frantically into the darkness, eventually hitting the ground; then the owl would come down and kill him.

During this before-dawn hour, the great owl had seen the White Gobbler looming and had landed by him and had begun to shove him, inch by inch. Suddenly, the fear that had turned the great gobbler's blood to water left him and he stood up at the very end of the limb and hit at the owl in the darkness with his wing, fortunately hitting him in his great round face. The owl said "kruuk" and spread his wings for balance, and at this moment, the gobbler flew at him and, with his long, sharp spurs, hit one outspread wing at the first joint, and it went limp, but they both lost their balance and fell to the ground. The owl instinctively turned over on his back on hitting the ground and spread his sharp talons to protect his body, but the gobbler thought only of getting away. He ran blindly, first into a bush, and flopping, freed himself; then he ran into a tree trunk and he was dazed for a few seconds. Finally he sat down and froze, again forgetting that he was white.

When dawn came, he got up and walked dazedly. Soon the other gobblers began to call and he answered. The owl, with his forewing dragging, climbed into a fallen treetop and sat blinking in complete puzzlement.

Each year the White Gobbler of Rancho Seco strutted on the gobbling ground he shared with two other gobblers, and each year there were poults that were mottled, but none pure white. Just as years of domestication and soft-mindedness had been displaced by species instincts and memories of the wild, so did the descendents of the White Gobbler go back to the original bronze-grey and rusty-bordered feathers, eventually.

Chip noticed these mottled young birds every year, and each year some of them were killed, but White Gobbler lived on and each hunting season he was the subject of conversation around the fireplace at the ranch house. Each hunter talked eagerly of his hope that he might get a shot at him, and the hunter who had actually had a chance at him became more and more unhappy about his miss.

Now it was the year of few live oak acorns and kinikinik berries, and the gobbler flock ranged far to find sufficient food. Also, it had been a cold, wet summer and there were no grasshoppers. Each night the gobbler flock roosted in a different tree, and their search for food led them beyond the boundaries of Rancho Seco, and one day they crossed a paved state road. They had stepped across it daintily, saying "perk, perk," and had found grain on the other side. As they ate, a pickup came roaring at them and standing back of the cab was a man-animal, and he was firing into the air. The flock arose as one bird and flew back across the state road, but just then a truck came along and at the precise moment White Gobbler was over the road, he and the truck met, and he fell to one side, his white feathers settling after him. The driver of the truck looked back through the rear-vision mirror and said to his companion, "Musta got some ole boy's white turkey."

There was no racial memory concerning paved roads and great, roaring trucks to warn the White Gobbler of Rancho Seco.

The Royal of Glen Orchy

THE DEER FOREST OF GLEN ORCHY in Scotland was not really a forest but a great expanse of low mountain ridges covered with bracken and heather and strewn with great granite boulders left there by the great ice sheet which had spread over Scotland many thousands of years ago, from the north. When the ice sheet melted, it left these great granite boulders. Now they were covered with lichen and sometimes in the vaporous light of the late afternoons they looked like great grey-flecked beasts asleep on the mountainsides.

It was a dreary land if you didn't happen to love it. All the animals and birds seemed to have such sad voices. The voices of the lost lambs were like the weeping of lost children and the voice of the lapwing seemed to be sad, even when he himself was happy. The call of the curlew was the cry of a ghost. You seemed to hear so many sad voices and were unable to see the animals and birds to whom they belonged, in the watery light. But once you saw the black grouse in the spring dancing, you couldn't possibly believe that such a strangely beautiful bird could have a voice that would have the sound of a boulder being pushed across a frozen pond, and once you saw the lapwing fall from the sky like a falling leaf, singing his love song, which wasn't much of a song but certainly a gay, wild, and exciting call that sounded like "hoo-*oo*-oo-*oo*-oo-ee," you thought no more of the moon's sadness. The curlew filled the sky with crazy mating flight and his mournful cry, and of course when you could see the lambs playing about their mothers, you immediately forgot the sadness of their bleating.

The treeless land, with its moss and bracken and heather and its great granitic boulders in an afternoon mizzle, was both romantic and mysterious, and you had to love it.

One early summer day, the "royal" of Glen Orchy was born. His mother had stood over him where he lay in the heather and had washed his face and his neck with her tongue, then had left him to go out and browse and graze. He lay full length on his belly and stretched his neck out so that his chin lay flat on the moss. He was hidden by the heather, and the dappled light that shone down through the leaves and the branches of the heath was blended with his hair. The fawn's body was so spotted and marked that you couldn't know which was a light spot and which a real spot on his coat, and since he did not move he was invisible.

He was only a few hours old and yet he felt he must lie absolutely still so as not to attract the eagles or the wildcats. There was not so much danger from wildcats since they hunted mostly during the night, but the golden eagles often chose the granite boulders for their hunting stations, and their eyes were sharp.

This protective immobility was as much as a heritage from red deer ancestors as the protective coloration of his body. The baby hair he would shed and he would become reddish-brown to blend with the landscape, but the protective immobility which he had received from his ancestors as a species memory, he would never abandon. When he grew up, he would be standing or grazing among the bracken and the heather and among the great boulders, and his coat now would be different from the fawn's spotted coat which must blend with light spots filtered through the heather.

When he heard his mother approach at nightfall, even though he was very hungry, he wouldn't even open his eyes if they happened to be shut until he felt her nose on his neck; then he would get up, shakily at first but with more assurance later, and have his dinner.

When he was a few days old, his mother allowed him to follow her as she grazed, but only during the night. At dawn she would give him his breakfast, lead him to some spot where the cover was sufficient, then she would push him down with her chin, and he would assume his old familiar position, flat on his belly with outstretched neck and chin on the ground. In this position he would lie all day until she came to touch him with her nose.

One day when the Gulf Stream brought heavily laden air over the mountains, the rain came down heavily and began to run under Royal's belly and he arose and shook himself and stood shivering. This was a breach of protective immobility as well as protective coloration, but it was raining hard and there would be no eagles on their hunting stations and no wildcats certainly. This was not a species memory, urging that he might be safe in a rain squall, but merely a matter of avoiding discomfort.

One night when he was out with his mother, she gave the alarum bark and stood like a statue, staring at a growth of bracken and birch sapling in a corrie. Royal stood still and cocked his great ears and waited. Nothing happened, and his mother grew impatient and stamped the ground sharply with a front foot and barked again. Then there was another long wait, and his mother repeated her stamping, with the other foot now, and barked again. The wildcat crouched in the bracken and spat at the hind and growled, then shifted his savage eyes to the fawn again.

After a short time, the great round-faced wildcat slunk away, looking back over his shoulder; the hind's bluff had worked.

The female red deer of Scotland is called a "hind," and the Scotsmen say she "barks" when alarmed or when she bluffs. It is certainly not like the "whistle" of the whitetail deer of America, and it does sound something like the bark of a little dog, perhaps like a Chihuahua.

There were many experiences during the summer since now he was allowed to accompany his mother wherever she went, and he played around her, running and jumping, and teasing the mother blackgame, called "greyhen," and her chicks, or blowing at the tail of a mother red grouse as she fluffed her feathers and walked away, looking back at him with great annoyance. One day a mother greyhen flew at him, and thereafter he didn't come so close to them. He would run at them, then stand on his hind legs and pretend to strike at them with his front hooves. This angered the greyhen until she almost lost her wits. She would send her children scampering out of the way, and she would fluff her feathers and curse the fawn.

The summer passed and there were red and brown tints over the moors, and one October day a great antlered stag approached him and his mother. Royal wanted to run away since he had seen only hinds all summer, and this great stag with the swollen neck and the great antlers might be dangerous. His mother stood still and waited for him, and when he came close, the great stag and his mother touched noses, and all during the autumn Royal traveled with his mother as a member of a band, under the eye of the stag. There were several hinds besides his mother, and there were other fawns, and soon they were playing together. They would put their heads together and push each other around in a circle, just as two fighting stags might do, and like two quarreling hinds they would stand on their hind legs and strike at each other.

That winter the wildcat stayed close to the band and managed to kill the weak and sick fawns, and when spring came there were only four fawns who had survived, out of the eight.

The old Marquess who owned Glen Orchy deer forest had neglected to introduce new red deer blood often enough from the Continent, and inbreeding had caused certain weaknesses, and half the deer did not get beyond the fawn stage and the eagles and wildcats were well fed, but the vigorous ones escaped and Royal was among the most vigorous and alert. Soon he must face the dangers of the forest alone since his mother left him one day when he was dozing, sheltered from the wind on the mountainside in a small corrie, and he never saw her again. This was in the spring when he was just a year old.

As he wandered in search of her, and in his bewilderment he became careless, an eagle saw him and swooped over his head, striking halfheartedly, then shot higher and turned to make another dive, and this was a savage one. As Royal ran toward cover in the bottom of a corrie, the eagle clutched at his neck and shoulders and the fawn stumbled and fell and began to bleat for his mother.

The eagle shot into the air again and made another dive, but Royal was on his feet now and he stood on his hind legs and with his front hooves struck at the eagle, who, unhurt, veered off and up again. This was possibly the first time this had ever happened, especially within the experience of the eagle. He sailed now in narrow circles above the fawn but Royal stood and watched him with his ears back. He was only a yearling and the fawns of the red deer had been eagle food through the centuries. As a matter of fact, fawns from birth until they became too large to handle were eagle food, but there was something here that was not within the balance of moorland struggle—the attack on a yearling.

Soon the eagle circled higher, and it might be suspected that he was not intensely hungry or he wouldn't have given up so easily. As he circled, he screamed from frustration.

Royal walked then to the cover at the bottom of the corrie, watching the eagle over his shoulder.

Lying on his belly on "the tops," hidden by the cottongrass and bracken, was McCarricker, the gillie. He said in his native dialect that he had come that morning to be at the dancing ground of the "blackgums, whan you coom to lek," which means he had come to watch the blackgame in their mating dances, and also to count the fawns that had survived the winter. He must keep the Marquess informed as to the possibilities of good shooting the next autumn.

As he lay on the tops waiting for the blackgame to "coom to lek," he saw the eagle make his dive at the back of Royal, and his whole attention was centered on the little drama. When the plucky little fawn struck at the eagle, McCarricker was filled with pride. He carried an old telescope and, resting it on a small boulder, he watched the fawn until he entered the cover. He wanted to remember this courageous fawn, and when he saw the blood streaming down his shoulder he knew that this particular fawn would carry a grey scar the rest of his life. He also noted that the fawn was quite large for a yearling, and he knew by the way he carried his large ears that he was a stag.

McCarricker was gnarled like an old oak, and he could go all day stalking deer and say not a word to the sportsman he attended. He would simply point a crooked finger and say, "Ken yon stag; try 'im."

That late afternoon he went back to the lodge, thinking of "yon fawn."

After his shoulder healed, Royal came across another little male whose mother had left him and they played together and grazed together and teased the blackgame together. When the cocks were dancing with their lyre-shaped tail feathers curved to each side, and were unaware of anything except their own glory, the young stags would come up behind them and blow at their spread tails, causing them to walk faster than they wished and making them very angry. Sometimes the young stags blew and pushed them out of their very dignified strutting before the hens, and blew or pushed them into a very undignified run.

The little stags, when they were satisfied with grazing or browsing, butted each other or struck at each other with their front feet, or they ran up and down the moors at full speed—back and forth, back and forth.

This was play. All young animals must play. This is demanded by nature. They must play at those things which they must do perfectly when they become adults, in order to survive in the harsh struggle of life. Stags must lower their antlered heads and fight each other so that the strongest will win and hand down his spirit and courage and his strength to later generations so that the red deer can remain in the struggle of life. Thus did the little stags of Glen Orchy practice those things in their fawnhood which they must use in later life. They must run from danger, freeze so that they would blend with their surroundings, learn to fight with their future antlers, and strike with their front feet.

So every day Royal and his playmate spent hours doing those things which their very existence would demand of them when they became ant- lered stags. They had never been taught to do this; it was a memory urge of the species.

As they grew larger and stronger and more courageous, the great golden eagle lost interest in them, and the wildcat sought his food among the weaker ones or the sick ones. The wildcat hunted now in the spring for the nests of the blackgame, the red grouse, and the curlew, hoping to find a brooding hen or a careless cock, and of course the easiest prey of all were the lambs and even their silly mothers.

The summer passed and the growths at the bottom of the corries had touches of red and yellow and there were odd little growths forming on the head of each of the little males, and by rutting season when the old stags were walking over the moors roaring, Royal's playmate had two sharp spikes sticking up on his head, but something more had happened to his own head. He not only had the spikes but they were forked, and this was unusual. The two little stags would be called "prickets" now in their second year, but a pricket was not supposed to grow more than his two spikes.

McCarricker was the first to notice the forked spikes of Royal, and he could identify this large second-year fawn with his forked spikes as the one he had seen the eagle attack. He could even spot the wound, now healed, on his shoulder but remaining a grey scar.

And McCarricker was more than just an ordinary gillie and a man filled with emotion over the fact that he was a part of the great brooding moors and the wild life they supported. He couldn't possibly speak of that which he felt since he had no words either in Gaelic or English that could express his thoughts and emotions, even to himself, so he remained silent, and his emotions bubbled within him. The silent, gnarled gillie would play an important part in the life of the fawn with the forked spikes.

The years passed and each year McCarricker made it a point to locate the now full-grown stag who had had a forked antler when he was only a pricket and now carried great antlers, and when guests came to the lodge to shoot deer, McCarricker guided them away from the tops and corries used by Royal. But one October when the gillie was out with a guest of the lodge, a deep roar came out of the mists, like the roar of a leopard, and he knew instinctively that the roar could only come from Royal. Royal had wandered away from his home heath. When the guest became excited, McCarricker told him that it was impossible to crawl through the wet bracken within rifle shot of the deep-voiced stag. He knew that which no one else knew. He knew that his fawn of nine years before was now a great "royal," which meant that he had at least twelve points to his antlers. He had just finished convincing his sportsman that a crawl was useless when there was a stag's roar from behind them, and then from the great royal came an answer and soon they saw him standing on the tops, clear-cut against the horizon. His head was high and his great royal antlers against the horizon startled even the gillie, and the guest tried to keep his hands from shaking.

McCarricker noted the shaky hands and he also noted the distance. He also knew that Royal had not even seen them down the mountainside, and that he might not care much if he did since he was filled with the arrogance of rut and since he had never been shot at due to McCarricker's contriving.

Even in the cold October mist, McCarricker began to sweat under his cap, though he knew the nervous guest would probably miss, but the point was that he could no longer keep the fact that there was a mighty royal in

Glen Orchy a secret. Every guest who came to the lodge would want that famed royal, and he would be compelled to guide them.

Then a bright idea came to him as the guest stood watching the mighty stag gazing across the corrie to the tops back of them. He made his decision and at that moment became false to his trust. He instructed the guest to try him from where he stood, assuring him it was his only chance.

The report of the rifle was deadened by the heavy air, and the great stag didn't move. McCarricker muttered something under his breath, and he could feel the sweat dripping onto an ear now. Maybe the shaky guest would hit the stag by accident if he had several chances, and McCarricker was wondering what he could do to frighten the stag when a hind appeared from under the brow of the hill. She had heard the shot and had come to the tops to investigate, and she stared down into the corrie, unable to make out the stalkers in the blurry light, but she stood and stared, and when the second shot missed, she needed no more; she barked twice in the direction of the shots and turned and disappeared and the great royal followed, his antlers seeming to swim over the tops when his body and head were out of sight.

The guest had a shot at another stag and got him, and he would never know why the gillie should be so happy about it.

But the secret was out, and McCarricker was heavy-hearted. He knew that the highest prize of a deer stalker was a royal. He had heard the guests talk. He knew that royals' heads hung in the German and Austrian castles and in lodges in Scotland, and that the royal of Glen Orchy, *his* Royal, was doomed.

The old Marquess asked him about this magnificent royal, and he had to tell the truth but only the bare facts, pretending that he was just an ordinary red deer stag, with antlers that might have as many as twelve points, which would make of him a royal. All the time he was telling the Marquess about him, he saw in his mind again the majestic stag against the skyline, waiting for another challenge to his kingship.

McCarricker worked out a plan. He would slip away with a rifle, without the gamekeeper or anyone else knowing about it, and he would stalk his royal, and when close enough he would fire at the ground just in front of him and then just behind him. He would do this several times and this would teach the great stag that man was a dangerous animal. And Royal, even in the high emotion of rut, would remember.

But he had no time in which to do this. The Marquess had invited some special guests to try for the only royal that had appeared in his forest for many years.

McCarricker stalked for a European nobleman for two days looking for the great royal. Each day the nobleman killed a stag, and McCarricker saw with dejection that he was a fair shot.

Then in the blurry light of a late afternoon they heard the voice of Royal, like the roar of a hunting leopard. He was not cutting the skyline and he was protectively blended with the wet, lichen-covered boulders and the bracken and heather. They located him by his voice; then they began the laborious crawl toward him, through the wet heather and bracken.

When they got within three hundred yards of him, McCarricker pulled some bracken and held it before his face and slowly raised his head. The great stag was standing, looking across at the distant hills—a perfect shot. McCarricker lowered his head and turned around to the nobleman and pointed his finger in the direction of the royal. There were hinds with him, and they knew danger to be somewhere near, but they were depending more on their noses and their ears rather than their eyesight, which was strangely limited. Perhaps their ancestors had lived in forests like those of Germany and Austria and they had not lived on the moors long enough to develop the power of eyesight necessary to all dwellers on the plains and the moors. But this was not to say that the red deer eyesight is not keen; it is to say that it is not as highly developed as their hearing and scenting powers.

And this worried McCarricker. There was no moving air, and they had made no noise, and though one large hind was looking at them, she would not know exactly what species of animal they might be in the dull, watery light if they made no startling movement. He was thinking fast. He knew that his nobleman could stand up and have a better chance at the royal, especially if he had to shoot him on the run. If the guest rose slowly under his instructions, the hind, who was standing like a statue looking in their direction, would probably not see him. It was almost certain that she would be unable to make out the nature of the danger down on the hillside if he instructed his gentleman to rise to his knees very, very slowly.

He had just finished these thoughts when the nobleman whispered, "Perhaps you can crawl in front of me, then kneel, and I can have rest on your shoulder."

McCarricker was horrified. This was "not done" in the British Isles. This sort of bad sportsmanship was of the Continent. Gillies have privileges, and on the moors stalking, they are in command. He was rather brusque in his disgust and distress, and he assured the nobleman that if he knelt or stood, the hind would see him and sound the alarum. He would have to shoot from his prone position. This McCarricker knew would place him at a disadvantage, shooting through the heather. He could suggest this now, with a clear conscience, since his gentleman had made the unsportsmanlike suggestion.

McCarricker watched him wind the sling around his arm and poke the rifle barrel through the heather, then take aim, and he wished fervently that "yon hind" would bark the alarum. He thought of rising so that she could see him, but it was only a fleeting thought, and he was immediately ashamed of it. He lowered his head and almost touched the earth with his nose in his despair. Then the shot came and when he raised his head there was nothing on the tops, and he was filled with happiness. Then the nobleman, with a wide grin, said, "With only one shot; we must step it off." McCarricker took the five-pound note his gentleman handed him, without knowing what he was doing. He felt weak-kneed, and he convinced his gentleman that they ought to sit and wait for the stag to lie a few moments since if he was only wounded he would get up when they appeared too soon and run off and perhaps be lost. The nobleman was so filled with emotion that he obeyed and sat on a boulder and failed to see the tragedy in McCarricker's face.

They paced the distance up the hillside where Royal had stood and found it to be three hundred yards, but when they reached the tops, there was no royal stag lying dead. McCarricker smiled with happiness; then he thought that the stag might have been wounded and might have staggered off to die. He began to examine the ground for blood spots but found none, though he did find a few stiff neck hairs, and his happiness had to be kept in control.

He knew what had happened: Royal had been "creased," and after lying for a few moments had revived and run off in full vigor. He explained this to his gentleman and then handed back the five pounds. His bullet, he explained, had just touched the nerve on the back of the neck and had momentarily paralysed the royal. If McCarricker had been a talkative man, he would have talked now in his happiness. There was only the deep contentment within him. He was smiling inside.

As they slogged back to the lodge at dusk, the roars came from all around them but came out of the watery light disembodied. Suddenly they both stopped and listened as the deep roar of Royal came to them from far across the moors.

After being creased, Royal lay as if he were dead, but he was only paralysed, then revived and got up and ran down the other side of the mountain. He ran until he came to a ridge. Here he stood for some time, looking back over the way he had come; then he walked quietly down under the ridge. The slight air movement came from behind him and flowed over him and he could scent anything that approached. He could see far over the heather and bracken in front of him. He lay for some time under the command of his racial instincts. He would be able to hear the man-animal if he approached from behind and be able to see him if he came from the direction which he faced.

He lay for some time, switching his great ears, his sound detectors, back and forth, one forward as the other moved backward; then in the distance he heard a stag's roar. He cocked both ears in that direction, then rose and answered, and this is the roar McCarricker and his gentleman heard as they slogged through the wet heather.

Royal walked downhill to a peat bog and, stepping out into it, he lay down and rolled in it; then he came out and stood for some time, looking in the direction from which the challenge had come. He walked stiff-legged, with mincing steps, and attacked a whinbush, threshing it viciously with his antlers. He stood then and gazed in the direction of the challenge, and when it was not repeated, he thought of his hinds, and he extended his muzzle and roared, then waited. Soon there was an answer, and he trotted off in that direction, the peat muck making of him an angry black stag.

Then came the end of the rut, and the stags were thin, and the swelling had gone from their necks, and the trophy hunters would not be as interested in Royal, and this made McCarricker happy again. No more guests came to the lodge to try for the famed royal of Glen Orchy that season.

Although Royal was thin and disinterested after the rut, he lost none of his vigor. That winter he joined the other stags, and they formed a sort of bachelors' club. There were no hinds or fawns in this band.

Spring came and he lay for hours watching the blackgame in their mating dance. The blackgame and the red grouse had become his friends now. When the red grouse or the blackgame flew low over the moors, whether he was banded with his autumn hinds or with the winter and summer stags, he and others all turned at the same time and gazed in the direction from which the birds had come, looking for the approach of the man-animal.

Royal was a marked stag now; they knew about him all over Scotland and on the Continent, and McCarricker, despite the love of stalking and his love of the autumn colors and the crisp air, found himself dreading the coming season. He saw Royal often during the spring and summer. During April he shed his magnificent antlers, and with his antlers he had shed his glory. McCarricker hunted until he found them in a corrie. One of the tines had been chewed rather badly by red deer, perhaps by Royal himself, before he found them in June, but he carried them back and showed them to the Marquess, hoping that he would not want to hang them in the lodge.

The Marquess was astounded by their beauty, and during the summer he mentioned them often.

By September, Royal had grown another set of antlers, exactly like the ones he had shed, and then one October day the old Marquess called for McCarricker and they went out onto the moors to stalk Royal. McCarricker now gave up. It was no use. He would guide the Marquess to the hills used by Royal, watch him fall before the rifle of the Marquess, then dutifully gut him, and pull out his red flag to be left by the carcass so that the men with the wagon could pick it up. After all, Royal had lived for how long? Twelve years, and soon he would decline, and his antlers would be smaller year by year and thinner and more delicate, and there would be strange little points at the tips growing in circles and called "cupping." McCarricker made himself a little more comfortable with these thoughts as he and the Marquess set out.

The sun was shining, and when they crawled up the side of a ridge to peek over, there, one hundred and fifty yards on the tops, stood Royal watching them. There were no hinds with him at the moment to warn him. His fear was completely drowned in the emotion of rut, and he looked almost black in the bright light of the morning sun, just having rolled himself in a peat bog. His rut-fever even drowned for the moment the memory of the paralysing bullet.

McCarricker handed the Marquess the rifle and stood filled with the wonder of Royal. His antlers were greater than ever; he must have fourteen points now. He held his head high, with majestic arrogance, and watched them.

The two men stood for some time, each filled with the incredible dignity and beauty of the famed stag. Then the Marquess handed his rifle back to McCarricker, and without taking his eyes from the magnificent creature, he said, "He must not be shot by anyone."

There was a long silence, and finally McCarricker said, "'Tis a guid day." The Marquess looked at him sharply and understood quite well.

Old Three Toes
of Buffalo Fork

T HE BIGHORN HUNTERS had their camp high up near the divide but some distance from the sheep country so that the great rams might not discover them and wander to the other side of the range. It was a warm- ish night for October and several times they were awakened during the night by the howling of wolves. This meant that there was low pressure in the mountains and this was the time of year when the large watery flakes of snow fell. The snows didn't last long but the hunters were on the Pacific side of Two Ocean Pass, and if the snow was heavy, they might not be able to get back over the pass for several days.

They had haunches of wapiti hanging from a tree, and the skin of a black bear was stretched and pegged to the ground near the tent. He had been seen by chance when the hunters had brought the packhorses up the moun- tain to bring down the meat and the great heads of the wapiti. The wind that afternoon was blowing down the canyon, and he failed to hear or scent the hunters. He was very busy fishing about in the carcass of one of the bulls for delicacies since it had been gutted rather carelessly.

The young hunter was very proud of his bear, even if he had forgotten to bring the heart and liver of the wapiti to camp. He defended himself with the idea that if he had thought about them he wouldn't have had a chance at the bear.

Every time he heard the long-drawn-out howl of a wolf that night, he got out of his sleeping bag and went out to see if the bearskin was still there. He had been told that there wasn't the least danger that the wolves might come close to camp, but he had to go out for a look anyway.

When he was sound asleep again in the early morning hours, one of the horses whistled through his nose, and he sat up in his bedding roll just as the guide and the horse wrangler sat up, with dazed expressions. There was another explosive nose-whistle and then the trampling of the pack- and saddle horses straining at their pickets.

They all three ran out into the darkness, the young hunter, the guide, and the horse wrangler, but half of the horses were gone. However they had not gone far and stood some distance away wide-nostrilled and wide-eyed with heads high. They snorted and whistled through their noses, and in the stillness and in the heavy air of early morning you could hear fading hoofbeats down the canyon. Some of the horses had broken their picket ropes and some had pulled the picket pins up, but the one they heard pounding down the canyon had kept going.

After they got the horses in and they became quiet, except for two or three of them whose flanks still quivered, the horse wrangler said, "Guess ole Hammerhead's just about reached the Hole by now; he's the only one missin'."

"Better saddle up and take in after 'im," suggested the guide.

"Huh un'h, no use; he'll never stop 'fore he gits to the home corral," said the horse wrangler. "Lucky if he stops there; we just got one less pack-horse—that's the size of it."

He stirred the fire, and put another log on it; then he turned to the guide, "Figure on gettin' outta here 'fore it sets in to weatherin'?"

"Yeah, we oughta get over the pass anyway."

"Well, I guess somebody'ud better set up and kinda watch for the rest of the night so we'll have something to get out on. When ole Three Toes gets horse hungry, he's got the brass of a gover'ment mule."

The young hunter spoke. "Who's ole Three Toes?"

The wrangler got up and crooked his finger at him to follow. He took a flashlight and walked into the lodgepole pines for a hundred yards, then stopped and pointed to the soft earth behind some young firs.

There were the large paw imprints of a mountain lion, and in the print of the left front paw, there was a toe missing. The prints were so fresh that you could see little particles of earth fall into one of them.

On the way back to the fire, the young hunter asked, "What happened?"

"'Bout his toe?"

"Yeah—what happened to 'im?"

"Mighta lost it in a trap, or some dude hunter mighta aimed at his head and shot off his toe when he was treed. I dunno; all I know is if it was either one, a trap or a dude's bullet, they ain't nobody gonna get 'im in a trap er git a shot at 'im treed. Yu notice how we bin a-picketin' our outfit? Most outfits tie a bell on a mare and turn the string out to graze all night. Not when you're in ole Three Toes' country. They mostly do like we bin a-doin'—grazin' 'em in the daytime, and bringin' 'em in at night. 'Course yu never know when he's to home. He ranges in 'bout a thirty-mile circle, but we know where he is, don't we?"

"What we gonna do without ole Hammerhead?"

"We'll just hafta distribute his pack amongst the rest, I guess."

"You say he'll go all the way home without stoppin'—maybe he won't. Maybe that picket pin he pulled up will catch in the bushes, and we can find him down the canyon."

"Huh un'h. He'll go so fast that picket rope'll float back like a twine string. I ain't a-woofin' when I tell yu ole Hammer's had enough sheep huntin'. Ever notice that white scar on his shoulder that looks kinda like a wa'r cut? Well, that ain't no wa'r cut, but ole Three Toes' brand. I guess ole Hammer was a two-year-old when the herd was grazing at the north end of the mesa where the foothills begin and all them junipers is, and ole Three Toes jist happened to be there in the early mornin', and he musta made a pass at ole Hammerhead, only then, like I said, he wasn't old, but maybe a two-year-old. He wasn't even called Hammerhead then 'cause he had the makin's of a sure good cow horse, but ever sense then he'll spook at his shadder and wasn't no good fer nothin' 'cept packin'. He's strong as a bull and ain't so spooky under a pack and when he's with other horses. Don't ast me how he got away from ole Three Toes that time; I'll never tell yu."

The young hunter asked, "How'd yu know it was Three Toes?"

"Yu seen that track out there? Well, we found it at the edge of the junipers, and the ground was soft enough that we could tell where ole Hammer had fell."

"Didn't yu do something?"

"All we done was to borry ever' lion dog in the country and git together a bunch of men and go after 'im. Yu see that peak there that looks plumb black? Well, them black rocks is big slabs, and that's where we lost his trail. Yu might say that's *his* country 'cause that's where he goes when things get too hot fer 'm. They ain't no horse can make it up there and the dogs cut their pads, and men sweat and cuss. He never treed once, I guess 'cause the trail was kinda cold; it took a day to git the pack and the men together."

There was a long silence as the fire blazed up; then the young hunter said, "Guess I'll sit up with yu."

"Sure, that's fine, but leave that gun in the tent. A man's liable to kill a horse in the dark thataway. Jist listen for the first snort; then we'll run out a-hollerin' and maybe pick up a burning stick from the fa'r."

Both fear and a buzz of thrill came over the young hunter. There seemed to be something alive moving about in his stomach.

The horse wrangler went a little way out into the darkness and came back with wood. While he fed the fire, he said, "We don't hafta stop talkin'. It jist might help some."

But Three Toes didn't come back to frighten the horses of the bighorn hunters. He had wandered away when the men had come out of the tent. Not that he was frightened, but because he had been foiled by the men and the nose-whistling of the horses. He wanted horse meat, the food he loved, but when he failed at the first rush, he went on about other business. This was his pattern of hunting. When he stalked a band of deer or wapiti cows, he didn't jump on a deer or a cow wapiti from a cliff or a tree but rushed from his cover and attacked the shoulder, holding on with one paw over the shoulder and the other under the neck while he bit into the neck vertebrae.

However, when he missed, he stood and watched the band of deer or wapiti or bighorn run off, wrinkling his lips and growling, annoyed, perhaps with himself.

So tonight when he failed in his plans to stampede the horses and single out one of the pack- or saddle horses, he wandered away like a shadow, like a small cloud shadow on a mountainside, and climbed to a rock ledge among his basalt slabs and sat for an hour watching the campfire in the canyon and the two shadowy figures about it. Since he had no urge to make another attack on the horses, he sat with mild curiosity, a sort of playfulness. But he was tired of bighorn and wapiti and deer meat.

He slipped down from his ledge among the basalt slabs with a grace that was exciting, his long tail curled at the end so that it was kept off the ground.

He had been gone from the basalt domain for a week or more, so he suddenly had the urge to make a "scratch." This was to indicate to other male mountain lions that this was his territory and therefore a warning to them to get out of it or they might have the famed Three Toes to deal with. Of course he didn't leave the famed trademark, the imprint of only three toes in the soft soil he had disturbed in making his scratch, since lion scratches are made with the hind feet, never with the front ones. A domestic dog or a wolf or a coyote will scratch the earth with his hind feet as a message to all others that they have come that way, but they don't scratch the earth and small twigs and pine needles into a neat little pile as the lion does. These others will scratch with their hind feet but may never look back to see what they have accomplished. But the tom lion is very proud of his little pile of soil and twigs which are the results of his scratch. He will nose it, as if admiring it.

This is what Three Toes did this early dawn as he seemed suddenly to remember that he had been gone from his domain for more than a week. He very deliberately made a scratch; then when he had a little pile, he examined it, then lifted his leg, much as a dog or a coyote or a wolf might do, and left his musk message for all to read. The message could be translated by all other toms and wolves and coyotes and black bears and grizzly bears thus: "You mountain lions are trespassing; get off my domain. You others, leave my wapiti, deer, and bighorn carcasses strictly alone until I am finished with them. To female lions: I am Three Toes, the mighty tom of the Buffalo Fork. Stay within calling distance; I shall return."

This was the true translation of that little pile of soil and twigs and pine needles sprinkled with the musk of Three Toes.

He glided on down the canyon, and when he came near to the carcass of the deer he had killed the day of his return, he stopped, screened by the willows of Pilgrim Creek. It took only a moment for him to understand the situation and he understood it so well, and all that might pertain to just such a situation, that he sank his belly and his tail thrashed in anger. He wrinkled his lips and growled and then spat like a fireside cat. He spat again and growled at the great bulk that bent over his deer carcass, but he came no nearer.

On hearing the growling and the angry "sphifft" of the lion, the great bulk straightened and then, with front paws over his chest, he stood like a man and tried to make out the form of the lion hidden by the screening willows. He was quite unconcerned, and there was a piece of venison hanging from his mouth as he looked intently at the willows. Then, as if the whole business concerned him very little, he let his upper body down again and with paws on the carcass began to tear again at it, ignoring the lion completely.

He was a grizzly bear, and he should have been in hibernation, but the unusually warm October had delayed the beginning of his long sleep. He couldn't quite make out the lion crouched in the willows, but he could smell him, even above the gamy odor of the carcass. He had no fear of an attack by the lion; as a matter of fact, he feared nothing in all the world, not even man. And besides, he liked venison and had it very rarely, as a matter of fact only when Three Toes made a kill. He himself was not quite as clever as Three Toes in ambushing deer or wapiti, and most of the time he had to eat tubers and grubs and berries and rob pine squirrels of their hordes of acorns and nuts. Only in the spring did he feast bountifully on wapiti and deer and sheep; after his hibernation he hunted the remaining snowdrifts for carcasses of animals that had failed to survive the winter.

Both the lion and the bear understood that there would be no attack by the former, so the bear went on pulling at the carcass, and the lion continued to growl and "sphifft-sphifft" for some time and his tail thrashed in anger. You could hear the leaves of the willows that had already fallen being disturbed by it.

Soon the lion became quiet and rose and walked off, turning back to have a last look at the feasting grizzly. He glided up the side of the canyon and halfway up he seemed to remember his frustrations, not only that of the hunters' horses but his deer carcass, and he stopped and looked back down the canyon in the direction of the bear and the carcass; then his lips wrinkled again, and his tail writhed like a dying snake, and he scream-growled, then stood a moment longer and went on.

The dawn was coming, so he climbed to his lying-up place in the slabs, and there he would spend the day.

He became hungry before nightfall, so he arose from his lying-up place and walked out onto his favorite ledge of rock surrounded by the uptilted basaltic slabs. Here he stretched to his full length and yawned with his great mouth wide open; then he sat back on his haunches and looked over his domain below. He had already forgotten the humiliation caused by the grizzly, who should have been in a cave in his long winter's sleep.

There was a shadow across the face of the uptilted slabs and a golden eagle dived at him. This was play they both understood, and they played this game quite often. The eagle would mock-dive and the lion would raise a paw and pretend to be angry. He would sometimes roll over on his back with all four feet in the air, and the eagle would zoom, make a circle, and come back for another mock-dive.

But during this late afternoon, the lion was in no mood for play. He was hungry. The eagle on the other hand had just feasted on a weak five-month-old bighorn, which he and his mate had managed to separate from the band of ewes and rutting rams. He wanted to play.

However, he soon learned the mood of the lion when, instead of raising his paw in mock anger, the lion rose on his hind legs and struck viciously at the eagle, missing him with his terrible claws only by inches.

The eagle zoomed and then continued up to circle so high that his scream of displeasure could scarcely be heard.

Hungry though he was, Three Toes sat on his ledge of rock for more than an hour looking down on the lower ranges and into the canyons. He had no particular plan in mind, and though he kept perfectly his protective immobility, he was conscious of no purpose. Even when not deceiving their enemies or their intended prey with their protective coloration and their immobility, animals and birds can sit for hours without moving. Their necessity to survive through blending with their backgrounds and keeping completely motionless has colored their whole existence.

Without definite plan, Three Toes moved off his ledge like a cloud shadow and glided down the side of the canyon. Before he had gone three hundred yards, he seemed to have a definite idea. He changed his course when he got to the bottom of the canyon and turned sharply up the dry watercourse, and when he came near the campground of the hunters, he lowered his body so that his belly almost touched the waterworn stones. When he came close to the camp, he went up the side of the canyon a little way and crouched behind a boulder. He raised his round head above it ever so slowly and looked long in the direction of the camp.

He saw nothing; then he raised his nose to get a scent, but all he got were the mixed acrid odors of charred wood of the dead campfire and the droppings of the pack- and saddle horses. There was no fresh scent of either horse or man. The camp was deserted.

He moved cautiously up to the place where the fire had been and sniffed there for some time. He struck viciously at a chipmunk but missed it, yet paid no attention to the Rocky Mountain jay who scolded him. He sniffed long at the place where the tent had been, then went over and sniffed at the stale horse droppings. When he was satisfied, he sprinkled one pile with his musk, then followed the scent of the horses up Two Ocean Pass Trail.

On Two Ocean Pass, he stopped very suddenly and sank to his belly and listened. Then he knew what the sound was. He knew it well; it was a rutting mule deer buck thrashing a sapling with his antlers. He slunk out of the trail and crouched behind a fallen Douglas fir.

The noise of thrashing ceased, and the lion waited. Soon the buck came from the growth of saplings, and with his nose to the earth crossed the trail and passed the fallen fir at a distance of perhaps fifty yards. He was too interested in the trail of a band of does to be cautious.

And Three Toes understood quite well, so instead of trying to get a position ahead of the buck, he slunk along the ridge parallel to the trailing buck. The buck stopped suddenly and held his wonderfully antlered head high, looking intently in the direction of a small park-like opening in the pines. The lion followed his gaze, and there were the band of does and their last spring fawns.

He fell to the earth on his belly; then, crawling with his shoulder blades visible and working until he was hidden by the ridge, he loped now parallel to the ridge's crest, then sank again to his belly, and crawled up the ridge to a growth of saplings. When he slowly raised his head and looked over, he was below the band of does and they were all looking at the statuesque buck.

Like the man-animal hunter, the great hunter-cat knew that he must escape the notice of the does, who would whistle and stamp a front foot, then all flee, and he would have no chance. He never raced after his prey, but charged it from hiding.

The buck came with great dignity toward the band of does, almost stiff-legged with rut pride and taking mincing little steps. The does and fawns watched his approach, and when they were thus absorbed, Three Toes crept as close to the band as his cover would allow, then lay motionless on his belly; not even the very tip end of his long tail moved.

When the buck was among the does and fawns, he slanted his shoulder toward a doe and stood motionless, and the doe flirted by making ridiculous little jumps. A fawn, having never seen such a magnificent creature as a full-antlered buck, came close to examine him, and the buck lowered his antlers and bluffed it away. As the fawn avoided the buck, it came within charging distance of Old Three Toes and he rushed out and caught it. The band fled in terror, with the buck behind the fleeing does and the only one of the band who dared to even look back.

A black bear had also been watching the does and fawns, but not with much hope. It was late in the season and the berries were gone. He was fat in preparation for hibernation, but he wanted one more feast before filling his belly with grass in readiness for his long winter's sleep.

He was behind a boulder, hoping that a fawn might come close and he could break its back with one blow of his paw.

When Three Toes made his kill, the bear came and sat near a dead lodgepole pine and waited. Three Toes saw him and his growl was a long rumble.

After eating, Three Toes walked down to the watercourse in the middle of the canyon until he found water, where he drank. Instead of washing his bloody mouth in the water, he rubbed it in the grass tussocks. He wandered up the opposite side of the canyon and lay down with profound contentment. He had forgotten that he had set out on the Two Ocean Pass trail on the trail of the packhorses of the hunting party. He would doze and keep an eye on the carcass of the fawn. The bear would not dare to come near it. There wasn't much left, but he hated coyotes and wolves and bears, and even grizzlies, even though he couldn't do much about the latter. Just after sunset, he became nervous and went back down to the fawn's carcass to scratch pine needles and twigs over it.

The coyotes yelped and a lone wolf howled from high up on the rimrock, but none came near. Before morning, the wind changed into the north and the large, heavy snow of October began to fall. The great cat glided down to the carcass of the fawn and ate the remainder of it, with the snow falling softly about him. He had another drink in the bottom of the canyon; this time he had no need to wash his face in the grass tussocks since the carcass had become drier.

He looked about him, then climbed up to the black slabs of basalt and curled up in his lying-up place and slept.

Again he became restless before nightfall, and he came out onto his ledge, now covered with snow. He again glided down the side of the mountain and then turned up the canyon. He came to the Two Ocean Pass trail, but there was no scent of horses or men now in the snow, but he could follow the trail since there was an impression of it indicated by the trough-like depression in the snow and the twisting lane between the pine and fir saplings.

He had no idea where he was going. He felt no hunger since finishing the mule deer fawn of last night. He kept up the steep, twisting trail to the Pass. He would stop occasionally like a true stalker and remain immobile for perhaps as long as a minute.

The sun was out and there was no wind, but there was movement in the white world. The heavy, watery snow would slide from the pine branches and thud on the ground snow. At every thud he turned his small, round head and gazed at the place where the snow had fallen.

When he came to the Pass and during one of his stationary moments, a pine squirrel barked at him. As he stood, he got the very faint scent of horse, not from the snow-smothered trail but it seemed to come over the air above the snow. It was very faint, so he raised his head high in order to catch more of it, then walked a few steps in the direction from which it came, and suddenly his nose seemed to be pulled to the snow and he began to dig.

He uncovered a horse blanket, and a surge of excitement came over him. He felt a profound urge to do something about this scent of horse on the sweat-stained blanket, and he began to play with it as a kitten plays with a spool. His claws got hung in the weave and when he jumped back, it was almost like something alive trying to follow him, and he became more excited and filled with emotion. He was completely absorbed by this play-thing so wonderfully scented with his favorite odor.

He would sit back on his haunches and look at it; then, as if remembering the earth struggle, he would look around him at the white world in which there was no movement except the snow sliding off the flexible branches of the pines during periods separated by as much as thirty seconds or more. He then approached the blanket and lay on his belly, pawing at it, as the black tip of his tail writhed.

Suddenly he rose and jumped backward away from it, then pounced on it and rolled over on his back with the blanket on top of him, like a puppy playing with an old scarf.

Soon he tired of his play and sat back on his haunches for a few moments, then rose and walked into the shadows of the pine forest.

He remembered the blanket and stopped and looked back in the direction from which he had come; then he made a scratch in the snow. His hind claws reached down to the soil and the pine needles and twigs and pine cones and when he had finished he had a neat little dark pile that could be seen very plainly on the snow. He sprinkled it with his musk.

He had left the snow-covered trail and wandered along the backbone of the ridge which ran down from the caprock. He may have had bighorn in mind. He wasn't hungry, of course, but he loved to be near bighorn sheep, to frighten them and to catch one if possible. He stopped suddenly and smelled of some tracks in the snow. He looked quickly in the direction toward which they were leading, down the flank of the ridge, but seeing nothing he followed them. He trailed them very carefully since there were rams with the band and their eyesight is almost perfect. He could trail the band by sight; even their bellies made an impression in the deep snow.

Suddenly he froze; then slowly, slowly, he lowered his body to the snow and gazed intently forward. He had caught the scent of man. He lay there on his belly for several minutes, and when he got no more scent of man, he rose and continued his trailing, and almost immediately there were the tracks and scent of man mixed with tracks and scent of the bighorn.

The sun had gone behind the ridge now and the canyons were gloomy and becoming colder. The hunter-cat left the visible trail of man and big-horn and glided low to the snow, up the ridge among the thick growths of lodgepole pine, and then loped along parallel to the trail. There was still no wind, but the air was heavier with the sun gone behind the ridge, and it car-ried scent much better.

He came to an outcropping of granite overlooking the canyon, and there he waited for the man to come along the trail. The sheep had passed, but now he was only interested in the man anyway.

Soon the hunter came with his rifle over his shoulder, walking slowly and looking ahead at the tracks in the snow, and the great cat couldn't control the tip of his tail.

Then the man—he was the young hunter of the bighorn hunters' camp, which now had been moved to the Atlantic side of the Two Ocean Pass—the young hunter stopped and looked at his wristwatch; then he looked long at the tracks of the bighorn leading on and on in the thickening gloom of the late afternoon.

He deliberately lit a cigarette and then turned down the canyon, leav-ing the bighorn tracks. When he had gone out of sight among the willows, Three Toes came down from his ledge and followed him. He crept along belly to snow and took advantage of every bush and sapling and growth of willows, but he came no closer than seventy-five yards to the hunter.

Darkness fell and the beam of the hunter's flashlight darted here and there, but soon the moon came up and flooded the snow and there was no more need for the flashlight. The moon was full and brilliant—the wapiti moon—and as if to confirm this, a bull wapiti challenged. The wapiti bugle built up into a high pitch that was almost like a scream, or like certain notes in a jackass's bray, then ended in a leopard's grunt. When the echo died, the hunter who had stopped moved on, and Three Toes followed.

Down canyon the bottom widened and the hunter-cat left the water-course and the tracks of the hunter and climbed the side of the canyon, and there he loped along parallel until he came to a tremendous Douglas fir no more than fifty yards from the canyon floor, and here he waited. The tip of his tail was perfectly still now. The young hunter made quite a lot of noise, and Three Toes could hear him before he saw him. Man-like, being a little frightened, he depended on man noise to gain the respect of the wild.

When he approached the Douglas fir, Three Toes became excited but he remained absolutely immobile. His gaze was so intense that the hunter must surely have felt it, as there were little prickles on the back of his neck as he walked on down the canyon.

Three Toes, when he had passed, was about to glide back up the canyon and, loping parallel to the hunter's course, take up another position and wait for him to pass again. He had no intention of attacking him; this was an exciting game, but just then he got the scent of the campfire at the mouth of the canyon, and he climbed back up the side of the canyon and found a place from which he could watch the hunters' camp.

He lay there for several hours watching. The moon climbed higher, and the bull wapiti challenged each other from across the canyons. The light in the tent went out and the fire died, and the hunter-cat glided down to near the place where the horses were picketed. There was not the least movement of air, and they failed to scent him, so he made a complete circle of the camp, and when he was east of the camp down canyon, the warmer air from the lower river valley began to flow up the canyon, and the horses smelled him and one whistle-snorted, and on this signal Three Toes ran through them, not stopping to attack, but loped on up the ridge paralleling the canyon.

Some of the horses pulled their picket pins again, or broke their picket ropes and ran into the pines, and a young saddle horse galloped down the canyon, just as Hammerhead had done two nights before on the Pacific side of the Pass. That night curiosity had interfered with Three Toes' plan, and he failed to parallel the mad gallop of Hammerhead. Now he did parallel the runaway saddle horse, then getting ahead of him running along the ridge while the horse ran along the dry, rocky course of the canyon stream. He crept down the canyon side and crouched behind a large granite boulder on the very edge of the course and waited.

But the frightened horse stopped before he came to the granite boulder, in a wide spot on the floor of the canyon, and his moon shadow was black on the snow. He raised his head and whinnied, then waited.

Three Toes crept up under cover of the willows and rushed him. As he bit into the back of his neck, he clawed his belly with his hind claws.

He lived on the horse carcass for a week, and by now the grizzly bears had gone into hibernation and did not disturb his feasting. He lost all interest in the bighorn hunters, the man-animals. The snow that came again covered the tracks of the runaway saddle horse and Three Toes, and the hunters made no search for the horse but instead packed and went down the mountain with their bighorn and wapiti heads and meat.

After Three Toes had finished the horse carcass, he went back to the Pacific side of the Pass and, on the headwaters of the Buffalo Fork, killed a mule deer buck. He looked about him into the white silence and growled at nothing, then proceeded to lick the hair from the carcass in a certain area so that he could begin his feast without being annoyed by the buck's stiff hair.

The fame of Old Three Toes was great, but it became greater, and for two years lion hunters came with their horses and hounds and ran him, but he would not stay treed long enough for the hunters to get within rifle range. He would watch for the hunters and when they came in sight, he would back down the tree and then spring far out onto a ridge side and run again until he became winded; then he would climb another tree and, instead of looking down at the dogs and spitting and growling, he would ignore them completely and watch for the hunters. When they came in sight he would jump out again and run until his short wind failed, but always he ran toward his slab rock refuge and then the hounds lost him and the hunters could not follow on horseback and lost themselves afoot among the wild, uptilted slabs of basalt.

Three Toes had only to look down at his three-toed left foot to remember that he must never wait for the hunters to come near the tree. He had been treed as a young tom years before, and a dude hunter had missed his head in his nervousness and had shot off his toe, just as the horse wrangler had guessed.

Now hunters came from all the mountain states to hunt the famed Three Toes. They brought with them the best-trained lion dogs in the west and rode their broad-chested, great-muscled cow horses to hunt him, but only one or two hunters ever caught sight of him, and always their hunt ended on the canyon floor at the bottom of the great pile of uptilted basalt. The tired hunters took off their hats and lay flat on their backs and cursed their luck, while their hounds lay panting with great noises in their throats and with their tongues touching the pine needles. The horses, with their bellies like bellows, stood on three legs resting the fourth and, with lowered heads, dozed.

The hunters secretly admired the great cat, but they pretended to hate him because they said he was menace to their horses. He got credit for every colt that disappeared, when as a matter of fact he killed not more than three horses in his long life, and one of these was a colt who was too weak to keep up with the fleeing herd or too stupid to stay at his mother's shoulder. He lived on deer and wapiti and bighorn, porcupines and marmots.

The ranchers became aroused, and they got together and made up a sum of $2,000 for the scalp of Three Toes, but no horseman with his hounds could take him.

They all knew his habits of course and they could not come within range of him when he treed, and they tried to outwit him by stopping some distance from the tree and having one of the party crawl toward it, acting as much like a dog as possible. He always spotted the clumsy figure on hands and knees, even when it tried to bark like a dog.

Then one day a man came with a helicopter, and the plans for Three Toes' destruction were laid. Twenty-five hunters rode to the canyon at the foot of the basalt slabs, then left their horses and climbed to positions overlooking all escape routes from Three Toes' refuge. There they sat with their rifles and waited for the roar of the helicopter.

From the helicopter you could see the much-used lying-up place of Three Toes, and the first bomb was dropped here, then a second, but he was not there. The pilot and his rancher guide saw him loping among the slabs, and they came over him and followed him and when he was turned back by a rifleman, they dropped another bomb. It missed him, but the blast knocked him down and he got up from the cloud of dust and standing on his hind legs he struck with a front paw at the helicopter, which was perhaps a hundred feet above him.

He then ran to the highest point of his refuge, a sandstone outcrop, and here he decided to fight. He crouched and waited for the attack which never came. His racial memories urged him to take this position and fight for his life, but there was nothing in these memories about the attack of mechanism. The bomb killed him instantly.

The men came up afoot to carry him down, and they had to gut him first since he was too heavy to carry down the rough mountainside.

Even in death he threw the horses into a panic, but their owners held them, and after much trouble they got the body across a saddle after allowing the horse to smell the carcass. But still the horse didn't like his burden and he drew his ears back, switched his tail in annoyance, and refused to move until someone got behind him with a quirt and another pulled him by the reins.

Two years later the ranchers were urging both the state and national government to do something about the overpopulation of mule deer and the epidemic which was the result. The deer had transmitted the disease to their cattle.

Three Toes had killed a deer every week on his domain, and for three years no tom mountain lion came to claim Old Three Toes' domain. When he came, the Airedale pack of a government hunter treed him and he was hit with a .38 Smith and Wesson pistol as he nervously watched the dogs chewing the bark of the pine in which they had treed him. The next winter the man-protected mule deer had overrun their range and had to be scientifically slaughtered.

Notes to the Stories

Singers to the Moon

3 *Cedar Canyon heads* . . .
To head is to have an upward inclination or slope; or to go round the head of (a stream or lake); of a stream, to have its head or source, to take its rise, to rise.

3 *. . . the watercourse in the bottom of the canyon flows into Bird Creek.*
The locations referred to in this story appear to be located west, northwest, and southwest of Pawhuska, Oklahoma, in the area centered around Bluestem Lake. Cedar Canyon and South Bird may be found on the Bluestem Lake U.S. Geological Survey topographical map.

6 *He refused to roach her mane,*
To roach a horse's mane is to cut it so that the remaining hair stands upright. Mathews uses the noun form of this term in his other works to refer to hairstyles worn by certain Osage men.

7 *Sheb said as they rode along, "They's a lineback whelp uses* . . .
To use is to frequent or haunt a place.

9 *. . . their fright was effecting their cunning as well as their speed.*
Possibly "affecting their cunning as well as their speed," but Mathews might have meant either.

10 *. . . the earth where they had trampled was hot and heavy with beeby scent,*
Possibly referring to a breed of cattle known as Red Angus. One of the better known breeders of these cattle was one Roy Beeby of Oklahoma.

20 *. . . the cyanide exploded into his mouth and he had died within a few yards.*
Cyanide guns are no less hazardous to pets and other species than poisoned horse meat. They also constitute some risk to humans and continue to target coyotes for both real and imagined attacks on healthy livestock, despite the minimal nature of the losses.

Grus, The Sandhill Crane

21 *. . . the scientific name for the species is* Grus tabida,
Originally written as *Grus Canadensis.* There are six subspecies of *Grus Canadensis*: *G. c. canadensis* (Lesser Sandhill); *Grus canadensis tabida* (Greater Sandhill); *G. c. rowani* (Canadian Sandhill); *G. c. pratensis* (Florida Sandhill); *G. c. pulla* (Mississippi Sandhill); *G. c. nesiotes* (Cuban Sandhill).

31   *They were fed on cornflakes and lizards and meat balls and kaffir . . .*
Kaffir is also known as kafir corn. Kaffir is a grain sorghum, *Sorghum bicolor caf-frorum,* having stout, short-jointed, leafy stalks, introduced into the United States from southern Africa.

Alfredo and the Jaguar

33   *Padre Francisco, the priest, came to see them, and to eat with them.*
Padre Francisco was originally Padre Edwardo. Mathews changed the name for unknown reasons.

34   *. . . he, Carlos Predregales, had shot El Tigre.*
Although Los Predregales appears to be a term in use in Mexico, referring for example to a location within Coyoacan, Mathews may have meant *pedregales* which means "Terreno cubierto de piedras sueltas" or terrain covered with loose rock. That is, scree or a talus field. Both spellings appear in this story.

35   *there was one which people called* jilguero,
This *jilguero* is probably the American Goldfinch (*Carduelis tristis*) or the Lesser Goldfinch (*Carduelis psaltria*). Mexico has several birds called *jilgueros,* including the Pine Siskin (*Carduelis pinus*), the Black-headed Siskin (*Carduelis notata*), and the *clarín jilguero.*

35   *The people called it the* clarín *. . .*
Mexico has three types of *claríns,* or Solitaires: the *clarín jilguero* (Brown-backed Solitaire, *Myadestes occidentalis*), the *clarín norteño* (Townsend's Solitaire, *Myadestes townsendi*), and the *clarín unicolor* (Slate-colored Solitaire, *Myadestes unicolor*). This one is probably the first.

35   *. . . the* coa *would sometimes call,*
This bird would be one of the many trogons that inhabit Mexico, known also as *coas.* Possibly the Coppery-Tailed Trogon (*Trogonurus ambigus*), the Elegant Trogon (*Trogón Elegante, Trogon elegans*), or the Mountain Trogon (*Trogón mexicano, Trogon mexicanus*). In the draft of a different story, in fact, Mathews wrote, and then crossed out again, the following addition to this story, apparently to be inserted at the end of the first paragraph: " . . . with the hoe. El Padre would be napping. He would glance over at him as he nodded, and as Alfredo pulled weeds and hoed, the copper tailed trogon called monotonously. The people called it 'coa,' since it seemed to be saying 'coa-coa-coa' for hours."

37   *He lost his sarapé,*
Serape. Mathews uses the Spanish spelling.

38   *. . . now he can't catch deer and javelinas . . .*
A javelina is a peccary (probably *Pecari tajacu*), a mammal that looks like a furry grey-brown pig, or a little like a smaller, friendlier boar.

39   *An Aztec thrush . . .*
This bird is known in Spanish as the *mirlo pinto* (*Ridgwayia pinicola*).

40   *Down the canyon, a Mexican jay . . .*
Sixteen species of jay inhabit Mexico, including the blue jay known in the United States. None is called the Mexican jay, so which species Mathews refers to is a mystery.

40   *He knew that El Tigre was watching him, . . . and he knew if he turned his head to see, El Tigre would spring.*
Mathews originally wrote, "He knew that El Tigre was watching me . . . "!

The White Sack

43   *It was obviously an animal, but it could never be taken for a wild one because it moved slowly, clumsily, more like a broken-winged eagle at a distance than anything else.*
Mathews originally wrote, "but it could never be taken for an indigenous one."

52   *. . . the rimrock of Santiago Canyon.*
Santiago Canyon is located near Jemez Pueblo, about fifty or sixty miles west of Santa Fe. So this story takes place within about one hour's present-day driving distance from Los Alamos, New Mexico, where the atomic bomb was created. It would be considered central New Mexico, though slightly west of center.

Arrowflight, The Story of a Prairie Chicken

55   *his pinnate feathers would be erected . . .*
If pinnate is a word normally used to describe something that "resembles a feather," a pinnate feather would be one that has lateral parts or branches on each side of a common axis or that is long and symmetrical. Pictures and drawings of male prairie chickens during their mating dance show several of these feathers of varying lengths standing nearly erect and coming toward a common point.

61   *They flew together and hit at each other with their wings, since they had no spurs . . .*
Prairie chickens have natural spurs on their feet, so Mathews must be referring to the artificial, metal ones used in human-staged cockfighting. In early high school, he participated enthusiastically in these cockfights, writing in his autobiography, "I was almost completely absorbed by my knight errantry, my quail and prairie chicken hunting, and my taxidermy, and my discouragements in the science of ornithology. Also some time before entering High School I had sent away for pit game eggs, and the success of my cocks in defeating the community's dung-hill cocks, inspired other little barbarians, and these others were raising their pit games and we staged cockfights first in one chicken pen and then in another, often to the dismay of our mothers, but protected by the indulgence of our fathers.

"My pit games fascinated me with their red saddles and hackles and their eyes that were embers from a fire. Even after some of my cockfighting companions had dropped the pit game hobby for High School dancing and hay rides, I carried on with mine."

62 *No coyote would try to go through such a spiny plum thicket . . .*
The word "spiny" here was handwritten into the manuscript and may be erroneous. In a different draft, this reads as "spinneyplum [*sic*] thicket," a spinney being a thorn hedge or a small wood or copse, especially one planted or preserved for sheltering game birds.

64 *But at the end of the first week of her brood, there was fortunate activity in a blackjack that had ventured out to the edge of the sandstone.*
This sentence originally read, "But at the end of the first week of her brood, the hen prairie chicken, there was fortunate activity in a blackjack that had ventured out to the edge of the sandstone." It is unclear what Mathews intended by this extra, possibly unfinished phrase.

66 *As a matter of fact, such clouds are called botryoidal, which means kidney-like,*
Most dictionaries say that botryoidal means "like a cluster of grapes." Either Mathews was working from memory, or he saw some resemblance between grapes and kidneys, perhaps on the inside of the latter.

The Last Dance

75 *. . . they stamped the ground with their feet.*
The heath hen is an eastern relative or subspecies of the prairie chicken.

77 *. . . shot by some boys from Tisbury.*
Tisbury is a town near the northern tip of Martha's Vineyard.

79 *The species called heath hens was dying out:*
Mathews crossed out the word "race" here to substitute "species" for it. The same substitution was made in the very last sentence of the story.

80 *. . . the cock of destiny became the Last Cock,*
Throughout the uncorrected manuscript, Mathews referred to this cock as "the cock of fate" or "a bird of fate," later deciding to use the word "destiny" instead.

The White Gobbler of Rancho Seco

83 *There was one who raised White Holland turkeys for the market.*
It is fairly well known that Benjamin Franklin once advocated making the wild turkey of North America the national bird. What is less well known is that turkeys, which are indigenous to North America, were brought to Europe early on to be bred and were later sold back to farmers in the western hemisphere. White Hollands were some of these, first brought to the United States in the early 1800s. The Aztecs and other

American Indians bred white turkeys, so the White Hollands may have been derived from this already domesticated stock.

83 *only a few feet from him, he saw something ashen . . .*
The last word here is handwritten and nearly illegible; in the second draft of the story in the same folder, the word reads "white," so "ashen" is likely correct.

84 *he . . . trotted over the saddle.*
Saddle is a term for the low part of a ridge between two peaks or hills, so called because it looks like the saddle for a horse.

85 *Chip, the rancho foreman,*
Mathews originally named this character Hal.

85 *Then suddenly Grulla snorted,*
Grulla is the Spanish word for crane, as well as being the name of a small town in Texas (La Grulla) and a wildlife refuge in New Mexico that is overseen by the Muleshoe Refuge mentioned in the previous story, "Grus, The Sandhill Crane." *Grullo* is a color of certain horses in the dun family, referring to their greyish coats.

The Royal of Glen Orchy

99 *The deer forest of Glen Orchy in Scotland . . .*
Glen Orchy is a long, deep valley about twelve miles long, in Argyll and Bute on the inland, western coast of Scotland. It follows the River Orchy, which flows between Loch Tulla in the north and Loch Awe in the south. The river's mouth is about sixteen miles north of Inveraray and about seventy-five miles northwest of Glasgow by road.

99 *. . . low mountain ridges covered with bracken . . .*
Bracken is a genus of ferns, large and coarse, often found on the moors.

99 *. . . the voice of the lapwing seemed to be sad,*
This bird is possibly the Northern Lapwing (*Vanellus vanellus*). Mathews might have been familiar with English translations of Ovid's *Metamorphoses,* which refer to this bird.

99 *The call of the curlew . . .*
This bird is probably the Eurasian Curlew (*Numenius arquata*). In Scotland, it is sometimes referred to as a "whaup." Curlews are wading birds. Mathews might instead be referring to the Whimbrel (*Numenius phaeopus*), which can also be found in Scotland.

99 *But once you saw the black grouse . . .*
The black grouse is *Tetrao tetrix.* Males are sometimes referred to as Blackcocks and females as Greyhens.

100 *One day when the Gulf Stream brought heavily laden air . . .*
People living in the western hemisphere may feel a bit disoriented by this description.

The Gulf Stream is a warm ocean current that flows from the Gulf of Mexico along the U.S. coast, but eventually reaches the British Isles. Its North Atlantic Current and the strong winds produced by it keep the western coasts of these isles and the west coast of Norway warmer than the east coasts. This ocean phenomenon was first noted by Juan Ponce de León in the sixteenth century and was later charted by Benjamin Franklin and others.

101   . . . *a growth of bracken and birch sapling in a corrie.*
Mathews embeds a note here after the word "corrie" to define it: ravine.

101   . . . *blowing at the tail of a mother red grouse . . .*
The red grouse is *Lagopus lagopus scotica.*

102   *The old Marquess who owned Glen Orchy deer forest*
A marquess (or marquis or marques, or perhaps *marqués* as in the Mexican Spanish Mathews would have used in the 1930s) is a member of the nobility of the United Kingdom, ranked below a duke and above an earl. Mathews refers to Gavin Campbell, for whom the title of Marquess was briefly revived from 1885 until his death in 1922. John Campbell, who died in 1862, had been the last Marquess of Breadalbane in the original line and was previously known as Lord Glenorchy (or the Laird of Glenurquhay). His ancestor Sir Colin Campbell built the Castle of Kilchurn or Coalchuirn at the east end of Loch Awe in 1440 (though it may have been erected by his wife during his absence during the Crusades). The castle was memorialized by William Wordsworth in "Address to Kilchurn Castle, upon Loch Awe."

103   *hidden by the cottongrass . . .*
Cottongrass is a type of sedge that grows in wetlands and bogs.

103   . . . *McCarricker, the gillie.*
Mathews embeds a note here after the word "gillie" to define it: guide to deer stalkers for shooting in general.

103   . . . *dancing ground of the "blackgums, whan you coom to lek,"*
A "lek" is a booming or mating grounds for grouse, prairie chickens, and other similar birds. It is also used to refer to the communal, competitive mating dance that takes place on the lek. Here McCarricker is using the term "to lek" as a verb meaning "to dance" and/or "to mate."

109   . . . *attacked a whinbush,*
Also known as "gorse" or "furze," whinbush is a variety of evergreen shrubs with an abundance of yellow flowers. These shrubs thrive through fires, which usually accelerate their germination from seed and can allow their ability to sprout from the stem to give them dominance for a time afterwards.

Old Three Toes of Buffalo Fork

113   *... the Pacific side of Two Ocean Pass,*

Two Ocean Pass is a pass that crosses the Continental Divide in the Teton National Forest about fifty miles northeast of Jackson Hole, Wyoming. North Two Ocean Creek divides in two here to flow toward both the Atlantic and the Pacific oceans. A National Natural Landmark designates this point on the Divide.

113   *They had haunches of wapiti ...*

Pronounced WAH-pi-tee. This is *Cervus canadensis*, or the elk of North America. It is the second-largest animal in the deer family, surpassed only by the moose. Wapiti are related to the red deer of Scotland, but constitute a distinct species. Different sources give the origin of the name as Cree or Shawnee, both of which are Algonquian languages.

114   *"Guess ole Hammerhead's just about reached the Hole ...*

Jackson Hole, Wyoming.

128   *Two years later the ranchers were urging both the state and national government ... mule deer had overrun their range and had to be scientifically slaughtered.*

In the manuscript from which this version was verified, Mathews crossed out these last two paragraphs, which form the ending of the story. It is common to find such excisions accompanied by handwritten revisions, which indicate that clarification rather than excision was intended. Other drafts within the same folder contain the apparent clarification, but this version has been preferred as more powerful, so these paragraphs have been let stand. The word Airedale is an uncertain inference from Mathews's handwriting, made by comparing his mentions of Three Toes in this piece to his autobiography.

Afterword

JOHN JOSEPH MATHEWS'S lifelong interest in wildlife is evident across the pages of these stories. All his life he observed and studied the habits of hawks, panthers, and other wild animals. Through the stories, he passed his knowledge on to all his grandchildren, and indeed to the world. His granddaughters Sara, Laura, and Christine, who lived in Maryland with his son, John, and daughter-in-law, Gail, he saw occasionally, usually when he went on business to Washington, D.C., but sometimes in Pawhuska, Oklahoma. There he introduced them to his world, a world very different from their own. When apart from the girls, he sometimes sent them stories and drawings of the animals he had observed around his home in the blackjacks. The grandchildren of his second wife, Elizabeth, whom he called Dibbs, were a greater presence in his life. Diana and Mead lived in Paris with Elizabeth's son, John Hunt. Diane, Peter, Henry, and Sammy lived in California with her daughter, Ann Hunt Brown. He wrote these children long letters illustrated with scenes of wildlife from his home, The Black-jacks, visited the Browns in California, and looked forward to Diana and Mead's visits to Oklahoma. Once he even recorded one of their visits on his tape recorder, saving for posterity amusing exchanges and the delights of reunited family. He regaled these many young ones with missives from The Blackjacks. So when, in 1962 or thereabouts, he approached or was approached by the *Atlantic Monthly Press* to work on a children's book, it is certain that these children were uppermost in his mind.

Although few of them have ever been published, Mathews wrote at least thirty-four short stories during his long career.[1] The nine collected here are unique in that he intended from the beginning to publish them together, in a book he increasingly envisioned as a boy's book. Despite the evident

interest of his granddaughters Diana Hunt and Diane Brown in his stories, he could not in November 1963 imagine their appeal to girls as well as
boys. Nor could he have predicted the dawning of widespread concern over
threats to wildlife worldwide which make this collection most relevant and
highly anticipatory of emerging views of animal behavior and intelligence.
During the two and a half months of their composition, he imagined for the
first time a specific audience for his writing: boys aged nine through twelve.[2]
His impulse to look to "[Ernest Thompson-] Seton, [Charles G. D.] Roberts,
and [Rudyard] Kipling for hints as to how I might be getting along" suggests
that it was himself as a boy of that age to whom he was trying to appeal.

"I am not sure of myself in writing my boy's book," he confessed. Yet
when he told his first-written story, "The White Sack," to Ann Hunt Brown
and her husband and to her children in separate sittings in August 1963,
the grandchildren clearly understood something about the story for which
the adults had little appreciation. Diane, Peter, and Henry Brown were all
held spellbound while "later when Diane told the story to her parents, they
thought it 'grim.' This is very interesting, especially since the two, Peter and
Diane who can read, have one of the most sensational papers in the United
States, the San Francisco Chronicle available . . . yet Ann and Tony gag."
Perhaps it was the story's ironies that caught the attention of the young, or
perhaps Mathews's intricate description of the information being exchanged
among the species of the "ravine that was not yet become a canyon" about
the intruder in their midst. Whatever it may have been, the kids certainly
knew a good story when they heard it.

"The White Sack" had actually been written long before the other eight
stories, during one of the most distressing periods of Mathews's life. His
initial impetus toward short story writing had come just after World War
II and had been motivated by financial exigency. Perhaps that exigency
rather than the love he brought to the task nearly twenty years later explains
the different quality of these "boy stories" as compared to the remaining
twenty-five. While his first fourteen or more stories were written under
considerable duress, in the hopes of financing his long-delayed work on *Life
and Death of an Oilman*, a biography of oil magnate Ernest W. Marland,
his return to short narrative fiction in the early 1960s came on the heels of

the success of *The Osages: Children of the Middle Waters* and the return of "pleasant" years to Mathews's life.

Although he mentions in January 1963 that he has already agreed to write a children's book for the *Atlantic Monthly Press*, he is also already disappointed that he hasn't started it. His trip to San Francisco that August appears to have given him the push he needed, though by June he had already been reading a book by Lawrence H. Walkinshaw on sandhill cranes. In addition to enhancing his own experiential knowledge of these cranes, he used the book to prepare pen-and-ink sketches that he intended to accompany the story. In fact, by December, Mathews would have 112 original pen-and-ink sketches prepared to accompany the book as a whole out of 120 that he ultimately made, illustrations which have unfortunately been misplaced or lost since his death.[3] He may have started "Grus, The Sandhill Crane" during this same month of June. He then moved on to "The Last Dance" on September 1, which he seems to have intended originally to place last. This story and its title were, he felt, "dramatic enough for 12-year-olds" and "based on articles and monographs by" Dr. Alfred O. Gross of Bowdoin College in Maine. At first entitled "The Dance of Death," it was the only story not based on Mathews's personal experience as a hunter and observer of his fellow animals, and he remarks that he felt clumsy in the writing of it. Perhaps he never knew how superb the story really is.

"Alfredo and the Jaguar" came next, then the simplifying of "The White Sack" for his young audience. This story had likely been composed in 1948 or 1949, judging by the entries Mathews made in his diary about it. All this work was done in early September. By the seventh, he was emending the Rancho Seco story, then almost a week later working on "Arrowflight." He comments that he finds the sketches he is making simultaneously with the stories more interesting than them. "The Royal of Glen Orchy," "Old Three Toes of Buffalo Fork," and "Grus" came next. Mathews had heard from a friend, Frank Spencer, about an article that Spencer had found on the designers of airplane wings getting their ideas of feathering from the sandhill crane, but we don't know if he ever found this piece. He finished the longest story, "Singers to the Moon," on October 14th. The following month as he was preparing the drafts for publication and apparently rearranging their order, he was also deciding to narrow the book from an intended ten stories to nine.[4] He had meant to write an "Osage story" and wanted "to talk with someone like Harry Redeagle about his boyhood, as the basis for" it. Unfortunately, if the known manuscripts are complete, it appears that he never wrote this story at all, much less included it in his publication attempts.

By July 1964, he had received a rejection from Doubleday of the book which he may have tentatively titled after "Old Three Toes of Buffalo Fork."[5] There is no trace of what happened to it after that. He had predicted in late November 1963: "All this so some old mis-informed gal in the children's department of Little, Brown & Company can turn it down. I'm casting real pearls from the prairie, the blackjacks, the mountains of Mexico and North America." Or perhaps this was no prediction at all. Mathews's last draft was completed on the eighth of that month, and his contact Seymour Lawrence was by now the embattled editor of the *Atlantic Monthly Press*, having staked his longevity in this position on the publication of *A Singular Man* by J. P. Donleavy. When that work was rejected on grounds of pornographic material by the management at Little, Brown, which had acquired the *Atlantic Monthly Press*, Lawrence ended up leaving the publisher. This drama was playing out during the same months as Mathews's attempts to get his boy book published, and he may indeed have received a short, curt note from "some old mis-informed gal in the children's department" within a few weeks of having sent off the manuscript. It may have been these events which turned Mathews against the eastern publishing establishment in his later life, complaining in his diaries about the "sexualism" and "vulgarity" of what was getting published and writing publicly about the neglect of southwestern regional literature. Yet this timeline seems off. Despite the notes on his manuscripts, his diary indicates that he was still finalizing the untitled draft in December, with Elizabeth preparing the final typescripts based on his edits.

The last we hear of the book's fate, Mathews is working with a literary agent, Robert Center, to try to place it with Viking. He is still convinced "it is really worthy of publication" but worries that it may not sell. Perhaps he became halfhearted about the project's marketability and gave up. Given the gaps in his diary between July 1964 and January 1966, we may never know. Perhaps he decided to publish the book privately among his immediate family only. In June of 1965, he is hosting his grandchildren Diana and Mead Hunt at The Blackjacks. In his sound diary for June 17th, we hear the young Mead saying, "I wanna hear the coyotes," and his older sister, Diana, echoing, "I want to hear them too." Mathews replies with ebullient teasing, "*I'm* not in control of the coyotes. . . . You think you can get a coyote chorus by pushing a button, don't you?" Later he remarks that he finds them "tremendously charming" as well as "tremendously interested in the story of the spider" which he had reread from *The Osages* a few days before so that he could tell it to them. Several days later, he can be heard telling Diana, "You know you can add anything you like to that spider story," to which she replies, "Did you write it?" Hilariously, he responds, "I don't know, I must have." So by this next year, the apparent unsuccess of his efforts at publishing the boy book seems to have left little mark. He basks in the "very, very pleasant visit" of the Hunts and laments that the "children have left a vacuum here on the ridge," missing their European naïveté, "unsophistication," and graciousness. But he says not a word about the manuscript, Robert Center, Viking, or the work's ultimate landing spot.

One clue to that landing place may exist in the first story. "Singers to the Moon" features a ranch bird dog named Spot and a young observer named Sammy who rides across the blackjack ridges on his loyal horse Peg. In *Twenty Thousand Mornings,* Mathews tells us that after the colt who would become his best companion was born, he might have named her Pegasus rather than Bally had he not become annoyed at his older sister's didactic monologues about the winged horse of Greek mythology. So at first glance, the story merely disguises young Jo Mathews as Sammy, his mare Bally as Peg, and his first dog Spot as the scared-to-death ranch dog Spot. But the choice of the name Sammy may have had valence, given that Samuel Brown was the name of one of his younger grandchildren. Perhaps it was this grandson who was the ultimate recipient of the boy book. The story's "Sammy" seems to be younger than the Jo who in high school and during World War I hunted coyotes with his cousin's husband, who marketed their hides. Yet he is also more mature, in his recognition of the individuality of Lineback (the coyote protagonist of "Singers"), than the twenty-something aviator Mathews who buzzed bewildered coyotes in the mesquite deserts of Texas and remembered that the air service cadets used to "playfully" throw fire extinguishers at them while circling the Brush Country. He is most like the boy who sometimes used to guard his solitude from his best friend, Tom Mitscher, because he preferred on occasion to imagine himself a contented wolf.

Readers already familiar with Mathews's works will recognize interesting connections between some of the stories in this volume and his previously published works. The most evident literary forebear of the stories is *Talking to the Moon.* Though the style and genre of the two books are quite different, their purport seems quite similar. Both aim to provoke readers to think carefully about their relationship to nonhuman animals and the natural world and to consider themselves as biological creatures rather than merely as entities caught in the flows and throes of a merely human civilization. Mathews wrote in that 1945 work: "I had come to the blackjacks to live, as one climbs out of the roaring stream of civilization onto an island, to rest and watch" and that he was "disturbed by something deeper, and I wanted to get my feet on my own bit of earth. . . . I wanted to express my harmony with the natural flow of life on my bit of earth" where "physical action and living to the very brim each day in harmony with life about me were exhausting and therefore completely satisfactory." Here, that particular Mathews disappears. He removes himself as the center of the seeing and the living to put in his place those individuals struggling each minute and hour to survive and flourish, often against remarkable odds. It seems he took to heart at least three remarks of his own boyhood favorite.[6] Ernest Thompson-Seton said in *Wild Animals I Have Known* that he wanted to write about the life of the individual animal "rather than the ways of the race in general" as it was so much more "profitable . . . to devote that space to the life of some one great" individual and his or her real personality; that "the life of a wild animal *always has a tragic end*"; and that "man has nothing that the animals have not at least a vestige of, the animals have nothing that man does not in some degree share." Though Mathews's stories do not always have a tragic end, he was well attuned to the common loss suffered, shared amongst us, when an individual animal is lost, especially one with a large personality, and to the fact that wild animals almost never see old age or die without violence.

Sundown and *Twenty Thousand Mornings* also have their shadows in at least one of the feature stories of this volume. If Mathews finally found his inspiration to write the planned collection through reading about the sandhill crane, readers will perhaps find it interesting to note that in his autobiography, *Twenty Thousand Mornings,* Mathews refers to himself as a sandhill crane and notes that others saw him as such too. "I played fullback, despite the fact that about this time I was built like a sandhill crane. Our coach Jake Duran once said: 'Whenever I see one of them big tackles get into the secondary and blast yu, I shut my eyes and pray; the good Lord musta put your joints together special, with some kind of extry wir'in'.' The sandhill crane had the advantage of wings, and I had to remain on the ground." Many have attributed too much autobiographical likeness to Mathews in his character Challenge Windzer from *Sundown,* but it is fascinating that a major focus of Mathews in "Grus, The Sandhill Crane" rests on the cranes' dancing and the moment when Grus feels a tremendous thrill, his blood surging with emotion, and he "had to dance." Although there is no suggestion that Grus is unhappy like Chal, the passage reminds us of moments in *Sundown* when Chal feels the urge to dance. "Then, very suddenly, that mysterious feeling came over him. A mild fire seemed to be coursing through his veins and he felt that he wanted to sing and dance; sing and dance with deep reverence. He felt that some kind of glory had descended upon him, accompanied by a sort of sweetness and a thrilling appreciation of himself. He wanted to struggle with something. His body seemed a wonderful thing just then, and he had a feeling that he could conquer anything that might stand in his way. There seemed to be intense urges which made him deliciously unhappy."

We might also compare Mathews's prose to the direct and indirect literary antecedents of this particular set of stories. Having never been published, they have as yet no literary descendants, but can and will also be compared and contrasted to many who wrote after 1963. Four of the turn-of-the-century writers Mathews loved wrote animal stories: Thompson-Seton, Roberts, Kipling, and Jack London.[7] Of these, his stories seem most to resemble Roberts's. His *The Kindred of the Wild* probably furnished both philosophy and instruction—a model. People began late to observe, he wrote, "with the wonder and interest of discoverers, the astonishing fashion in which the mere instincts of these so-called irrational creatures were able to simulate the operations of reason. . . . The drift of all these data was overwhelmingly toward one conclusion. The mental processes of the animals observed were seen to be far more complex than the observers had supposed. Where instinct was called in to account for the elaborate ingenuity [with which animals approached problem-solving], it began to seem as if that faithful faculty was being overworked. . . . Men were forced at last to accept the proposition that, within their varying limitations, animals can and do reason." While Thompson-Seton impressed Mathews with his powers of pictorial illustration compared to Roberts, Mathews as an adult wrote that he had realized that the man could not really write. "His dramatics were stiff but apparently pleasing to himself" and both Thompson-Seton and Roberts were "observers of nature, and loved it, yet were they under the influence of 19th Century man-smugness." It is important that we look with complex and skeptical eyes, then, on those who doubt that Mathews saw through the harmful colonial affinities of London and Kipling, or think he engaged in any kind of imperialist nostalgia for hunters who were themselves nostalgic for what people like them had destroyed. Though Mathews wore a safari-style pith hat while on his Guggenheim Fellowship in Mexico, the mind that that helmet protected was of a far different kind of hunter than those who had invaded the great expanses of Africa, destroyed the buffalo of the Great Plains, pushed the wolves of the Great North to the brink, or had it out for the coyotes of greater North America.

Among contemporaries, Mathews shares the most with three powerhouses of the environmental movement: Aldo Leopold, Sally Carrigher, and Rachel Carson. Matthews's *Talking to the Moon* had been published four years before *A Sand County Almanac* came out posthumously. It would be difficult to trace whether Mathews influenced Leopold, though the structure of the almanac's first part resembles Mathews's monthly and seasonal organization in *Talking*. The strong kinship between the men's visions, particularly when comparing this 1963 volume to Leopold's now universally influential environmentalist classic, is everywhere evident, so a point-by-point comparison of *A Sand County Almanac* (or even its most famous excerpt, "Thinking Like a Mountain") with *Old Three Toes and Other Tales of Survival and Extinction* would be out of the question in such a small space as we have here. We have no evidence that Mathews read Leopold, though it would be easy to miss references in his voluminous and often illegible diaries. Mathews did record the title of Sally Carrigher's 1944 *One Day on Beetle Rock* in his 1955 diary and hers is by far the closest of these three writers to Mathews's creative approach and use of perspective. There is more humor and irony in Mathews's stories than in many of Carrigher's and he ranges over different terrains rather than remaining in one place throughout his nine narratives. It appears that Mathews had read a short story about a grouse entitled "Spinster of Beetle Rock" from Carrigher's upcoming book in the *Saturday Evening Post* in early December 1943. It remains unclear whether Mathews read the full book, merely recorded the title as one he intended to buy or borrow, or having bought or borrowed it never read it. He usually recorded the fact of his reading any book along with his impressions of it in his diaries, yet there is no further mention of Carrigher beyond this title among a list of other books. So it seems unlikely that he knew it fully, unless it lies within one of the now gaping holes in the diary record. Carson's *The Sea Around Us,* on the other hand, he found "fascinating" and recorded it in 1952 as "one of the most exciting books I have ever read," later tempering that handwritten exaggeration to "one of the most exciting books I have read this year" in the typescript of the diary. We see Carson's concerns in *Silent Spring* echoed by Mathews in "Singers to the Moon" and "Arrowflight" with regard to inorganic poisons. We don't know if he had read that particular work of hers, but that brief intersection with her passions is telling of a nascent spirit of the era.

These stories probably benefited from Mathews's wider reading, beyond animal stories and works by environmentalists, though two other authors whom he complimented overtly in his papers deserve mention as potentially interesting to compare to him in their focus on wildlife. He "grazed" T. H. White's *The Goshawk* over and over again, and also read *The Once and Future King*. In June 1963, he singled out *Wild Lone: The Story of a Pytchley Fox* by "B. B." for praise as well.[8] Beyond these two, and beyond his readings about the extinction of the heath hen of our eastern coast, he had also read (or at least intended to read) A. W. Schorger's *The Passenger Pigeon,* as well as an article called "Extinct Animals Live Again," so he had been thinking about species extinction in the years leading up to these stories' composition. Traces of his friends Paul B. Sears's *Deserts on the March* and J. Frank Dobie's *The Mustangs* and *The Voice of the Coyote* (which he read in 1955), might also be discernible. Always an aficionado of technology, Mathews listened to records of bird songs from the Cornell Laboratory of Ornithology in 1956 and 1957 and probably watched early television shows such as *Mutual of Omaha's Wild Kingdom.* He may have gathered cues for what to do or not do from his readings of Mary Austin's *Land of Little Rain,* Farley Mowat's *People of the Deer,* John A. Hunter's "How Wild Animals Behave," and even Gontran de Poncins's *Kabloona,* Alice Marriott's *The Black Stone Knife,* Lois Crisler's *Arctic Wild,* or Robinson Jeffers's poems.

Of course, we necessarily also think of Mathews's American Indian forebears and how they influenced his outlook on nonhuman beings. Mathews knew and read several of his contemporaries, including D'Arcy McNickle and Lynn Riggs, but for works such as these short stories, they seem to have had little impact on him. Literary records of tribal animal stories, such as Zitkala-Ša's and Ella Deloria's Iktomi stories, and very early treatments of animal-human relations, such as David Cusick's narration of the Haudenosaunee creation story or Jane Johnston Schoolcraft's "The Origin of the Robin," if he knew them at all, bear very little resemblance to his outlook and purposes. It seems more likely that Mathews learned aspects of how he interacted with and observed wild animals from his father and unrecorded individual Osages with whom he grew up and conversed later as an adult and budding writer. When eighteenth-century Native Americans complained that their children were coming back to their tribes from colonial schools "useless," they were observing that their children were *uneducated:* illiterate in the language and body language of animals, among other things. Ancient American Indian traditions, as represented within contemporary books like *Yaqui Deer Songs* and its accompanying film, *Seyewailo,* demonstrate at least three fairly widespread aspects of an indigenous North American ethic toward animal observation and human-nonhuman relations.

Animals were and are watched and listened to carefully: to learn lessons from them about how to behave (or not behave) physically—how literally to move one's body or one's mind to effect a desired outcome, how to gather knowledge about the world; to learn better how to hunt, often through imitation of the sought-after prey or through mimicking of camouflages and freezing; and to gain powers and talents both natural and supernatural.[9] Mathews's stories show him sharing most in the heritage of the first two ethics. In particular, Mathews reverses the common literary trope—even in many American Indian stories—of humans inhabiting animal identities in favor of having humans see from an animal's point of view.

It will be hard to trace Mathews's American Indian antecedents, then, without being attuned to the stark differences among these antecedents in their anthropomorphizing and unwillingness to anthropomorphize nonhumans. We will perhaps more easily be able to see how Mathews's writing stands out, and is often quite different from those who have come after.[10] His literary treatment of nonhumans and his unique point of view diverges from contemporary Osage writers, including Carter Revard and Elise Paschen among others. His feline stories might be set against Tim Tingle's "Caleb," his way of writing about his concern for the dangers of modern technologies against Gerald Vizenor's vision of ecological apocalypse and tutorial renditions of various, contrasting human-nonhuman relationships in *Bearheart,* and his manner of expressing his ethic of living with rather than against canines against Paula Underwood's *Who Speaks for Wolf.* Of course there are many others—Joseph Bruchac's many children's texts, Winona LaDuke's *All Our Relations,* Thomas King's Soldier from *Truth and Bright Water,* Linda Hogan's 317 dead eagles in *Mean Spirit,* Kateri Akiwenzie-Damm's poetic sturgeon, L. Frank-Manriquez's coyote of *Acorn Soup,* Louise Erdrich's bears, cranes, crows, and wolves—with which to surround, embrace, compare, and contrast Mathews.

In the pages that follow, I offer interpretive readings of each of the stories and illustrate their many connections and commonalities, concentrating in particular on the conservation ethic that unites them and recommends them to us as strong allies in the defense of wildlife movement. Given the diversity of the stories, no singular interpretation is possible, however, and because readers will wish to have read the stories prior to indulging in this interpretive analysis, we have placed this historical and biographical contextualization of each as an afterword. Readers will avoid plot spoilers and perhaps experience greater benefit from encountering the book as it would have appeared in the 1960s rather than first as mediated by this editor.

The first story, last written, is the perfect inauguration for a series advocating ecological sanity and the protection of wildlife from the injudicious behaviors of the human animal. Although *One Day on Beetle Rock* and *A Sand County Almanac* had been published as early as 1944 and 1949 and *Silent Spring* came out the year before Mathews completed his manuscripts, his vision remains prescient and his approach unique for the times in which he wrote. It will strike many as ironic that an avid hunter might emerge as a moral hero in the struggle for recognition of animal rights, especially in an era when artificially inflated political candidates rave about shooting wolves from helicopters and rant about their own "rights" to kill nonhuman persons, confusing state sanctions with Jeffersonian theories inadequate to the situation. But Mathews's deep empathy for other earth beings, his understanding of their individual consciousnesses and their intelligence both individual and collective, arose from his boyhood seclusion from the world of mankind, his early becoming embedded in the world of the birds and mammals with whom he engaged in the "earth struggle." His usually unconquerable urges to hunt were never to him a signal of his superiority, but evidence unremitting of our commonality with all life.[11]

Although he wrote many expository statements about survival, reproduction, and a mysterious third force that drives our behaviors, these never attain the heights of Mathews's *creative* narrative prose. This prose is the surplus of his conscious attempts—in his autobiography, in letters, in *Talking to the Moon*—to work out a theory for the determining limits of biological necessity on human and nonhuman behavior. When he tells a story, he exhibits an insight that he may not even have known that he had. Though barely distinct from his declarative prose, his narratives are a thing altogether extra. It is specifically his incredible ability to manipulate point of view, to move through a terrain with its inhabitants and through their thoughts and senses rather than apart from them, which creates this extraordinary surplus to his articulate knowledge, and thus to ours. It distinguishes him from the nature and conservation writers of his era, who rarely transcend the boundaries of their own flesh even when impassioned in the interest of species threatened by humanity.

Singers to the Moon

"Singers to the Moon" is the first of several stories in which Mathews draws upon these talents to invoke empathy with the coyote or another animal. He puts us and himself in Lineback's place as Lineback strategizes where best to locate his "lying-up" place for best sight and scent of the potential dangers around him. He teaches us that coyotes must close their mouths to listen when being chased, because the noise of their own panting overwhelms their sense of hearing. Even more crucially, we witness the young coyote crying from loneliness once after becoming lost from his mother and brother. Mathews despised anthropopathy, or the ascription of human feelings and passions to other species. But he was not so infuriated with the human arrogance of projection that he failed to ascribe logically to all species a unity of basic emotions. Mammals in particular, who spend the first year or more of their life under the protection of mother and family, must experience a sense of loss, if only a self-protective one, when deprived of their habitual companions.

As important as, perhaps more important than, his ability to create empathy in his readers for one of the most misunderstood predators of North America is his focus on the coyotes' intelligence. He shows us not only the individual intelligence of Lineback, but the passing of information from one to another that constitutes the species' collective and adaptive knowledge. Language is key to this focus. Historically, both intellectual racism and the denigration of the intelligence of animals ushered in the Amer-European invasion of the Mississippi and Missouri Valleys.[12] Language among nonhuman mammals was denied and North American human languages demoted in the effort to assure the superiority of the intrusive culture. So when Mathews has his audience listening to the inner speech of Lineback as he runs for his life and both coyotes and other canines "reading" musk messages and learning the "news" in their visits to U.S. Geological Survey (USGS) survey pin number 12, it is far from a literary conceit. We are to question our association of human-articulated, tongue-carved language with the capacity for symbolic thought and behavioral signification that ranges beyond one order, family, or genus of sentient life. After all, following the death of Lineback's mate, the canines quickly learn through Lineback's musk message—symbolic communicative behavior—about the dangers of the tainted horse meat.[13] Significant too is the contrast between the ending of this story and the final lines from "Alfredo and the Jaguar." By having the coyotes (ky-oats in Mathews's pronunciation) laughing at the end, even after Lineback's ignominious murder, he suggests that El Tigrero's view of laughter may not be Mathews's own. It is as much as saying, "We will not be moved." And indeed all assaults on this population have failed to diminish their presence. They have escaped thus far the fate of the equally outraged wolf.

The impetus for these assaults lies with their bad reputation for killing the calves of human-protected livestock. Mathews debunks that reputation with the authority of observation: "Sometimes the cows would give birth to weaklings, and they were never able to rise to their feet to suckle. The wise pair knew about such calves, and when they came upon a range cow standing over a sick calf, they sat in the grass and waited for it to die; then they must wait for the cow to leave before they could feast. When these carcasses were found, Sammy's father and other ranchers jumped to conclusions and cursed all coyotes as eternal enemies." Mathews had personally witnessed the "efficient" and indiscriminate poisoning which the story condemns. During his college years, one of his good friends, Floyd Soderstrom, had staked a precarious claim in South Dakota and survived his first winter by poisoning coyotes and wolves with "dough balls filled with strychnine" and selling the hides for money. In January 1945, Mathews railed in his diary against a "barbaric coyote hunt" to be held in Osage County, which he considered to be an "organized attempt at mass murder." He clearly saw the ties to English foxhunting and it is a measure of his determination to educate people on the stupidities of government efforts to control and eradicate particular species that coyote-poisoning appears not only here in "Singers" but returns to us in fine Leopoldian form in "Arrowflight." What distinguished these activities from the sport hunting in which he engaged, at least in his own mind, was the detachment from even the vicarious experience of interspecies rivalries aimed at survival. Dogs must be trained against their inherent fear to attack wild canines while neither humans nor bovines are at grave risk if we refrain from the speciecide such training often serves.

It should hardly go unmentioned that "Singers to the Moon" is a story about a coyote by a part-Osage writer that is definitively *not* a trickster story. Mathews's en-characterization of Lineback, his family, and his larger pack defies the pigeonholing that American Indian writers have suffered in having all their narratives stuffed into the same trite, collapsible sack. Even the most complex understanding of trickster discourse cannot do justice to this story from the point of view of the animal and his thoughtful, experiential behavior: not because trickster discourse is beneath it but because it is simply apart from it, having nothing to do with what Mathews was after. Importantly, in contradistinction to the genre, Mathews individualizes coyotes in such a way that his narrative highlights just how anthropopathic many indigenous North American narratives about "the coyote" are. He wrests the perspective away from both Amer-Europeans and Native Americans, from humans, and restores it to the central figure of the story. To borrow an idea from the expert critic of the cheapening of the genre, Mathews's story is about survivance, but not of some segment of humanity. It is about the awesome survivance of *canis latrans*.

Grus, The Sandhill Crane

Appropriately, Mathews begins his collection in the blackjacks, writing about *God's Dog: The North American Coyote* there, and perhaps snidely and subtly contrasting them to the "time efficient" Red Angus cattle bred by Roy Beeby and others for the convenience of multitasking farmers. "Grus, The Sandhill Crane" is a more optimistic story of human-nonhuman interaction and is based on Mathews's own witnessing of the biannual Greater Sandhill Crane migration from a site about four hundred miles north. In his youth, the author had toyed with the idea of becoming an ornithologist, but eschewed the "scientific card-indexing" associated with the pursuit. "I wanted to play it by ear," he wrote. "I wanted to play natural science, where it dealt with sentient beings, by ear" rather than becoming comfortable with "formality, the scientific necessity; the birds imprisoned both as to image and character on glossy pages." He wanted to go so far as to learn their Latin genus and species names, but not so far as to make human fixations his focus.

It was observation of birds that drew Mathews to aviation and the opportunity to learn how to fly during World War I. Given his witnessing of the meek beginnings of that technology, he must have had an immense appreciation for a bird that could sustain itself at fourteen thousand feet, an altitude which cripples many a human being and requires artificial pressurization of commercial airplane cabins to sustain both life and comfort. (Indeed, this height is surpassed by the Greater Sandhill Crane's distant relative, the Eurasian Crane, who can sustain themselves above thirty-two thousand feet in their Himalayan traverses.) But even more captivating for Mathews is the crane's dancing. In a collection which focuses four of nine stories on specific birds, three of these stories center around their dances. Once again, this is Mathews drawing our attention to the *joie de vivre* experienced by those outside the human circle. While the dances have both survival and reproductive functions, there is a superfluity of emotion and artistry that we tend to reserve for ourselves. Thus, the Grus story in particular opens our eyes to the culture of beings in the natural world, because the cranes' dance often appears to have no direct or immediate purpose aside from joy and welcoming. These dances have been filmed and can now be watched online by interested readers. Indeed Mathews himself spent time capturing footage of sandhills and various other animal expressions.

The story is also remarkable for the way it effortlessly eliminates the political boundaries between Canada, the United States, and Mexico. Mathews had visited each of these three nations by 1963. In his own memoir, he reminds us that he had not been born in the United States but in the Osage Nation, only later becoming an avid American. Thus, during his early childhood, he only visited the place rather than living there. His entry into the nation at the exact age of thirteen far from eliminated his penetrating critiques of Amer-European behavior. As author of *The Osages,* he had a profound historical comprehension of the contingencies and newness of French, Spanish, English, and U.S. efforts to carve the continent according to "I, me, mine." So perhaps there is a hint of irony in the fact that Grus, who ignores international borders and shies away from mushrooms among the grasshoppers and marsh lilies, becomes the tutor of aggressive humanity in its nationalistic race for aeronautical superiority. Nicely, however, Mathews hints at the international cooperation of ornithologists and other scientists as well as politicians in establishing protected wetlands for the cranes.

He specifically honors Muleshoe National Wildlife Refuge and Bitter Lake National Wildlife Refuge, which had been established in 1935 and 1937 respectively to protect the central flyway. Although Grus's family seems more at risk once they land in northern Mexico, our two countries signed a Treaty for the Protection of Migratory Birds and Game Mammals in 1936. Within the past twenty-five years, Laguna de Babicora in Chihuahua has become threatened and in need of renewed conservation efforts, but so far the *Grus canadensis tabida* has remained off the threatened and near-threatened species list. While the Greater Sandhill Crane is not itself at greatest risk, its relatives the Florida and Mississippi Sandhills are threatened or endangered, and preservation of habitats remains a constant concern. The pilgrimage to the Platte River site, where the migrating birds rest on their way north or south, continues to draw hundreds of Audubon Society members each year as they and other organizations work to reverse conditions similar to those that wiped out the heath hen.

One notices in this story and others Mathews's curiously imprecise use of the term "racial memory," a characteristic wielding of this term during the time when he was growing up, under the influence of Jack London and other writers. In one location he will use it to refer to instinct or capabilities inherent from birth or shortly thereafter. In another, it seems to mean behaviors learned by the collective sharing of knowledge among members of the species, as when the redwings and marsh hawks "remember" that sandhills once but no longer ate their eggs and nestlings. A second conflation, of race for species, also makes Mathews's analogies to human interactions cryptic. "It is like the ancient Indian sanctuaries of the pipestone quarries in Minnesota and the Great Salt Plains in Oklahoma," he says of the sandhills' undisturbed mating by a great highway with cars speeding past. "There seems to be an understanding among sandhill cranes, as well as between man and sandhill cranes."

What makes the pipestone quarry sanctuaries "like" the sandhills stopping at this Platte River way station (or the way station itself) remains a mystery, particularly because Mathews never indicates whether the pipestone important to many midwestern people is protected by law or by tacit agreement. He refers perhaps to Pipestone National Monument, established like the wildlife refuges, in 1937 (adjacent to where a federal boarding school for Indian children was also located). If so, the analogy of "an understanding . . . between man and sandhill cranes" does not hold. More likely he refers to the earlier sanctity of the pipestone among indigenous North Americans, in which case it does hold. Or is it possible that he refers to the boarding school itself as an "Indian sanctuary"? If so, Mathews would be internalizing some of the theories and habits of thought from the early twentieth century and the preceding centuries, which placed American Indians and animals in the position of "scientific" objects to be studied by Euro-humans. Much of his life's work debunked the idea that the Osages were anything less than students and scholars of the natural world themselves along with debunking the conceptualized superiority of humans to other animals. There is much truth to his observation that all species native to the western hemisphere including *Homo sapiens* were threatened by the European invasions. Yet he repeatedly resorted to a falsely holistic analogy between nations and races threatened with genocide and species threatened with extinction. Present-day students may be critical of these ideological fallacies, but they cannot know what it was like to live through the nadir of Osage hegemony. As a mixed-blood man, Mathews personally witnessed the demise of so many old men who were also his friends that we will never understand why he and those around him resorted to thinking in particular ways, or needed to explore particular ways of thinking, in order to survive or to comprehend their own survival. For his time, his efforts to work out a theory of biological determinism have no less integrity than early efforts toward theories of economic determinism, mechanistic though they now seem.

Alfredo and the Jaguar

We may also miss the significant critique of human arrogance embedded in this slippage between species of animals and human collectives. In "Alfredo and the Jaguar," the Mexican Indian man Carlos Predregales imagines that "El Tigre must certainly have informed all the cougars and jaguars of that part of the savage Sierra Madre Mountains" that his death by firearm was a warning to them. Though framed as being only in his imagination, Mathews has the Indian man making a wiser, more scientific, better informed observation about animal behavior than the higher ranking mestizo or Spanish-American don. It is one that he has already reinforced in both two preceding stories featuring coyotes who spread musk messages and cranes who walk out of range of shotguns. In other words, in these stories, species respond to threats from humankind in similar ways to human responses to threats from other humans: by spreading information and forming collective strategies to maintain their communities even in the face of individual deaths. Perhaps Mathews saw lessons to be learned from other species' defenses against extinction. What we certainly know is that Western science has followed the lead of Mathews, Predregales, and others. Wildlife scientist Gordon Haber studied the individuals of the Denali Toklat wolf pack from 1966 to 2009 and identified the social organization of wolves as consisting of "high levels of altruism [and] cross-generational learning" which make individual wolves and not just their overall population important to consider in managing the human-wolf relationship.

This story about an individual jaguar appears to take place in a region of Mexico that Mathews came to know in 1940, during the Guggenheim Fellowship that allowed him to write *Talking to the Moon* and other works. In June of that year, he moved from Cuernavaca in the state of Morelos to the Hacienda Santa Engracia in Tamaulipas. Though none of his diary entries correspond with any precision to this particular story—unlike a story outside of this collection which transposes directly one of his own experiences into the life of a fictional character—he did hunt with two young men on whom he may have modeled the character Alfredo as well as discussing with the Hacienda's don possibilities for hunting the wild cats that were

killing domesticated animals on his property. Although he also visited Aca-
pulco, driving over the Sierra Madre del Sur to reach it, these scenes are
more consistent with his residence north of Mexico City. For the first several months of his stay in Mexico, Mathews suffered from not being able to
locate guidebooks to the local birds, a lacunae that was filled partly but not
completely through his many talks with his host in this particular locale. He
mentions in particular in January 1940 that he cannot identify a species of
jay for lack of a guidebook.

This story is particularly intriguing because of the centrality of jaguars in
Mesoamerican literature. The *Popol Vuh,* the *Chilam Balam,* and the *Can-
tares Mexicanos* or *Songs of the Aztecs* all make significant references to the
animal. In fact, *Chilam Balam* means literally "Jaguar Interpreter (of the
Gods)" or "Prophet of the Title 'Jaguar.'" So that work itself associates jaguars with sacred, symbolic language. In the *Popol Vuh,* the only surviving
text of which was copied by a friar named Francisco Ximénez, three of the
four first mother-fathers to be created from corn dough are Jaguar Quitze,
Jaguar Night, and Dark Jaguar. And the highly honored Plumed Serpent has
the capacity to manifest himself as "a snake, an eagle, a jaguar, or a puddle of
blood." It is wholly unclear whether Mathews had read or was familiar with
any of this literature, particularly the Mayan texts, given his greater proxim-
ity to Mexico City than to the Yucatan. Certainly, as in his other works, he
"humanizes" the jaguar and the other animals. We see what he sees as he
sees it, as though we are him, as we would with any human character. He
has the jaguar thinking, becoming angry, anticipating. So his use of the species is somewhat consistent with those Mesoamerican representations that
feature them prominently. But it is the prominence of Christianity in the
story that gives us a clue to what Mathews might be doing.

As a young boy, Mathews was horrified by an image of the crucifixion of
Jesus represented to him on a holy card given to him by his father's cousin.
He cut from the card the figure of the Roman soldier who slashes Jesus's
side and buried it out in his yard. As a young man visiting Oberammergau,
Mathews was transfixed by the Passion Play and remarked particularly the
scene of the crucifixion. So Alfredo, in addition to being likened very subtly to Jesus through his innocent attraction to Padre Francisco's stories of

the Boy in the manger and his saving presence at El Tigrero's side, is also an image of the young author uneasy with the torture of a man whose life had enthralled him. Mathews wrote in his diary about the efforts of Cortez to eradicate Mesoamerican beliefs through the imposition of Christianity: "When Cortez conquered Mexico, he attempted to have the cathedrals built in certain well-chosen spots, away from the concentration of life around the old temples—away from the influences of the Aztec gods. But the conquerors [sic] plans were never successful. Where the Indians built their homes, there they stayed and the cathedrals came to them, and displaced their temples." These comments reconfigure the placement of the churches away from the assumed agency of the Spanish—in "chopping off" the temple tops to surmount them with Christian symbols—to the agency of the Indians. As Dennis Tedlock has also observed, they "learned to use the symbolism of Christian saints as masks for ancient gods [and] the Roman alphabet as a mask for ancient texts."

So it may be significant that laughter and the devil figure prominently in the Mexican Indians' reaction to El Tigre's reappearance. When Alfredo's father, Carlos, learns from his son that the jaguar has killed Macho, the burro, he seeks out not the jaguar hunter but Padre Francisco, never for a moment believing that his aim was not true. It is Don José who calls in the specialist, ignoring Carlos's equation of the wounded jaguar with El Diablo. But Don José misses the potential complexity of Carlos's beliefs, which fit not only a straight Catholic interpretation, but one informed by the history of the religion in Mexico. When the Catholic priests and monks suppressed the divinities and lords of indigenous Mexico, they were symbolically associating jaguars and shape-shifting with the devil. So not only does the jaguar's return from certain death constitute a reincarnation rivaling that of Jesus; it also represents the precarious re-ascendency of Mayan beliefs and loyalty to their patrilineal forefathers. In addition, El Tigrero has taken the priest's place both physically and spiritually. And it should not be forgotten that the Mayas may have been enemies with the tribes in the mountains of Tamaulipas. In the fourth book of the *Popol Vuh*, the Jaguar *gentes* imitate jaguars in order to kill people from other tribes to sacrifice to their gods.

It is also significant that laughter is what saves El Tigrero from attack by the much more mundanely and realistically broken-ankled earth jaguar. Mikhail Bakhtin has pointed out the suppression of laughter during the era of medieval Christian seriousness, and recent Native American writers like Sherman Alexie have picked up the theme of ancestors laughing in the trees. El Tigrero tells Alfredo that El Señor the Lord sent down the laughter as a weapon to defeat the Jaguar. The reader might note that he also decides to be practical, thinking of some way to escape *before* praying to the Lord, and that we have no way of knowing whether the lord he credits is Indian, Christian, or both. Mathews was well aware of the feudalism of the hacienda (land grant or plantation) system in Mexico, and its federalization in 1917 during the Mexican Revolution. He also would have noted the similarities of Mexican social structure to the social structure of mixed- and full-bloods that he witnessed growing up in a region only a century removed from Spanish influence and the influence of the growing métis Creole communities formed as a result of French-Osage intermarriages. His focus in the story on the thoughts and activities of the Mexican Indians, despite his greater familiarity at Santa Engracia with the Hacendado's family, is consistent with his efforts to trace Osage full-blood resistance to and accommodation of Christianization.

The White Sack

The laughter that ends this last story also sets the tone for the next. "The White Sack" is by far the funniest story in the collection. On a first read, it evokes emotions that are terrifying, ominous, annihilative. In particular, there is nothing in the least funny about the last two paragraphs. It is only when we read it again after some reflection that the hilarity of the situation emerges. Mathews's timing and phrasing is perfectly staged. He features an overweight, perhaps obese, "dude" who seems to know little to nothing about hunting, eating apples to loosen his belt while trying to take down a mule deer buck probably at least his own size. While "stalking" the deer, he not only "wears" the insane white of his enormous laundry-turned-lunch-sack, but his thoughts are deflected far away from the world around him to his self-pity and envy of good-looking politicians. Despite this, he is bloated with self-confidence at the sure prospect of winning the upcoming election for governor, in a state where skill in hunting can form no small part of the voters' judgment of their candidates.

It is fantastic the way Mathews paints such an accurate portrait of what he called "earth-detachment," the pure out-of-it-ness of the human animal, who is there with all the other alert and wary animals, but is not really there. He is capable of sight, but sees nothing around him. He lives inside his own mind, not in the world. He is conditioned by his complacent condition out of all alertness, all useful use of his senses. Mathews stokes the laughability of the prose to a high heat, and then pricks the balloon. First, the man hears nothing in the "godforsaken" country and believes himself to have been tricked by the men at camp. By this time, the reader has seen at least sixteen species (not including judges and witnesses and jurors and lawyers), a land filled with life. Then, he hears the "clack, clack, clickety-clack" of a bounding pebble and feels nervously for his safety catch. He can hear his heart pumping in anticipation of his imminent glory and his vision of what he wants to see blurs his view of what is right in front of him. Finally, he fails to "hear the bullet that whizzed past his own head because of the blast of his own rifle." How ironic too that the nearly identical noncom (the other man on the mountain), who at least knew enough to wear protective red, goes down, while the fool in white who can't hear his own death in his ears survives!

Though Mathews wrote this story only a few years after the culmination of the Manhattan Project and set it only a few miles from Los Alamos, the 1963 manuscript shows that he originally intended the district attorney's victim to be "a philosopher of a great university." It is unclear when he made the change to a nuclear physicist, though the fact that the trace may be found in this version suggests that it was sometime after his August rehearsal of the story for the Hunt Browns. Only a year before had been Kennedy's standoff with Khrushchev over nuclear missiles in Cuba. So this narrative allegory of Mutually Assured Destruction could only have been perfected by the timely change, which raises the stakes and drives the point home. Must the reader reconcile her strong sense of jeopardy and loss at the death of an "innocent" man with her joy that the dead man could one day have meant her own extinction? With her disappointment that the story is one of Mathews's few fictions that is not also nonfiction? Perhaps it is the tension among these emotions which brings out the hilarity. Mathews himself must have derived great pleasure in shooting by proxy the man who represents forces against whom we can never defend ourselves. How well too he catches his surrogate in the trap. A man who is responsible for prosecuting crimes against the state, like involuntary manslaughter, lives to face his voting public while the man he kills might have been more "necessary" to perceived "national security" than any governor or DA could ever be.

Mathews had visited New Mexico four times in the 1930s, each visit relatively brief. It is not clear that he ever visited Jemez Pueblo, which would be only a few miles from the apparent setting of this nuclear deterrence narrative. In January 1935, he was in Tucumcari on his way to Prescott, Arizona, for a meeting with a man from Los Angeles having something to do with a "Trust Company." This would have been at least five years after his residence in Los Angeles. That August, he attended the "College of Indian Wisdom," a title he may have facetiously given to "Earnest" Thompson-Seton's Camp in Santa Fe, which appears to have had the goal of bringing together mostly non-Indian intellectuals for the purpose of strategizing the preservation of Indian cultures. His mentor W. S. Campbell (Stanley Vestal) was also in attendance, along with Laura Adams Armer and Ellsworth Jaeger. While in Taos, Mathews visited with the artist W. Herbert "Buck" Dunton, whose work he greatly admired. He also visited Navajo lands before returning to The Blackjacks. Mathews wrote from Seton's Village of his boyhood hero and his idea: "Seton is about what I expected and his idea of nurturing Indian Culture is good but I am afraid, useless. . . . I am sorry that the carrying out of his idea will fail, but being an old man and yearly growing older he will never know that it is so fated[,] . . . that which certainly is a great idea but ought to remain one. . . . Dorothy [Campbell's daughter] calls the whole thing 'goopy' and that expresses as nearly as any other thing what I feel about it." In October of the following year, he spent some time at the Runyan Ranch, not far from the White Sands Missile Range where the Trinity test of the first atomic bomb would later take place. He was apparently there to hunt, as on his final known New Mexico visit of that decade, to Magdalena, also proximal to White Sands, in October 1938. He would return to Runyan Ranch and other New Mexico locations several times in the 1950s and 1960s with his wife, Dibbs.

Arrowflight, The Story of a Prairie Chicken

With "The White Sack," "Arrowflight, The Story of a Prairie Chicken" forms an interesting fulcrum in Mathews's approach to perspective and narration. The preceding stories have either remained within the perspective of a single nonhuman species or ranged from the humans' perceptions to the animals' and sometimes back again. With these two central stories, Mathews not only concentrates on the perceptions and experiences of the animals, but travels among animal consciousnesses. The move further decenters and displaces the importance of the human as narrator as well as human as observer. In the nuclear story, the beginning is all from the center of the animals and we see individuals of one species reading the cues of the others to obtain information about their environment. We are let into the emotions of the wolf and we witness the nutcracker rehearsing what he will say to other nutcrackers up the mountain about the man-animal. As a result of this not-reserved-to-humans rehearsal of a speech or performance, the buck mule deer figures out that the "strange unknown" is approaching the mouth of the little canyon. This interspecies communication and, in effect, cooperation takes place despite the fact that the mule deer buck has "no friends." Yet the reactions of seven other species—including two predators—save him from his two enemies.

In "Arrowflight," Mathews also turns his attention to the ecosystem rather than simply the individual animal or species. The narrative features no less than forty-five species interacting with one another, including *Tympanuchus cupido pinnatus, Canis latrans, Bubo virginianus, Quercus stellata, Quercus marilandica, Spilogale gracilis, Procyon lotor, Microtus pennsylvanicus, Neotoma cinerea, Falco mexicanus, Accipiter gentilis, Buteo jamaicensis, Circus cyaneus, Equus caballus, Equus caballus* Spooky, *Sigmodon hispidus* or *Sigmodon fulviventer, Homo sapiens, Lycopersicon esculentum, Canis familiaris, Ambrosia artemisiifolia, Andropogon gerardii, Tyrannus forficatus,*

Dermanyssus gallinae, Triticum, Tradescantia ohiensis, Quercus palustris, and *Buteo swainsoni.* Of course, the most memorable interaction takes place among the coyote, the cotton rat, the stored grain, the green tomatoes, and *Homo sapiens,* who foolishly "overdid . . . with a sort of American business efficiency" the murder of the cotton rats' natural predators with poisoned horseflesh.

As Mathews encourages us to "Think Like a Prairie," he extends our view of the imbalance caused by the act even further than Leopold. Beyond the overrunning of the prairie with the cotton rats and the devastation wrought back on the ranchers who were supposed to benefit, even the prairie chicken ("arrowflight" to the Osages) is affected, by the marsh hawks who come in to fill the vacuum left by the decimated coyotes. "During the second April of the invasion, there were fewer cocks dancing on the booming grounds and they were molested. Swarming harriers, with their hunger satisfied and feeling quite playful, would dart at the dancing cocks and annoy them. They had no intention of eating them; they only wanted to tease them, many of them coming from parts where there were no prairie chickens, and this dance on the high prairie was fascinating to them and they had to do something about it." So even while we are invited in to the "playful" emotions of one species, giving us insight into the fact that interspecies play without predation exists at all, we also see that the teasing threatens to interfere with successful mating among the arrowflights of the narrative, so that the poisoning has far-reaching effects on the region's stability.

Perhaps the point is also driven home by the "soft sounds of encouragement" that Arrowflight's mate gives to her hatching chicks. We see mother's love here expressed. And although Arrowflight's death arises in part from his relaxing from constant alertness in the company of this loving hen ("there is no keener hearing and sharper eyes than those of a hen prairie chicken who has brought to adulthood eight children out of ten"), there is a subtle emphasis on the nine who survive. Yet Mathews doesn't fail to stress the idiocy and sheer ignorance of any boy who could possibly confuse a prairie *chicken* for a "chicken *hawk.*" We can imagine him laughing up his sleeve while staging this tragedy, a man who had served in one world war and volunteered to serve in a second. If "chicken hawk" is an epithet for someone who advocates war but avoids serving in the military, for a coward, a hypocrite, one who lacks the judgment and experience necessary to bear arms, how better could Mathews emphasize the passing down of ignorance and hypocrisy from poisoning father to guessing son? Neither is truly intimate with their "earth struggle" nor has the judgment or experience necessary for the war against coyotes, chickens, and hawks which they advocate implicitly and explicitly, yet neither has any compunction about propelling it along toward an end that is ultimately self-destructive.

"Arrowflight" is the second of only two stories to take place in Osage country and the first of three consecutive stories about Galliformes (quails, turkeys, grouse, pheasants, ptarmigans). It is a sad commentary on where we have come since 1963 that an article entitled "Save the Last Dance" was published in the *Missouri Conservationist* in 2004 by the Missouri Department of Conservation. Kathy Love reports that the number of prairie chickens in Missouri has gone from tens of thousands in the 1860s, to thirteen thousand in 1944, to a devastating five hundred at the time of writing. Although hunting them was banned in 1907, Missouri's meager population is not all native to the state, but partially the product of reintroduction from Iowa. Indeed, all subspecies of prairie chicken—Greater, Lesser, Attwater's, and of course the Heath Hen—are either vulnerable or endangered if not already extinct. There is no mistaking that Mathews saw a connection between his beloved prairie chicken and the heath hen of "The Last Dance," which disappeared in 1932, the same year in which his *Wah'Kon-Tah* was published. By placing these stories in a cluster, he hammered home the continuum of abuses the birds have suffered on the same east-west trajectory as traditionally associated with Manifest Destiny. Importantly, in a book directed toward boys, he places in both these stories the only negative views of boys in the collection. They serve as cautionary tales for the young reader, warning "him" of the cost of immature arrogance. Like the boy in the previous story, the murderer in "The Last Dance" thoughtlessly misidentifies the species of his target. Unlike that character, these boys at least know shame in their deed, though it comes far too late and is expressed through deception and denial.

The Last Dance

Tympanuchus cupido cupido, the heroes of "The Last Dance," once inhabited the entire eastern seaboard from New England through the Carolinas. Despite dense human populations in these areas prior to the European invasions, the heath hen thrived. Within two and a half centuries of successful British settlement and three centuries of Spanish, there were no heath hens left anywhere but the island of Martha's Vineyard. Mathews takes the story from there, telling quite accurately the final twenty-six years of their existence. One of the implicit lessons we learn from the story is that endangered species cannot always be saved without isolating them for a time away from natural predators, natural threats, and added human-introduced dangers like the domesticated cat. Mathews must have derived little recompensatory pleasure in having one of the two *felis catus* who spells the demise of the last female heath hens fall victim to a great horned owl. The tone of the passage is grave and ironic: "The noise of the spitting and the yowling was so frightful that the heath hen, in making herself small, pressed too hard against her children and there were peeps of pain. The remainder of the night she hovered her brood, frozen, waiting for death. Death did not come to her, but when she left the spot where she had hovered, another of the little females was dead."

Without a doubt, Mathews's main "tactic" in this story is love. To prevent the further degradation of species diversity, we must come to love that which we have hitherto neglected and killed. Renewed is the image of the mother encouragingly clucking to her "downy little ones." Though fated to fail, her vocal and body languages are crafted to shape her progeny with courage against the odds they are about to face. She moves slowly so that they do not get lost. And it is partly from her loving perspective that we see "the splay-toed little male running jerkily and the other three, strung out behind, struggling with every weed stem and falling over every stone and fallen branch." Mathews makes us love the little heath hen cock of destiny from the first page in a way that is special and unlike our appreciation of the others' quirks. We love him the instant he is not frightened at being called back sharply by his mother to the protective fold after exploring on his own, but comes "running back . . . with the joy of being alive surging within him." Our own joy of being alive responds to his empathically. The relative loneliness of his life and his childlessness are harder to take because in him overflowed the innate enthusiasm to plunge deeply into existence which seems to be missing from his siblings. His boldness goes unrewarded.

To some extent, Mathews's insecurity in writing this story out of his direct experience shows through. It is overbalanced with theory, straying from principles he elsewhere had observed, captured, and knew to be true. Darwin is too much in it, too little critiqued. In all of Mathews's other stories, he shows species faced with danger and extinction becoming smarter as a result. Both collectives and individuals pick up cues that allow them at least a fighting chance. However, in "The Last Dance," rather than having the heath hens still learning, being very good at survival but nevertheless endangered, he falls back on the Darwinian (or pseudo-Darwinian) assumption that if a species truly edges toward extinction, it is partly because it is not fit, is weaker, stupider, has less energy for life. Rather than becoming stronger, the fictionalized heath hens in this story become weaker and die out because of their own actions or inactions. The mother can't count (in apparent contrast to Arrowflight's mate); the sprouting wings of the little female weighs her down, making her seek food halfheartedly and murmur with discontent and lazy complacency. Mathews implicitly attributes their demise not to the surrounding forces and a throwing out of balance of the natural world by humans, but to their own inadequate reactions to overwhelming odds having little to do with their "fitness."

The fact that he seems to have drawn a connection between the hens and Native Americans makes this resort to theory over experience more disturbing.[14] In his draft, Mathews has added in handwriting the paragraphs that explain the establishment of reservations for the birds. "The people of Massachusetts had become concerned about the heath hens of Martha's Vineyard," he writes, "and had raised $70,000 to set aside a special reservation for them, and then had appointed special wardens to protect them." He was quite familiar with such reservations for human beings *and* such special wardens (under whom frighteningly this eastern grouse goes extinct anyway). He, in fact, erased from this draft some of the traces of that familiarity.

His last two references to species had originally been references to the "race" of heath hens. As with the fourth bird story, "Grus," the analogy in all parts that he started to draw here and then stepped back from seems to exhibit a kind of internalization of the savagist myths that blamed the anticipated extinction of Native tribes on their behavior rather than the behavior of their antagonists. We must also wonder, given the interesting parallels to the story of Ishi in the fact that the cock of destiny is studied to death, whether Mathews knew of or considered that example when conceiving this story.

Yet we must acknowledge, despite the book-learned, Darwin-bound limitations of the story, that Mathews is again here as always on the side of survivance. When the cock of destiny is left finally alone in the world, his responses are more than adequate. In the years before his last dance, he arrives at the empty dance grounds, moving with great dignity. As if knowing the danger of satisfying his urge on the open, vulnerable ground, he flies to a tree limb and performs his booming there. Then he disappears, as though refusing to satisfy the curiosity of the human onlookers. We, after all, have come to his rescue far too late and after our murderous urges have made mockery of the impotent, bystanding pretense of wanting to save him, to study him. Then the year the observers last sight him at those dance grounds, he dances quite passionately, perhaps defiantly, as though he knows very well the meaning of this last dance and feels to the full the sadness of the disappearance of the hens and the last two cocks he once knew. Perhaps too he dances from the *joie de vivre* that has characterized his entire existence. Well aware of the transience of all historical moments, and of all cultures, Mathews could bestow no higher compliment nor present any fiercer statement of the strength, intelligence, learning capacity, and wisdom of this fated last survivor.

The White Gobbler of Rancho Seco

It is unlikely that Mathews imagined the White Holland gobbler of "The White Gobbler of Rancho Seco" as one of the threatened species of larger concern in this book. After all, how could a turkey popularly raised and bred for Thanksgiving and Christmas consumption go extinct? Nevertheless, fifty years later, some are calling for conservation efforts to preserve the purebred white turkeys, which are rare and often confused with more plentiful white turkeys that do not "meet breed standards." His emphasis instead seems to be on the wild turkeys of the gobbler's adoptive family and the adaptive skills learned by this anomalous poult as a result of his conspicuous appearance. Mathews revised his early drafts of this story, which had originally begun with the first sighting by Chip, the foreman, so that the persistent coyote who acts as catalyst for all the subsequent action would receive the honor of first perspective. This shift also allowed him to emphasize the intelligence of birds who in popular terminology have become synonymous with stupidity, clumsiness, ineptitude, and failure. Simply by showing us the turkeys flying from danger, he dispels the myth that they cannot fly and reminds us that their grounding is a result of our self-serving fattening of them for market, not a result of nature.

The scenes of this story derive from Mathews's experiences in Texas with his friend and fellow author Frank Dobie. He may mean in his first lines to displace it from its actual location. Dobie's mother had grown up on a Rancho Seco about twenty-five miles west of Corpus Christi. Dobie himself had moved in 1959—around the time of Mathews's visits—from the Cherry Springs Ranch outside of Marble Falls, about fifty miles northwest of Austin, to the Paisano Ranch on Barton Creek just southwest of the city. In his diary, Mathews referred to a deer and turkey hunting retreat he enjoyed with Dobie as Rancho Seco, the ranch house of a mutual friend, Ralph Johnston; there is no Hondo River in these parts of Texas, in fact no Hondo River in Texas at all. He refers instead to the Hondo Creek and State Route 173 near Hondo, Texas, in Medina County west of San Antonio and a location he also knew as Arroyo Seco. In any event, the two men had much in common. Both served in World War I, both spent time at prestigious English universities, both wrote about the southwest and saving species or breeds from extinction, both pronounced against the fascism they detected simmering beneath U.S. politics, and both of course were serious hunters. At the end of his life, Mathews owned seven of Dobie's books, including *Apache Gold and Yaqui Silver, A Texan in England,* and *The Voice of the Coyote.* He frequently reminisced about the times he had spent hunting with

Dobie and his friends, replaying for himself repeatedly a tape he had made on November 16 and 17, 1960, of this group of self-described freethinkers.

The story itself is almost more depressing than the story of real extinction that precedes it. The white gobbler's end is sudden, unexpected, brutal, and disrespectful, but Mathews is not the source of this disrespect. After a lifetime of learning quickly and skillfully how to avoid the unusual hazards to which his difference subjects him, this hardy father who has eluded the aspirations of every hunter on the Rancho is laid low by an indifferent truck. The driver's careless reaction, his misplaced assumption about the insignificance of the event, again reminds the reader of the increasing ignorance of human beings regarding the environments they move through and affect, and by which they are sustained without reciprocal gratitude. Mathews once wrote that when automobiles were first introduced, hunters "could not really be accused of unsportsmanlike behaviour, since the danger to the hunter over hunting from horseback was much greater in the high center of gravity cars of those days." He noticed at the same time how cars "were rolling over the prairies, running over prairie chicken nests, and during August and September loaded with gunners, who shot from the cars . . . [and] could cover many a section in a day." He observed the thousands of doves who were killed before they learned to fly to safety, but also the way they and other animals did learn so that not even the sophomore coyotes were hit by the "strange beast" that provided the vultures and them with road-killed food.

In this story, he emphasized instead the skill of the prey over the predators. As in "The White Sack," we see cross-species warnings. The flag of the whitetail buck alerts the flock to danger as does the death of one of their number. They learn to avoid blinds and succeed by and large, and ironically, in escaping conscious attempts on their lives. We also see both the conscious forethought of an owl and the success of the gobbler's fear-driven defense against him. It is a captivating scene, heightened by our appreciation of the emotion that suffuses the gobbler as our emotions suffuse us and by Mathews's careful reproduction of the sounds of the two enemies and particularly the owl's startled reaction to the easy mark, who fought back and got away. Mathews had by this time spent hours with his tape recorder catching the familiar sounds of The Blackjacks around him as well as the primordial and disturbing challenge of the bull wapiti, which he could never adequately describe, and other animals from ranges farther away from his home.

The Royal of Glen Orchy

Mathews went far back in time and farthest away in distance to create the story of "The Royal of Glen Orchy." In June 1921, after his first term at Oxford and at the age of twenty-six, he had toured Scotland by motorbike with his friend W. J. Hobbs riding in the sidecar. After traveling from Edinburgh to Inverness and then all the way up the northeastern coast to Wick, they had returned south past Loch Ness and via Fort William to Glasgow, following the road through Bridge of Orchy around where the story is set. On July 6, he wrote from Glasgow, "When we reached the south end of the Glen the skies had cleared and the sun came out. At Bridge of Orchy we got some good Kodak pictures of highland cattle and also, at 'Auch Lodge,' the seat of the Marquis of Badalbin, I got in conversation with Mr. Tedcastle about shooting this autumn. Mr. Tedcastle has a lease on the deer forest and I have arranged to come up this autumn to shoot on the place. Cheers!—at last my hopes have been realized. If the skies had not cleared and the cattle had not been grazing the lush grass along the bottom of the valley as we came out of Glencoe I would not have seen Mr. Tedcastle and perhaps I could not have had an opportunity to shoot the great red deer of Scotland. As it is I shall bag a stag this October and perhaps get a chance at blackcock as well." The marquis to whom he refers would have been the Marquis of Breadalbane, Gavin Campbell. Although the title had gone extinct in 1862 after the death of the second marquis, it was recreated briefly for this seventh Earl of Breadalbane and Holland, who died the October after Mathews would have hunted on his lands. Auch Lodge is the same location where the famed author of *Peter Pan,* J. M. Barrie, had vacationed with the Llewellyn Davies children about seven years earlier.

The red deer is not a threatened species and this story is one of only two about survival rather than death, yet it enunciates important principles regarding human interaction with nonhuman species. Mathews introduces these ideas through the unusual character of McCarricker. The gillie (a "guide to deer stalkers for shooting in general") is unusual not only for this story but in the collection as a whole. He seems to be the one adult human being we meet whose "instinct" is to protect individual animals in whom he recognizes some uniqueness. Royal's specialness, his strong survival instincts induce in McCarricker equally strong feelings of both empathy and identification. The man seems based on two individuals Mathews met in the United States just before his move to Oxford: his guide at Two Ocean Pass near the Buffalo Fork of the final story, Bill Barron, and that team's wrangler, Wuff.[15] Bill on the one hand was a man of about sixty who had recognized in the young Mathews a person who lost himself in the hunt rather than the quick kill and who reminded him of a nobleman from the United Kingdom in his hunting-for-the-sake-of-hunting fever. Like McCarricker, he was skilled in assessing the capabilities of his clients and respected them or not accordingly. On the other hand, Wuff "was a derivative of the mountains, rugged, natural, granitic and illiterate, with a soul overflowing with poetry he couldn't express. Such esthetic urges imprisoned by the lava crust of complete ignorance, oafish peer conformity, and male pride, created frustrations which were poignant at times." McCarricker by comparison is "more than just an ordinary gillie and a man filled with emotion over the fact that he was a part of the great brooding moors and the wild life they supported. He couldn't possibly speak of that which he felt since he had no words either in Gaelic or English that could express his thoughts and emotions, even to himself, so he remained silent, and his emotions bubbled within him."

These esthetic urges are the higher of the two principles which Mathews sets out as standards for the human hunter. If the other principle is practical and somewhat self-serving—the protection of those individual stags and hinds who exhibit extraordinary strengths in comparison to the rest of the species and thus guarantee their future and continued improvement— beauty has no direct practical function. Like the love he tried to instill in us earlier, it is about subordinating our other instincts to a force greater than ourselves: our mysterious kinship with forms of life so different from ourselves that we are normally incapable of recognizing that mutuality. That ability is what brings grateful tears to the eyes of the sympathetic reader when the Marquess responds to the royal just as McCarricker has, ordaining his slaughter beyond the pale despite the imminent decline of his reproductive prowess.

Perhaps this story should be considered Mathews's triumphant anti-*Bambi*. If that narrative imposes a human-sanctioned monogamy on all the animals of the forest, "The Royal of Glen Orchy" teaches children the facts. Polygamy, or rather the sustaining of multiple female mates against weaker male rivals by the fiercest and most mature males, is simply a trait of this species. It is likely that Mathews saw it in Darwinian terms, but the larger point is that there is variety among species in their mating practices which the Disney film suppresses. The culture these false stories create, enforce, and reinforce adds to the increasing earth-detachment of the human species, alienating us from all but human-created cultures, and a select few at that. Interestingly, Mathews also features in this story the important role that the hinds play in saving Royal from gunfire. The contrast between the hinds' salvational role here and the role of the hen in "Arrowflight" in lulling Arrowflight into a false security should be noted. Mathews tended to be an androcentric writer. While women were important forces in his own life (in particular, his mother, his grandmother, his sisters, his wives, his daughters, and granddaughters), his understanding of, knowledge of, and interest in them was often limited. He frequently, perhaps too frequently, tried to get at their essentials through study of females among various species. So attending to his efforts to observe them and their interactions with males of their species helps us to identify intersections with his views of sex and gender among humans.

Old Three Toes of Buffalo Fork

Mathews could not have picked a more appropriate final story for this collection than "Old Three Toes of Buffalo Fork." The story is infuriating as it seems intended to be. It leaves any lover of cats great and small as impotent as Three Toes against the irrational forces of hatred against them. The great tom's last gesture appropriately links his irritation at the eagle earlier in the narrative with the United States itself, as represented by this helicopter out of all proportion (and so recently reintroduced into the national rhetoric by a deceptively, speciously attractive mouthpiece of neo-imperialism). Perhaps his failed last stand in self-defense also expresses Mathews's frustration, after repeated attempts to reveal the wrong and stupidity and hypocrisy and arrogance that he saw in humans' uncontrolled urges. "He then ran to the highest point of his refuge, a sandstone outcrop, and here he decided to fight. He crouched and waited for the attack which never came. . . . The bomb killed him instantly." To upset the balance of nature in this unconscionable way, to target predators because they are doing what they do best and exist for, is perfect immorality. Mathews pointedly reminds us that the bounty put on the "scalp" of Three Toes cannot be distinguished from the scalp bounties placed on human heads during earlier eras. Nor indeed can the $150 bounty some now want placed on the severed forelegs of the Alaskan wolf. In refashioning stories he had already told, in *Talking to the Moon, Twenty Thousand Mornings,* and even "Alfredo and the Jaguar," Mathews literally placed us on a Continental Divide. It is now up to us whether we will remain divided, or come together, under the extended perspective of the mountain lion of Buffalo Fork. To think like Old Three Toes, to think like a mountain, to think, for once. As though we might be worthy of that honor.

Notes to the Afterword

Numbered narrative notes are listed first, followed by source notes, which are tied to the corresponding paragraph text in the afterword by page number and key phrase.

Narrative Notes

1. If one includes the ten stories Mathews published in *The Sooner Magazine* between 1929 and 1933, the count would be forty-four ("Ole Bob" being already included above). However, several if not all of these seem to be more evidently nonfiction.

2. Yet, in an interview with Guy Logsdon in 1972, Mathews recollected that he had never had an image of a reader while writing. Interview with Guy Logsdon, March 14, 1972, Osage Tribal Museum, Pawhuska, Okla. (John Joseph Mathews Sound Recording 2281; hereafter JJM SR).

3. Today's publication costs make the formerly routine illustration of books rather prohibitive, so this present volume must do without their great enhancement of any text on nature and wildlife.

4. The order of the stories as they appear in this volume was determined by the dates on the drafts in the archive marked "copy made for publication" and Mathews's comments on his preferred order, as discernible: "Singers," October 21; "Grus," October 22; "Alfredo," October 24; "White Sack," October 27; "Arrowflight," October 31; "Last Dance," November 4; "Gobbler," November 6; "Royal," November 8; "Old Three Toes," emended "Friday 8, 1963" and November 9. The last was the only draft not marked "for publication," so the publication copy was determined by formatting similarities with the other drafts and priority placement in the archive folder. "Singers" and "Royal" were the only stories with only one extant draft. "Alfredo" and "Gobbler" were the only ones with as many as three. Given the clarity of Mathews's publication drafts, minor variations have not been noted. For descriptions of major variations, see the notes to each story.

5. On July 5, 1963, Mathews wrote that he intended to title his heretofore untitled book *Old Three Toes of Buffalo Fork.*

6. Mathews seems also to have agreed with Thompson-Seton when he wrote, "Since, then, the animals are creatures with wants and feelings differing in degree only from our own, they surely have their rights."

7. Mathews specifically mentions *All the Mowgli Stories* by Kipling and *The Call of the Wild* and *White Fang* by London.

8. "B. B." was the nom de plume of Denys Watkins-Pitchford.

9. I wish to distinguish here between stories that taught human beings how to behave morally—using animal characters, or characters with animal names or characteristics—from stories and discourses that taught them more literally to think about how animals saw, moved, responded, and interacted in the world, often as lessons to how human beings might see, move, respond, and interact. The former is, of course, a fourth widespread aspect of indigenous North American discourses involving animals.

10. Among non-Native writers, these might include Dian Fossey and Jane Goodall.

11. Mathews is not a "classic" animal rights writer. For example, there is certainly no "right to life" or vegetarian ethic for this writer who was known to shoot starlings as nuisances and colonial invaders in addition to engaging avidly in hunting his entire life. Mathews likely lived in part on the animals he hunted in the blackjacks. However, he certainly advocates here and elsewhere for an animal ethic and esthetic (perhaps comparable to Leopold's land ethic and conservation esthetic). There were lines in human behavior toward nonhumans that he saw as foolish, arrogant, and earth-detached to cross; increasingly he deplored the violating of

those lines separating the killing of individuals in honest, mutually hazardous earth struggle from the mass, indiscriminate killings of thousands and the targeting of individuals through a massively, unfairly increased human technological advantage. His was not just a utilitarian ethic for the survival of humans, but a deep recognition of a strong commonality of consciousness connecting human and nonhuman and a deep respect for the different ways of being alive and enraptured to be alive on this earth.

12. Mathews coined the term "Amer-European" early in his career to emphasize that most Americans of European extraction were really Europeans in culture, transplanted onto another soil but little changed in habit and outlook.

13. Some may argue that musk messages are merely sensory while language is symbolic, but Mathews's story clearly argues that the two are equally symbolic, while materialist theories of human language remind us that it is, at base, as fundamentally "merely sensory" as musk.

14. He was not the first to make this connection. In February 1791, a bill to preserve the heath hen and other game went through the assembly of the state of New York. When the title was read, the chairman pronounced heath hen "*Heathen* . . . which seemed to astonish the northern members, who could not see the propriety of preserving *Indians* or any other Heathen"! Alfred O. Gross, "The Heath Hen," *Memoirs of the Boston Society of Natural History* 6.4 (May 1928): 497–98. (Boston: Boston Society of Natural History, 1928).

    Ironically, the combination of having established a reserve for the birds and practicing fire suppression may have actually contributed to their extinction. After an inevitable fire broke out in May 1916, the heath hens had no cover in which to lay their eggs—that not burned had been removed in the effort to prevent fire—so predators destroyed them. The lack of cover also left the heath hen vulnerable to goshawk attacks (Gross, "Heath Hen," 507–12).

    Alfred O. Gross himself called heath hens a race: "Later the birds of the East became separated from those of the Middle West and this isolation resulted in the establishment of two races: *Tympanuchus cupido cupido,* the Heath Hen; and *Tympanuchus cupido americanus,* the Prairie Hen" (491). This may be a source of Mathews's original terminology.

15. Of course, the man could also be based on someone Mathews met on the hunt in Scotland. Unfortunately, there is no record of that experience in his extant diaries.

Source Notes

In the preface, I borrow some wording describing Mathews's writing from an anonymous reviewer of the stories, May 5, 2012.

137 *John Joseph Mathews's lifelong interest*
John Joseph Mathews, *Twenty Thousand Mornings: An Autobiography*, ed. and with an introduction by Susan Kalter (Norman: University of Oklahoma Press, 2012) (hereafter TTM), 62, 74; Laura Edwards to Susan Kalter, September 23, 2013; John Joseph

Mathews Collection, box 1, folder 34, Western History Collections, University of Oklahoma Libraries, Norman, Okla. (hereafter, JJM followed by box and folder number, as in JJM 1.34); Diary, July 4–18, 1962, August 3, 1963 (JJM 3.1, JJM 3.2); Diary, June 16–27, 1965 (JJM SR 2274, 2275); Diary, January 2, 1963 (JJM 3.3); Diary, August 17, 1958 (JJM 2.12). John Hopper Mathews's daughters were all born between the mid-1950s and early 1960s, while the eldest of the Browns and the Hunts had come into Mathews's life somewhat earlier (Laura Edwards to Susan Kalter, October 14, 2013).

137 *Although few of them have ever been published*
    (JJM 4.1–29, 42); Diary, December 31, 1949, March 5, 1952 (JJM 2.1, 2.3); Diary, September 1–December 10, 1963 (JJM 3.2); Diary, October 13, 1963 (JJM 3.2).

138 *"I am not sure of myself in writing my boy's book"*
    Diary, October 13, 1963 (JJM 3.2); Diary, August 3, 1963 (JJM 3.2).

138 *"The White Sack" had actually been written*
    Diary, December 31, 1949 (JJM 2.1); Diary, April 7, 1948–December 31, 1949 (JJM 1.50, JJM 2.1); John Joseph Mathews to Elizabeth Hunt, December 13, 1939 (JJM 1.9); Diary, February 21, 1943 (JJM 1.46); Diary, April 5, 1945 (JJM 1.47); Mathews to E. Hunt, June 27, 1940, Mathews to E. Hunt, July 17, 1940 (JJM 1.15–16), Diary, February 6, December 6, 28, 1943, June 21, 1945, May 22, September 7, 1948, December 19, 1949 (JJM 1.46, 1.47, 1.50, 2.1), Ann Hunt to Savoie Lottinville, July 5, 1948, Lottinville to A. Hunt, July 6, 1948 (Oklahoma University Press Collection, Western History Collections, box 103, folder 3, University of Oklahoma Libraries, Norman, Okla.) (hereafter, OUP followed by box and folder number); Mathews to John Hunt, May 10, 1940 (JJM 1.22); Diary, September 3, 1948 (JJM 1.50); Diary, August 7, 30, September 8, 17–18, December 31, 1961 (JJM 2.14).

139 *Although he mentions in January 1963*
    Diary, January 2, 1963 (JJM 3.3); Diary, January 2, 1963 (JJM 3.3); Diary, August 3, 1963 (JJM 3.2); Diary, June 17, October 9, 1963 (JJM 3.2); Diary, November 1, 8, 1963 (JJM 3.2, 3.3); Diary, October 25, 1963 (JJM 3.2); Diary, October 9–11, 1963 (JJM 3.2); Diary, September 2, 1963 (JJM 3.2); Diary, November 2, 1963 (JJM 3.2); (JJM 4.6), (JJM 4.10).

139 *"Alfredo and the Jaguar" came next*
    Diary, September 4–5, 1963 (JJM 3.2); Diary, September 6, 1963 (JJM 3.2); Diary, December 31, 1949 (JJM 2.1); Diary, September 7, 1963 (JJM 3.2), Diary, September 10, 1963 (JJM 3.3); Diary, September 13, 1963 (JJM 3.2); Diary, September 24, 1963 (JJM 3.2); Diary, October 3, 6–7, 1963 (JJM 3.2); Diary, October 1, 1963 (JJM 3.3); Diary, October 8, 1963 (JJM 3.2); Diary, October 13–14, 1963 (JJM 3.2); JJM 4.1, 4.4, 4.6, 4.8, 4.10, 4.18, 4.21, 4.22, 4.27, 4.28; Diary, November 8, 1963 (JJM 3.2).

140 *By July 1964, he had received a rejection*
    Diary, July 6, 1964 (JJM SR 2277), July 5, 1963 (JJM 3.2); Diary, November 24, 1963 (JJM 3.2); Diary, November 27, 1963 (JJM 3.2); Diary, November 2, 8, 1963 (JJM 3.2);

Diary, August 15, 1962 (JJM 3.1); Seymour Lawrence, "Adventures with J. P. Donleavy, or How I Lost My Job and Made My Way to Greater Glory," ed. David L. Hartzheim, published first in *The Paris Review* (Fall 1990), *The J. P. Donleavy Compendium*, n.d., www.jpdonleavycompendium.org/Adventures-With-JPD.html; David L. Hartzheim, "Seymour Lawrence, 1927–1994: A Tribute," *The J. P. Donleavy Compendium*, 2008, www.jpdonleavycompendium.org/Seymour-Lawrence.html; Diary, November 11, 1963, August, 7, October 14, 1967, January 9, February 19, March 6, 21, September 23, 1968 (JJM 3.2, 3.5, 3.6); Diary, October 10, 1967 (JJM 3.5); Diary, February 10, 1968 (JJM 3.7); Diary, June 12, 1962 (JJM 3.1); Diary, November 24, 27, December 6, 10, 1963 (JJM 3.2)

140   *The last we hear of the book's fate*
      Diary, July 6, 14, 1964 (JJM SR 2277); Diary, June 16–27, 1965 (JJM SR 2274, 2275)

141   *One clue to that landing place may exist*
      TTM 33, 35; Diary, June 30, 1964 (JJM SR 2276).
      Mathews talks in his draft autobiography about hunting coyotes with his maternal cousin's husband, Tony Fortune, and several cowboys during Christmas vacation of his sophomore year in high school "on the high prairie of the Elm Creek and Salt Creek drainage." He writes,

> "Forced by fate and circumstance [his cousin] and Tony had no free time from their struggle with the earth and against the elements, but in their deadly serious absorption by simple existence, they, in their practicality, could appreciate useless ornamentation in others, as well as laugh at Fate's malevolent whims. . . . Tony's wolf hounds were business partners, not a sporting man's hobby, and his ugly skunk hound was a necessity, since he marketed both coyote and skunk hides. But he was also an eager sportive hunter, and when we set out stirrup to stirrup with the running hounds strung out behind us, the little house on Elm Creek like an exotic, scarcely noticeable growth on the seemingly limitless prairie, with its problems of existence as well as the note at the bank were forgotten. . . . Our coyote hounds were unlike the English fox hounds; they were visual hunters and in England would have been called gaze hounds, like the stag hounds of Scotland. They were called greyhounds locally, but were only half greyhound; they were, as a matter of fact, a cross between the stag hound of Scotland and the common greyhound, hence they had the speed of the greyhound and the fighting ability of the staghound, and to successfully hunt the prairie wolf they needed both. They were high-backed with grizzle muzzles, and had the grace of a cheetah and the stupidity of a sloth." The dogs make Mathews's horse, Bally, nervous and her half-sister, Brownie, is a much better hunter than she, needing no cue to look for wolves and competing with the hounds in the chase. "She was frantic to join the hunt. . . . I believe she was the first to see every coyote we caught during that hunt. . . . When I got back to the barn at home, in the New Year's twilight, I thought little of having missed the holiday dances and parties; I had a fine dog coyote skin

tied behind my cantle." (TTM 88, 276n64 referring to *Twenty Thousand Mornings* manuscript, 87–89, found in JJM 4.32/33 [hereafter TTM MS])

In this excerpt, Mathews talks about hunting prairie chicken and quail with his dog and catching three coyotes with Tony Fortune, about the coyote horse Brownie's excitement about coyote hunting, and about a "sophomore" coyote who runs under the bellies of a team of horses pulling a buggy, startling the horses into a gallop, TTM 281n102, referring to TTM MS, 152–53; TTM 199–200, 208; TTM 62–63.

142   *Readers already familiar with Mathews's works*
Talking to the Moon: Wildlife Adventures on the Plains and Prairies of Osage County (Norman: University of Oklahoma Press, 1945), 11, 16 (hereafter *Talking*); Ernest Seton-Thompson [*sic*], *Wild Animals I Have Known* (New York: Charles Scribner's Sons, 1900), 9–10, 12.

143   Sundown *and* Twenty Thousand Mornings
TTM 100 and see also 102, 140–41, 191, and Bally as a shot sandhill crane, 31; *Sundown* (Norman: University of Oklahoma Press, 1934), 73.

143   *We might also compare Mathews's prose*
Diary, October 13, 1963 (JJM 3.2); TTM 106; Charles G. D. Roberts, *The Kindred of the Wild* (New York: Stitt Publishing Company, 1905), 22–23; Diary, October 13, 1963 (JJM 3.2); Diary, February 22, 1957 (JJM 2.9); Mexico Diary, January 2, February 9, June 23, July 3, 9, August 1, 1940 (JJM 1.37–38, 1.41–42, 1.17).

144   *Among contemporaries, Mathews*
Aldo Leopold, *A Sand County Almanac* (1949; New York: Oxford University Press, 1966), 3–98; Diary, February 7, 1955 (JJM 2.6, smaller diary book); Sally Carrigher, *One Day on Beetle Rock* (1944; Berkeley: Heyday Books, 2002), *One Day at Teton Marsh* (1947; New York: Alfred A. Knopf, 1972), *Icebound Summer* (1951; New York: Alfred A. Knopf, 1953); Diary, December 9, 1943 (JJM 1.46), Diary, February 22, 1952 (JJM 2.3), April 28, 1952 (JJM 2.3), May 13, 1952 (JJM 2.4), May 13, 1952 (JJM 2.3), cf. April 5, 1955 (JJM 2.6). Rachel Carson, *Silent Spring* (Boston: Houghton Mifflin, 1962). Another early writer in the conservation vein was Gary Snyder, who began publishing in 1957. Snyder and Mathews seem to have little in common, in the strict literary sense, beyond an interest in nature. Mathews's regionalism is not a political bioregionalism, so they also seem to form a contrast in this respect. Gary Snyder, *No Nature: New and Selected Poems,* (San Francisco: Pantheon Books, 1992), iv.

145   *These stories probably benefited*
Diary, December 8, 1955 (JJM 2.6), March 8, 1958 (JJM 2.12), February 21, 1959 (JJM 2.12), August 26, 1962 (JJM 3.1) and passim; Diary, July 14–15, 1961 (JJM 2.14); Diary, June 12, 14, 16, 25, 30, 1963 (JJM 3.2); Diary, October 26, 1955 (JJM 2.6, smaller diary book); Diary, June 14–15, 17, 1963 (JJM 3.2); Diary, March 26, 1953 (JJM 2.4), May 17, 1958 (JJM 2.12); Diary, July 1, 1956 (JJM 2.8); Diary, May 10, 1957 (JJM 2.9); Diary, May 16, 1953 (JJM 2.4); Diary, March 26, 1953 (JJM 2.5), August 28, 1955 (JJM 2.6); Diary,

July 10, 1956 (JJM 2.8) and passim; Diary, November 6, 1955 (JJM 2.6); Diary, March 26, 1953 (JJM 2.5), July 23, 24, 26, 28, 1956 (JJM 2.8) and passim; Diary, April 22, 1959 (JJM 2.12). On this date, Mathews bought his first tape recorder, a Wollensak, using it a few days later to record Osage songs from the Bureau of American Ethnology and to listen to drafts of *The Osages*; Diary, January 18, 1966 (JJM 3.4); Diary, February 6, 1955 (JJM 2.6, smaller diary book).

146   *Of course, we necessarily also think*
    Mexico Diary, April 20, 1940 (JJM 1.39), Diary, October 5, 1961 (JJM 2.14), January 7, 1956 (JJM 2.8); Zitkala-Ša, *American Indian Stories, Legends, and Other Writings,* ed. Cathy N. Davidson and Ada Norris (New York: Penguin, 2003); Ella Deloria, *Dakota Texts,* ed. Raymond DeMallie (Lincoln: University of Nebraska Press, 2006); David Cusick, *Sketches of Ancient History of the Six Nations,* ed. William Martin Beauchamp (1825; Fayetteville, N.Y.: H. C. Beauchamp, 1892); Jane Johnston Schoolcraft, *The Sound the Stars Make Rushing Through the Sky,* ed. Robert Dale Parker (Philadelphia: University of Pennsylvania Press, 2007); Larry Evers and Felipe S. Molina, *Yaqui Deer Songs / Maso Bwikam: A Native American Poetry* (Tucson: University of Arizona Press, 1987).

147   *It will be hard to trace Mathews's American Indian antecedents*
    Carter Revard, *How the Songs Come Down* (Cambridge, England: Salt Publishing, 2005); Elise Paschen, *Bestiary* (Los Angeles: Ren Hen Press, 2009); Tim Tingle, *Walking the Choctaw Road* (El Paso: Cinco Puntos Press, 2003); Gerald Vizenor, *Bearheart: The Heirship Chronicles* (1978; Minneapolis: University of Minnesota Press, 1990); Paula Underwood, *Who Speaks for Wolf* (Austin, Texas: Tribe of Two Press, 1983); Winona LaDuke, *All Our Relations* (Cambridge, Mass.: South End Press, 1999), Thomas King, *Truth and Bright Water* (1999; New York: Grove Press, 2001); Linda Hogan, *Mean Spirit* (New York: Ivy Books, 1990) 110; Kateri Akiwenzie-Damm, "Sturgeon," in *My Heart is a Stray Bullet* (Wiarton, Ont.: Kegedonce Press, 1997); L. Frank-Manriquez, *Acorn Soup* (Berkeley: Heyday Books, 1999); Louise Erdrich, *Tracks* (New York: Harper Perennial, 1989).

148   *The first story, last written*
    Diary November 1, 1961 (JJM 2.14), May 6, 9, 12, 13, June 3, 5, 8, 1962 (JJM 3.1); Amanda Coyne, "Palin and the Wolves: Inside Alaska's Aerial Hunt," *Newsweek*, April 10, 2009, www.newsweek.com/id/193370; Mark Benjamin, "Her Deadly Wolf Program: With a Disdain for Science that Alarms Wildlife Experts, Sarah Palin Continues to Promote Alaska's Policy to Gun Down Wolves from Planes," Salon.com, September 8, 2008, www.salon.com/env/feature/2008/09/08/sarah_palin_wolves/; "Alaska's Gov: Sarah Palin Farewell Speech—7-26-09," OnlineNewsPaper, *YouTube*, www.youtube.com/watch?v=W0b2NM2MYng.

148   *Although he wrote many expository statements*
    TTM 95, 275n61, referring to TTM MS, 76–77. "There could have been some sort of ontogeny here, since primitive man must have felt deep frustrations, watching the birds. Reason came to him, and he cooked his food and used articulate speech, took

the skins of animals to protect himself from the elements, but he was still earth-bound, and could only dream of flying as the birds could do. And flight being beyond him, in his dreams he would attribute such power to supernatural beings, such as angels, which his Force-inspired urge might lead him to create." (TTM 129–30); Lottinville to Mathews, November 9, 1943 (JJM 1.28), Lottinville to Ewing, November 10, 1943, Mathews to Lottinville, November 11, 1943, Ewing to Lottinville, November 16, 1943, Lottinville to Mathews, November 19, 1943, Mathews to "Heimer" (Lottinville), December 17, 1943, Lottinville to Mathews, December 21, 1943 (OUP 94.5); *Talking*, 214–33.

149   *"Singers to the Moon" is the first*
    TTM 40–41.

149   *As important as, perhaps more important than,*
    Diary, May 24, June 3, 1964 (JJM SR 2276).

150   *The impetus for these assaults*
    "That winter he got a job feeding for some rancher, and to supplement his wages, he made dough balls filled with strychnine, and scattered them over a wide area. He walked many miles over the snow and in blizzards to gather up the bodies of the poisoned coyotes and wolves, skinning them on the spot when there were too many to carry home intact. He got sufficient money from his hides to create comfort during the hard winter." TTM 280n97, referring to TTM MS, 139; Diary, January 14, 1945 (JJM 1.47); Mathews, *Talking*, 174–90; TTM 157–58; Theodore Roosevelt, "Wolves and Wolf-Hounds," in *Hunting the Grisly and Other Sketches* (New York: Review of Reviews Company, 1910), 229; "The Wolf, the Jackal, and the Fox," *The Menageries: Quadrupeds, Described and Drawn from Living Subjects*, vol. 1, 2nd ed. (London: Charles Knight, 1830), 95; "Fact Sheet on Hound Hunting," *Wildlife Abuse Campaign: Ending the Killing of Animals for Trophies and Pleasure*, Humane Society of the United States, 2009, http://www.hsus.org/wildlife_abuse/campaigns/bears/hounding/hound_hunting.html; "Wolf-baiting," *Wikipedia*, July 14, 2009, http://en.wikipedia.org/wiki/Wolf-baiting.

151   *It should hardly go unmentioned*
    Gerald Vizenor, "Trickster Discourse: Comic Holotropes and Language Games," in *Narrative Chance: Postmodern Discourse on Native American Indian Literatures*, ed. Gerald Vizenor (Albuquerque: University of New Mexico Press, 1993), 187–211.

151   *Appropriately, Mathews begins his collection*
    Hope Ryden, *God's Dog: The North American Coyote* (New York: Lyons Press, 1975); Hope Ryden, "God's Dog: A Celebration of the North American Coyote," *Hope Ryden*, n.d., accessed November 14, 2009, http://www.hoperyden.com/god_s_dog__a_celebration_of_the_north_american_coyote_1391.htm; "Red Angus Recognizes Industry Contributions from First 50 Years," *The Cattleman* (February 2005), Texas and Southwestern Cattle Raisers Association, bNet Business Publications, ProQuest, http://findarticles.com/p/articles/mi_qa5420/is_200502/ai_n21366289/; Department of Animal Science, Oklahoma State University, "Red Angus," *Breeds of Livestock*,

updated November 22, 2002, www.ansi.okstate.edu/breeds/cattle/redangus/; Betty
Irvan and Douglas Martin, "A Brief History," *BIM Red Angus: Quality Red Angus
Seedstock since 1986*, BIM Red Angus, 2009, www.bimredangus.com/a-brief-history-
of-bim/; Roy Beeby, "Time Efficient Cattle," first published in *Red Angus Journal*, n.d.,
University of Nebraska, Lincoln Extension, Knox County, accessed July 23, 2009,
http://www.knox.unl.edu/files/file061114132719; Diary, April 27, 1962, March 18, 1963
(JJM 3.1, JJM 3.3); TTM 106–109.

152   *It was observation of birds that drew Mathews*
    TTM 74, 107–108, 128–31, 166–67; TTM 167–230; Zoological Society of San Diego,
"Birds: Crane," *San Diego Zoo Animal Bytes*, 2009, San Diego Zoo, www.sandiego-
zoo.org/animalbytes/t-crane.html; TTM 70, 191, 206; Diary, June 15, 1940, March 18,
1963 (JJM 1.41, 3.3); Multiple authors, "Sand Hill Crane Dance" (September 2007) and
related videos, *YouTube*, 2009, www.youtube.com/watch?v=eAqcpMEoLao.

152   *The story is also remarkable for the way*
    Diary, September 6–16, 1952 (JJM 2.3); (JJM 1.7–18); TTM 88; "Sandhill Crane,"
compiled from P. A. Johnsgard, *Cranes of the World* (Bloomington: Indiana University Press, 1983) and C. D. Meine and G. W. Archibald, *The Cranes: Status Survey and
Conservation Action Plan* (Gland, Switzerland: IUCN, 1996), *International Crane
Foundation*, www.savingcranes.org/sandhillcrane.html; National Audubon Society, "Sandhill Crane," *Audubon*, 2005, http://web1.audubon.org/waterbirds/species.
php?speciesCode=sancra.

153   *He specifically honors Muleshoe National Wildlife Refuge*
    Jeanne F. Lively, "Muleshoe National Wildlife Refuge," *The Handbook of Texas
Online*, Texas State Historical Association, 2009, www.tsha.utexas.edu/handbook/
online/articles/view/MM/gkm1.html; "Bitter Lake National Wildlife Refuge," *U.S. Fish
and Wildlife Service*, n.d., accessed July 24, 2009, www.fws.gov/refuges/profiles/index.
cfm?id=22510; "Crane Information," *North American Crane Working Group*, 2009,
www.nacwg.org/craneinformation.html; "The Cranes, Status Survey and Conservation Action Plan: Sandhill Crane (*Grus canadensis*)," *Northern Prairie Wildlife Research
Center*, USGS, 2006, www.npwrc.usgs.gov/resource/birds/cranes/gruscana.htm; R. C.
Drewien, W. M. Brown, and D. S. Benning (Hornocker Wildlife Research Institute,
University of Idaho), "Distribution and Abundance of Sandhill Cranes in Mexico,"
Abstract, *The Journal of Wildlife Management* 60.2 (1996): 270–85, *CAT.INIST*, Cen-
tre National de la Recherche Scientifique, Institut de l'Information Scientifique et
Technique, http://cat.inist.fr/?aModele=afficheN&cpsidt=3054998; "Sandhill Crane,"
All About Birds, The Cornell Lab of Ornithology, Cornell University, 2009, www.all-
aboutbirds.org/guide/sandhill_crane/id; National Audubon Society, "Sandhill Crane,"
Audubon, 2005, web1.audubon.org/waterbirds/species.php?speciesCode=sancra.

153   *One notices in this story and others*
    TTM 38–39, 105–106, 109–10, 113.

154   *What makes the pipestone quarry sanctuaries*
    "Pipestone National Monument," *Pipestone: A National Register of Historic Places Travel Itinerary*, National Park Service, n.d., accessed July 24, 2009, www.nps.gov/nr/travel/pipestone/pnm.htm; Jim Northrup, *Rez Road Follies: Canoes, Casinos, Computers, and Birch Bark Baskets* (Minneapolis: University of Minnesota Press, 1997); John Joseph Mathews, *The Osages: Children of the Middle Waters* (Norman: University of Oklahoma Press, 1961), x, 785–86; John Joseph Mathews, *Wah'Kon-Tah: The Osage and the White Man's Road* (Norman: University of Oklahoma Press, 1932), 323n1. For Mathews's theories of biological determinism, see notes to paragraph beginning "*Although he wrote many expository statements.*"

155   *We may also miss the significant critique*
    Tracy Ross, "Dogs of War," *Backpacker* 37.1 (January 2009): 60–68, 94–95. Haber died in a plane crash on October 14, 2009, before this volume went out for peer review. Gordon Haber, "Alaska Wolves," 2007–2009, www.alaskawolves.org/Alaska%20Wolves.html.

155   *This story about an individual jaguar*
    Diary, October 13, 1939–July 31, 1940 (JJM 1.36–43); Diary, June 3–24, 1940 (JJM 1.40–41); Diary, January 2–9, 1940 (JJM 1.37); June 5–July 29, 1940 (JJM 1.40–43).

156   *This story is particularly intriguing*
    Dennis Tedlock, introduction to *Popol Vuh*, rev. ed., trans. Dennis Tedlock (New York: Simon and Schuster, 1996), 25 (hereafter PV and PV intro); Ralph L. Roys, *The Book of Chilam Balam of Chumayel* (1933; Norman: University of Oklahoma Press, 1967), 3; "Chilam Balam de Chumayel (manuscript)," *Princeton University Library Digital Collections*, http://diglib.princeton.edu/xquery?_xq=getCollection&_xsl=collection&_pid=c0940; PV 27, 44, 52; John Bierhorst, ed. and trans., *Cantares Mexicanos: Songs of the Aztecs* (Stanford: Stanford University Press, 1985), 35–41 and passim in multiple songs. The *Cantares Mexicanos* is a compendium of ceremonial songs collected in the 1500s by Spanish monks. A large number of these songs refer to jaguars, but it is unclear what the term connotes in each location, whether the animal itself or something metaphoric or metonymic.

156   *As a young boy, Mathews*
    TTM 6, 8–9; Diary, June 30, July 2–3, 1922 (JJM 1.45); Diary, November 9, 1939 (JJM 1.36); cf. Tzvetan Todorov, *The Conquest of America: The Question of the Other*, trans. Richard Howard (Norman: University of Oklahoma Press, 1999); Tedlock, PV intro, 25.

157   *So it may be significant that laughter*
    PV 145–75; PV intro 43–50.

157   *It is also significant that laughter*
    Mikhail Bakhtin, *Rabelais and His World*, trans. Helen Iswolsky (Bloomington: Indiana University Press, 1984), 59–144, 1–58; Sherman Alexie, "A Drug Called Tradition," in *The Lone Ranger and Tonto Fistfight in Heaven* (New York: Harper

Perennial, 1994), 13; Diary, June 4, 1940 (JJM 1.40); cf. *Wah'Kon-tah;* Mathews, *Osages,* 465, 525–38, 735–86 and passim; Mathews, *Talking,* 47–60, 75–94, 210–44.

159   *It is fantastic the way Mathews paints*
   TTM 19, 74, 91, 95, 128, 130–31, 166–67, 183, 186, 200, 204, 206–207, 218, 223.

159   *Though Mathews wrote this story*
   "Manhattan Project," *Encyclopaedia Britannica Online,* 2009. www.britannica.com/ EBchecked/topic/362098/Manhattan-Project; (JJM 4.28); "Cuban Missile Crisis," *Encyclopaedia Britannica Online,* 2009, www.britannica.com/EBchecked/topic/145654/ Cuban-missile-crisis; Diary, February 24, 1962, January 24, 1963 (JJM 3.1, JJM 3.3).

160   *Mathews had visited New Mexico*
   Mathews to E. Hunt, January 16, 1935; Mathews to E. Hunt, January 18, 1935; Mathews to E. Hunt, August 20, 1935; Mathews to E. Hunt, August 24, 1935; Mathews to E. Hunt, August 31, 1935; Mathews to E. Hunt, October 17, 1936; Mathews to E. Hunt, October 29, 1938; Diary, June, October 1956, November 1957, September, October, November 1958, November 1961 (JJM 1.2, 1.3, 1.5, 1.6, 2.8, 2.9, 2.12, 2.14). On June 9, 1956, on a trip through New Mexico to San Diego to visit historian Abraham Nasatir, Mathews writes, "Before we turned off on H-70, I looked intently at the western wall of the Sacramentos, and thought I could see the point on which I sat to look over the White Sands, while deer hunting, in 1934." The Runyan Ranch was by 1956 the ranch of his friend Bryan Runyan, though it is unclear whether Mathews met Runyan before or upon visiting the ranch in the 1930s. Mathews was briefly in Ojo Caliente, near Los Alamos, in September 1958. Diary, October 28, June 5, 9, 1956, September 26–27, 1958 (JJM 2.8, 2.12).

161   *In "Arrowflight," Mathews*
   Jerome A. Jackson, Walter J. Bock, and Donna Olendorf, eds., *Grzimek's Animal Life Encyclopedia, Volumes 8–10, Birds I, II, III,* 2nd ed. (New York: Thomson Gale, 2003); Devra G Kleiman, Valerius Geist, and Melissa C. McDade, eds. *Grzimek's Animal Life Encyclopedia, Volumes 12, 14, 16, Mammals I, III, V,* 2nd ed. (New York: Thomson Gale, 2003); Keith Rushforth and Charles Hollis, *National Geographic Field Guide to the Trees of North America.* (Washington, D.C.: National Geographic, 2006); Shirley L. Scott and Lise M. Swinson, *National Geographic Field Guide to the Birds of North America,* 2nd ed. (Washington, D.C.: National Geographic, 1987); Ben-Erik Van Wyk, *Food Plants of the World: An Illustrated Guide* (Portland, Ore.: Timber Press, 2005); Doug Ladd and Frank Oberle, *Tallgrass Prairie Wildflowers,* Falcon Field Guides (Helena, Mont.: Falcon and the Nature Conservancy, 1995); Fiona A. Reid, *A Field Guide to Mammals of North America North of Mexico,* 4th ed., Peterson Field Guides (Boston: Houghton Mifflin, 2006); Peter Ziegler, Greg Septon, and John E. Toepfer, "STCP: Society of Tympanuchus Cupido Pinnatus, Ltd.," STCP, 2008–2009; K. D. Thompson, R. G. Fischer, D. H. Luecke, "Determination of the Viremic Period of Avian Reticuloendothelioso Virus (Strain T) in Chicks and Virus Viability in Triatoma Infestans (Klug)," *Avian Diseases* (1968), American Association of Avian Pathologists; M. W.

Service and R.W. Ashford, *Encyclopedia of Arthropod-transmitted Infections of Man and Domesticated Animals* (New York: CABI Publishing, 2001).

162 *As Mathews encourages us to "Think Like a Prairie,"*
   Aldo Leopold. "Thinking Like a Mountain," in *A Sand County Almanac* (New York: Oxford University Press, 1949). On April 2, 1959, Mathews filmed a marsh hawk diving at dancing prairie chickens—"obviously in play." He writes that he would dive at a dancing cock and the cock would dodge without ever lowering his primate feathers or deflating his sac. "This is the first time I have ever seen this sportiveness on the part of a marsh hawk, and the unconcern of the chicken, even though they seemed at times annoyed" (JJM 2.12).

162 *Perhaps the point is also driven home*
   TTM 158–230; Mathews to E. Hunt, February 18, 1943, Mathews to E. Hunt, February 26, 1943, Mathews to E. and Ann Hunt, March 16, 1943, Mathews to E. and A. Hunt, August 5, 1944, Mathews to E. Hunt, September 24, 1944, (JJM 1.20, 1.21); Diary, February 19, 1943, (JJM 1.46); "Chickenhawk (politics)," *Wikipedia*, July 27, 2009, wikipedia. org/w/index.php?title=Chickenhawk_(politics)&oldid=324869339; Cheyney Ryan, *The Chickenhawk Syndrome: War, Sacrifice, and Personal Responsibility* (Lanham, Md.: Rowman & Littlefield, 2009); TTM 90, 140, 218, 229, 245.

163 *"Arrowflight" is the second of only two stories*
   Kathy Love, "Save the Last Dance," *Missouri Conservationist* 65.2 (February 2004), *Missouri Department of Conservation Online*, Conservation Commission of Missouri, 2009, http://mdc.mo.gov/conmag/2004/02/50.htm; "Tympanuchus cupido" and "Tympanuchus pallidicinctus," *IUCN Red List of Threatened Species*, Species Survival Commission, International Union for Conservation of Nature and Natural Resources, BirdLife International, 2008, www.iucnredlist.org/apps/redlist/details/141373/0 and www.iucnredlist.org/apps/redlist/details/141374/0; "Attwater's Prairie-Chicken: The Most Endangered Grouse in North America," STCP, 2008–2009; David Challinor, "The Last Heath Hen," *Spotlight on Birds* (January 2007), Migratory Bird Center, Smithsonian National Zoological Park, Smithsonian Institution, 2010, http://nationalzoo.si.edu/scbi/migratorybirds/science_article/default.cfm?id=32.

164 Tympanuchus cupido cupido, *the heroes*
   David Challinor, "The Last Heath Hen," *Spotlight on Birds* (January 2007), Migratory Bird Center, Smithsonian National Zoological Park, Smithsonian Institution, 2010, http://nationalzoo.si.edu/scbi/migratorybirds/science_article/default.cfm?id=32; "The Heath Hen Extinct in the Wild," *Bagheera* endangered species website, CKMC.com, n.d., accessed July 29, 2009, www.bagheera.com/inthewild/ext_heathhen.htm.

165 *To some extent, Mathews's insecurity*
   Diary, September 2, 1963 (JJM 3.2); Diary, September 26, 1943, August 30, 1946 (JJM 1.46, 1.48). In "The Royal of Glen Orchy," note that in-breeding does not lead to dullness or disaster as it here leads to demise.

165   *The fact that he seems to have drawn*

Alfred O. Gross, "The Heath Hen," *Memoirs of the Boston Society of Natural History* 6.4 (May 1928): 491–588 (Boston: Boston Society of Natural History, 1928); (JJM 4.6, 4.10); cf. *Wah'Kon-Tah*'s focus on Major Laban J. Miles; (JJM 4.6, 4.10); cf. Roy Harvey Pearce, *Savagism and Civilization: A Study of the Indian and the American Mind* (1953; Berkeley: University of California Press, 1988); Gerald Vizenor, "Socioacupuncture: Mythic Reversals and the Striptease in Four Scenes," in *The American Indian and the Problem of History,* ed. Calvin Martin (New York: Oxford University Press, 1987); "Yana," *Encyclopaedia Britannica Online,* 2009, www.britannica.com/EBchecked/topic/651663/Yana.

166   *It is unlikely that Mathews imagined*

"Turkey—White Holland," *Domesticated Birds,* Centralpets.com, n.d., accessed August 8, 2009, http://centralpets.com/animals/birds/domestic_birds/dbd4877.html; "White Holland Turkey," *The American Livestock Breeds Conservancy,* ALBC, 1993, www.albc-usa.org/cpl/wholland.html; (JJM 4.27); "Turkey History and Lore," *Turkey for the Holidays,* University of Illinois Extension, 2009, http://urbanext.illinois.edu/turkey/history.html; "Talking Turkey: A Bird's-Eye View of Wattle and Snood," as published in *Washington Post,* November 23, 2000, Encyclopedia.com, www.encyclopedia.com/doc/1P2-557794.html; Stephanie Watson, "Will a turkey really drown if it looks up during a rainstorm?" *HowStuffWorks,* 2009, http://animals.howstuffworks.com/birds/turkey-drown.htm; "Turkey," based on *American Heritage Dictionary,* 4th ed., *The Free Online Dictionary,* Farlex, 2009, www.thefreedictionary.com/Turkey.

167   *The scenes of this story derive*

(JJM SR 2280); "1562. J. Frank Dobie, *Ella Byler Dobie and Christmas,*" *Ranching Catalogue, Part 2 (Authors D–G),* Dorothy Sloan—Books, n.d., accessed August 8, 2009, http://sloanrarebooks.com/catalogues/RanchCat/RanchCat2/1540–1564.htm and http://www.dsloan.com/catalogues/RanchCat/RanchCat2/1540–1564.htm; J. Frank Dobie, *Cow People* (Austin: University of Texas Press, 1964), 85; Eldon S. Branda and Audrey N. Slate, "Paisano Ranch," *The Handbook of Texas Online,* Texas State Historical Association, 2009, www.tshaonline.org/handbook/online/articles/PP/app1.html; see also John Edward Weems, "The Texas Institute of Letters," *Dobie Paisano Fellowship Program,* University of Texas at Austin Graduate School, n.d., accessed August 8, 2009, www.utexas.edu/ogs/Paisano/til/; "2008–2009 Fellows," *Dobie Paisano Fellowship Program,* University of Texas at Austin Graduate School, n.d., accessed August 8, 2009, www.utexas.edu/ogs/Paisano/currentfellows.html; "Origin of the Fellowship Program," *Dobie Paisano Fellowship Program,* University of Texas at Austin Graduate School, n.d., accessed August 8, 2009, http://www.utexas.edu/ogs/Paisano/origin/; "Paisano Ranch," *Dobie Paisano Fellowship Program,* University of Texas at Austin Graduate School, n.d., accessed August 8, 2009, www.utexas.edu/ogs/Paisano/ranch/; Diary, March 13, May 1962 (JJM 3.1); "Yahoo! Local Maps," Yahoo, 2009, http://maps.yahoo.com/; James Baughn et al., "Hondo Creek Bridge, Medina County, Texas," Historic Bridges of the United States, 2002–2009, http://bridgehunter.com/tx/medina/151630AA0241001/;

"Outdoors," *Texas Hill Country Visitor Guide Online*, n.d., accessed August 8, 2009, http://www.hill-country-visitor.com/Texas_Hill_Country/Outdoors; Francis E. Abernethy, "Dobie, James Frank," *The Handbook of Texas Online*, Texas State Historical Association, 2010, www.tshaonline.org/handbook/online/articles/fd002; J. Frank Dobie, *The Longhorns* (1941; Austin: University of Texas Press, 2000); (JJM 6.1–7) and Diary, November 15–21, 1960 (JJM 2.13); January 9, 1962 (JJM 3.1); Diary, January 12, November 16–20, 1961, December 20, 1964, February 13, 1967 (JJM 2.14, JJM 3.4, JJM 3.5); (JJM SR 2280).

168   *The story itself is almost more depressing*
    TTM 157–58.

168   *In this story, he emphasized instead*
    (JJM SR 2276, 2277, 2274, 2275); TTM 239.

169   *Mathews went far back in time*
    Diary, June 24–July 10, 1921 (JJM 1.44); Diary, July 6, 1921 (JJM 1.44); Darryl Lundy, "Sir Gavin Campbell, 1st Marquess of Breadalbane" and "Sir John Campbell, 2nd Marquess of Breadalbane." *The Peerage: A Genealogical Survey of the Peerage of Britain as well as the Royal Families of Europe*, thePeerage.com, 2009, www.thepeerage.com/p15045.htm#i150444 and www.thepeerage.com/p2737.htm#i27362; "The Campbells of Breadalbane," *The Great Historic Families of Scotland*, ElectricScotland.com, n.d., accessed August 9, 2009, http://www.electricscotland.com/webclans/families/cambells_breadalbane.htm; Kennedy Hickman, "Glorious Revolution: Glencoe Massacre," *Military History*, About.com, 2009, http://militaryhistory.about.com/od/battleswars16011800/p/glencoe.htm; Andrew Birkin, *J. M. Barrie and the Lost Boys: The Real Story behind Peter Pan* (New Haven: Yale University Press, 2003), 219, 223. Michael Llewellyn Davies and his four brothers, the children of Barrie's friend Sylvia Llewellyn Davies, are said to have been the model for Peter Pan and the other characters in the play and novels about the character. Barrie became the children's guardian after they were orphaned when Michael was ten.

169   *The red deer is not a threatened species*
    "Cervus elaphus," *IUCN Red List of Threatened Species*, Species Survival Commission, International Union for Conservation of Nature and Natural Resources, BirdLife International, 2008, www.iucnredlist.org/apps/redlist/details/41785/0; TTM 236–52.

171   *Perhaps this story should be considered*
    Bambi, directed by David Hand (Walt Disney, 1942); see *Twenty Thousand Mornings* and Mathews's archived letters and diaries in the University of Oklahoma's Western History Collection for references to these women.

171   *Mathews could not have picked*
    Susan Kalter, ed., *Benjamin Franklin, Pennsylvania, and the First Nations: The Treaties of 1736–62* (Urbana: University of Illinois Press, 2006), 222n1, 286, 414–15; "Sarah Palin's Ongoing Wolf Slaughter" (January 2009), defendersactionfund, *YouTube*,

www.youtube.com/watch?v=yFdijgMytUA; Rodger Schlickeisen, "Palin's Resignation Leaves Wake of Wildlife Devastation" and related links, Defenders of Wildlife Action Fund, 2009, http://defendersactionfund.org; For populist sentiment regarding fore-leg bounties, see also TheYoungTurks, "Ashley Judd Takes on Sarah Palin" (February 2009), *YouTube*, 2009, www.youtube.com/watch?v=6LAiWmyTpAs&feature=related, PhotoAnimationGuy; "Save the Wolves" (September 2009), *YouTube*, www.youtube.com/watch?v=qHCcunc7SHo&feature=related.